Praise for *USA TODAY* bestselling author Julie Beard

"Wildly inventive, fun and fast moving.
I absolutely loved it!"
—*USA TODAY* bestselling author
Mary Alice Monroe on *Kiss of the Blue Dragon*

"Beard knows how to make the pages fly through
your fingers, not only with suspense, but also with
sizzling passion and exhilarating adventure.
A master of the craft, she creates memorable
characters and magical stories."
—Kathe Robin, *Romantic Times*

"Julie Beard is one of the few writers who takes the
concept of love and passion right to the brink! Keep
up the wonderful writing, Julie. I'm a fan for life!"
—*A Romance Review*

"Julie Beard writes intelligent romances
brimming with emotion and sensuality."
—*New York Times* bestselling author Joan Johnston

"There is a magical quality
to Julie Beard's writing."
—*Heart to Heart*

D1011809

Dear Reader,

Enter the high-stakes world of Silhouette Bombshell, where the heroine takes charge and never gives up—whether she's standing up for herself, saving her friends from grave danger or daring to go where no woman has gone before. A Silhouette Bombshell heroine has smarts, persistence and an indomitable spirit, qualities that will get her in and out of trouble in an exciting adventure that will also bring her a man worth having…if she wants him!

Meet Angel Baker, public avenger, twenty-second-century woman and the heroine of *USA TODAY* bestselling author Julie Beard's story, *Kiss of the Blue Dragon*. Angel's job gets personal when her mother is kidnapped, and the search leads Angel into Chicago's criminal underworld, where she crosses paths with one very stubborn detective!

Join the highly trained women of ATHENA FORCE on the hunt for a killer, with *Alias,* by Amy J. Fetzer, the latest in this exhilarating twelve-book continuity series. She's lived a lie for four years to protect her son—but her friend's death brings Darcy Steele out of hiding to find out whom she can trust.

Explore a richly fantastic world in Evelyn Vaughn's *A.K.A. Goddess,* the story of a woman whose special calling pits her against a powerful group of men and their leader, her former lover.

And finally, nights are hot in *Urban Legend* by Erica Orloff. A mysterious nightclub owner stalks her lover's killers while avoiding the sharp eyes of a rugged cop, lest he learn her own dark secret—she's a vampire.…

It's a month to sink your teeth into! Please send your comments and suggestions to me c/o Silhouette Books, 233 Broadway, Suite 1001, New York, NY 10279.

Sincerely,

Natashya Wilson
Associate Senior Editor, Silhouette Bombshell

Please address questions and book requests to:
Silhouette Reader Service
U.S.: 3010 Walden Ave., P.O. Box 1325, Buffalo, NY 142
Canadian: P.O. Box 609, Fort Erie, Ont. L2A 5X3

JULIE BEARD

KISS OF THE BLUE DRAGON

Silhouette®

BOMBSHELL™

Published by Silhouette Books

America's Publisher of Contemporary Romance

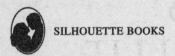

SILHOUETTE BOOKS

ISBN 0-373-51319-4

KISS OF THE BLUE DRAGON

www.SilhouetteBombshell.com

Printed in U.S.A.

JULIE BEARD

is the *USA TODAY* bestselling author of nearly a dozen historical novels who, with this action-adventure novel, makes a no-holds-barred debut in contemporary fiction worthy of a Bombshell heroine. She loves kickboxing, debating politics and being walked by her Basenji dogs. She lives in the Midwest with her husband and two children, one of whom was adopted from China. Julie is a former television reporter and college journalism instructor who has penned a critically acclaimed "how to" book for romance writers.

To my son, Connor, for having the spiritual insight and fortitude to make his parents go halfway around the world to China to adopt his sister, Madeline Jing. I adore you both.

ACKNOWLEDGMENTS

I would like to thank the following people for the support and help they gave me when I wrote this book:

Master David Blevins at Blue Wave Martial Arts Center, Shirl and Jim Henke, Amy Berkower and Jodi Reamer at Writers House, and especially Julie Barrett at Harlequin Silhouette. Without Julie's vision and enthusiasm, this book would never have been conceived, much less written. Thank you all!

Chapter 1

The Day From Hell

I like to make men sweat.

I like to tie a man in a chair and watch the beads of perspiration bubble on his upper lip one at a time, the air growing steamy from his nervous heat as I press the cold shaft of my Glock against his pulsating temple.

"You're gonna die, sucker," I whisper. "Too bad you had to be such an asshole."

That line works almost every time. That's because the world is full of Grade-A A-holes. Make that triple A. And I'm not just talking about men. I've seen women commit crimes so harrowing it would turn your blood into shaved ice. I blame part of that on the meltdown in the American justice system.

The Scientific Justice Act of 2032 ensured that no criminal could spend more than two years in jail without DNA evidence. God forbid they should suffer cruel and unusual punishments like their victims did. Naturally, what followed on the Internet were virtual manuals teaching criminals how *not* to leave DNA evidence at the scene of a crime. So now—more than seventy years later—executions, even for heinous serial murders, are so rare they make top ratings on pay-per-view. And punishment for run-of-the-mill murders? Forgetaboutit. Two years and you're out without that sacred DNA proof of a crime.

In too many instances, if victims and their families want justice, they have to hire a Certified Retribution Specialist like me—Angel Baker, CRS. I don't mete out vengeance myself. I simply haul in sorry-ass criminals so victims can have at it themselves. And the government looks the other way. It's cheaper than building new prisons.

So I shouldn't complain about all the jerks, creeps and sociopaths I have to deal with. Without them I'd be out of work.

Then again, I'm not in it for the money. But that's another story.

I knew this was going to be a tricky job. I had invited a ROVOR to meet me at a secluded green lot on Roscoe in the old Wrigleyville neighborhood on the north side of Chicago. I live close to Southport in a charming redbrick two-flat with a walled-in garden on a double lot squeezed in on either side by apartment buildings. I picked it up for a song—a mere two million—when the neighborhood went downhill. That was right after the Cubs relocated at the end of the twenty-first century to a TerraForma stadium in the middle of Lake Michigan.

ROVOR stands for Restraining Order Violator. A ROVOR is usually an abusive man who repeatedly violates court orders to stay away from his wife and/or kids until he kills them. I handle all kinds of criminals—rapists, thieves, white-collar criminals— but I feel especially sorry for domestic abuse victims and have taken on more than my share of cases to try to prevent tragedy.

I was doing this latest one pro bono. Call me a sucker, but I hate men who treat their loved ones like punching bags.

The ROVOR was Tommy Drummond, a ham-fisted laborer who liked to show his love for his wife and kid by breaking their bones in drunken rages. The family was hiding in an abuse shelter. Drummond had found out where they were and had violated his restraining order twice. I planned to let him know in no uncertain terms his visitor pass had expired.

It used to be that a job like this involved the usual tricks of the trade—some hand-to-hand combat, threats, smoke and mirrors and a little luck. All that changed two months ago when Chief Judge of the Circuit Court of Cook County, Able T. Gibson, started giving retribution specialists warrants to execute ROVORs who were repeat offenders. Instead of three strikes and you're out, now it was three strikes and you're dead.

Problem is, I've never killed anyone, even accidentally, and had no intention of starting now. Sure, I carry a semiautomatic pistol on occasion, but that's just the show part of my show-and-tell act. If retribution specialists were going to evolve into assassins, I would retire. Meanwhile, I wasn't above using the threat of a Gibson Warrant to my advantage.

The question I hadn't quite answered in my mind was how good of a liar I could be. In the past, my biggest challenge usually was figuring out how to scare the hell out of a man twice my size without shooting his nuts off. Now I had to confront Tommy Drummond and pretend that I had a Gibson Warrant with his name on it, then convince him to leave his wife and kid alone. Forever. And all this without ever showing him the warrant I didn't have. He had to *think* I was willing to kill him when I wasn't.

My door buzzer rang, jerking me out of my thoughts. I had no time for visitors, not when I only had fifteen minutes before I met up with Drummond. I raced down the stairs and opened the door to find none other than Lola the Soothsayer. She looked like a cross between a bag lady and the twentieth-century comedian Lucille Ball on a really bad hair day.

This I knew because I was a huge fan of old movies. While the jury was still out on how my own Technicolor life would turn out, I usually could count on a happy ending when I watched a classic film, especially those shot in black and white.

"Ah, Angel!" Lola said in that electrifying way of hers that always made me think she'd just discovered I was a reincarnation of Cleopatra or Catherine the Great. "Angel, Angel, Aaaaannnnggggeeeelllllll."

"What do you want? I'm meeting someone, and he'll be here any minute."

"*Someone?*" Lola adjusted the gold-lamé turban that was tilting to the right on her nest of brassy dyed-red hair and gave me a suggestive wink. "Glad to hear it, honey. It's about time you settled down."

I gripped the doorjamb instead of Lola's throat. "No, not that kind of someone. He's a ROVOR."

"A ROVOR? That means he's married, right?"

"Not always, but in this case, yes."

"He could always get a divorce."

"Lola! This is business. The guy is seriously dangerous."

Her red lips thinned in a grimace, revealing a lower row of tobacco-stained teeth. "O-oh, I don't like the sound of that, honey."

"It's all part of my job. And I can't be late because I don't want him to see where I live."

"If this guy is breaking the law, you should let the cops handle it. They don't like you horning in on their territory, believe you me. You'll have trouble on your hands."

I crossed my arms and leaned against the door frame. "You know more about trouble with the police than I do, Lola. You've got an arrest record longer than a roll of toilet paper."

"That's not my fault! Can I help it that the cops hate psychics?"

"They hate *con artists*." I started to close the door. "I'll call you tomorrow."

She stuck the toe of her scuffed boot in the doorway, stopping it with a thud. "Please, Angel." When I shook my head, she whimpered, "*Please*. I'm in trouble."

"With the cops?"

She shook her head. "They don't scare me. It's much worse than that." Instead of eyeing me cunningly, as usual, she looked at me as if I were some kind of savior. It creeped me out.

"Come on, Lola, it can't be that bad." I reached into the back pocket of my jeans and pulled out a thousand-dollar bill. "Here. Take it. It's all I have right now. Just don't drink it away."

Thankfully, her eyes hardened and she put her hands on plump hips exaggerated by a floor-length, confetti-colored gown. "I'll have you know, young lady, I've been sober for six months." She snatched the bill and stuffed it into her creped cleavage.

"Six months? Great." She could have taken a Z580 pill twenty years ago that would have stopped her drinking cold, but she'd refused. She said it would stifle her creativity and she wanted to sober up the old-fashioned way. Unfortunately that had never happened. "Congratulations. Now, goodbye, Lola."

"Please, honey." Tears puddled in her eyes, dripping over her garishly lined lower eyelids. She stole a nervous glance over her shoulder. "I'm in big trouble."

"What else is new?"

"Don't talk to me in that tone of voice."

"All right," I growled. "Come in, but make it quick. I have to dress fast."

There was no way I could face Drummond in blue jeans and a T-shirt. I breezed past the first floor entrance to my studio and bounded up the stairs two at a time to my living quarters, telling Lola over my shoulder to help herself to iced tea.

I dashed to my large bedroom in the back of the oblong flat, which faced the garden. I tore through my wardrobe, looking for the perfect costume. It was customary for retributionists to wear elaborate outfits on the job. That tradition was established in colorful New Orleans, where the first CRSs set up shop and established standards for the profession.

Most of us learn our trade on the street, and most come to the job with a background in martial arts or street fighting and a burning desire for justice. Actual certification is granted by a board of retired professionals. We're not recognized by any state or national organization, but so far no one has outlawed us, either. Government officials know that as long as the justice system is broken, someone has to make sure crime doesn't pay.

Enter *moi*—a five-foot-four chick with lots of muscle and even more chutzpah. But sometimes that's not enough. Clothing heightens the mystique factor and adds an element of danger. It also protects my identity. Not that I hide my profession from anyone, but I don't like the idea of being recognized on the street by someone I've recently hauled in for retribution.

I flipped past the Grim Reaper robe, my Crips gang wear and my nun's habit. Hmm. That had possibilities. Drummond was Catholic. Nah, I decided, moving on. While a white wimple and black habit might guilt him into good behavior, it wouldn't last. Better to scare the hell out of him, so to speak.

I briefly considered my Madame Dominatrix leather outfit. That would be a fitting irony since he obviously got off on dominating and abusing his poor wife, but I didn't want to turn the scumbag on. Better to assume the identify of what frightened him most—an intelligent, independent twenty-second-century woman. Besides, if Judge Gibson's warrants became protocol, I'd look like the Grim Reaper even without the costume.

I dressed in record time, pulling on flexible cobalt-blue pants over a paler blue crisscrossed spandex sleeveless shirt. Very feminine and conservative, but it also showed off my muscles and gave me complete freedom of movement. I snapped on spiked wristbands and a leather belt, and after serious consideration, put my Glock in the belt's holster.

Last but certainly not least, I applied a blue dragon easy-stick tattoo on my forehead. It was just bizarre enough that it sometimes intimidated my opponents. When I wore the sign of the dragon, I was telling the world, and myself, that I meant business. I grabbed the bogus Gibson Warrant I'd created on my computer and rejoined Lola.

"Oh, my God!" she barked in her post-menopausal smoker's voice when I emerged from my bedroom. And damned if she wasn't smoking a cigarette. "What is that *thing* on your forehead?"

"What is that *thing* in your mouth? Put it out!" I strode to the couch in the living room, my black ankle boot heels clicking on the polished wood floor, and grabbed the burning contraband dangling from her lips.

"Hey, hey, hey!" she cried. "Give me that!"

"No smoking, Lola! You're going to get me arrested." I went to the bathroom and flushed it down the toilet. "You know tobacco is illegal."

"If I wanna die, it's my right! What's this world coming to? You can't smoke. You can't even have sex anymore without a license. When I was young, we used to do it in the back of a hydro Chevy!"

Sex was not a subject I wanted to talk about with my sixty-year-old mother. "Intercourse licenses are required only for people who want good health insurance," I reminded her. "Now can we get back to your problems?"

She gave me a needling, curious look. "Do you have a sex license?"

I glared at her. "*Mo*-ther."

That pleased her enormously and I took the opportunity to change the subject. Pulling up an ottoman near her and taking a seat, I said, "Now, what's the problem? You need help?"

What followed was one of those rare moments when my mother's hard, scheming expression melted into something that looked suspiciously like maternal pride. Her rheumy-brown eyes puddled up. I tensed. I'd never been comfortable with her unexpected bouts of affection.

"Honey, I'm so proud of you."

I crossed my legs and adjusted the zipper on my boot. "Thanks."

"To think you're a retribution specialist! You actually do good in the world. Not like me. You're so strong, honey. You're such a good girl."

"Not everyone shares your admiration for my profession. And I'm twenty-eight. Hardly a girl." I nervously placed my hands on my slender knees. I was sure that wherever she was going with this, I wouldn't like it. But she was my mother. She brought me into the world. The least I could do was allow her to be proud, even though she had nothing to do with my success. "But thank you, Lola. That's nice of you to say."

"I just have one question, Angel."

"Yes?"

"Why in the hell do you have to ruin your beautiful face with that weird tattoo? I hate that Chinese crap."

I gave her a crooked grin. "Don't hold back, Lola. Tell me what you really think." Relieved by the insult, I stood and examined myself in the full-length mirror near the front entrance, trying to see myself through her eyes.

My white-blond hair stood straight up in short, soft tufts that tapered down the back of my head to the middle of my neck. My lips were curvy and naturally pink. My robin's-egg-blue eyes seemed almost innocent compared to the dramatic colors of my tattoo. Some women tried hard to be feminine. I tried hard not to be and was frustratingly unsuccessful, a disadvantage in my line of work.

That's why I needed a mean, green-eyed dragon with blue shimmering scales hunched over my brows. *Don't look into her soft azure eyes,* the dragon warned, *look into mine and meet your fate.*

Arched downward for the strike, the tattoo directed focus toward my neatly formed chin and, below that, a neck and body that was packed with more muscles than God had ever intended a petite, narrow-waisted, B-cup woman to have. I wasn't born that way, of course. I work out daily with Mike, my martial arts guru, and I'd started taking Provigrip as soon as the FDA okayed its use for policing agencies, bounty hunters and retribution specialists. Lola told me that when she was young, athletes took dangerous steroids to build muscles. Provigrip increased my strength by twenty percent at no risk to my health. I don't look like a body-building freak, but I can pack a punch.

"You really ought to dress normally, honey," Lola added as I turned back to her. "Best way to get a man."

I glanced at her outlandish everyday wear and shook my head. "I don't know what you're talking about. My outfit looks normal to me."

My whole body suddenly gave a quick shiver, like a divining rod honing in on water. My head jerked toward the window and a chill settled over my shoulders. "Someone's here."

It couldn't be Drummond. How would he know

where I lived? I'd given him a fake name and told him to meet me at the green lot down the street, luring him with the promise of a shady construction deal.

As I'd hoped, his desire to make some quick bucks had overcome any concerns he'd had about who I was and why I'd chosen him to help me with the scam.

The doorbell rang a second later.

Lola gave me a strange look. "How did you—?"

"Just sit tight. Don't worry if you hear anything…unusual. Not even if you hear gunfire. I'll be okay."

I skipped sideways down the stairs, pulled out my Glock and flung open the door. I took aim at a man who had slightly curly dark brown hair with a touch of premature gray at his temples. He wore a sleek, camel-colored sport coat that stopped at his knees. His wide stance and packed build made it clear he wasn't intimidated. He looked at me over the barrel of my gun with a deepening frown.

"Is that thing registered?" he asked in a deep voice.

"Yes. What's it to you?" I started to lower the weapon when I realized this man wasn't Tommy Drummond. "Who the hell are you anyway?"

"Detective Riccuccio Marco. I hope you're not going anywhere, Ms. Baker, because you and I need to have a little chat."

Chapter 2

The Wild, Wild Midwest

"Sorry, I've got plans," I said and shut the door. Another knock. I reopened it and smiled. "Look, Detective, I'm working."

"So am I." Eyes that had seen it all and questioned everything glanced down at my gun, which I'd put in its holster, and back up to my tattoo. "What exactly is it you do?"

I had the feeling he already knew, but I'd play along. "I'm a Certified Retribution Specialist. I'm getting ready for an appointment." I started to shut the door. He stopped it with a strong arm.

"It's important, Ms. Baker." With that he pulled out a hologram badge from inside his sport coat and flipped it open.

I watched with a sinking feeling in my gut as a three-dimensional display of his head pivoted for my benefit on the business-card-size disk. With his chiseled jaw and seductive, dark eyes, he was movie-star gorgeous, and I never trusted handsome men.

I turned from the hologram to the real thing, my gaze skimming over his bare ring finger. Even though he had to be at least thirty-five, he wasn't married. Why bother when he probably had women falling at his feet? I'd met men like him before. I'd almost married one, in fact. Fool me once, shame on you. Fool me twice…

I tipped up my chin and sneered. "Yeah, so you're a real cop with a real 3-D badge. I'm impressed. I still have to get going."

His exquisite mouth widened with a patient smile. "If I can't come in and chat, then I'll have to assume you're hiding something."

My jaw muscles tightened and I said in a low voice, "I'm not hiding anything, Detective. I'm a professional. I'm just doing my job. A job, incidentally, I wouldn't have to do if you and your brothers-in-arms were more successful at yours."

I glanced over his shoulder and saw a lumbering big blond man on the sidewalk across the street. He glanced from a piece of paper to the street sign. Oh, my God, it was Drummond. I touched the fake warrant tucked in my hip pocket. I couldn't whip this out in front of a cop. Marco's gaze followed my hand, which I then tucked into my pocket, pretending to strike a casual pose. From the corner of my eye, I saw Drummond get his bearings and head down toward the green lot. Somehow, I had to get rid of Detective Marco before Drummond got tired of waiting for me and left.

"Look," I said, clearing my throat, "I apologize for what I just said. I've been a little sensitive ever since the Gibson Warrant controversy blew up in the press. Some police officers seem to be blaming me and my colleagues just because a judge decided to start giving out death warrants. But I assure you, my profession is just as dedicated to law and order as yours. Now that you mention it, Detective, I would like to chat." I smiled like a Southern belle offering a mint julep. "Won't you come in? I'll be with you in a minute. Actually, maybe a few. I have to buy some, uh, sugar at the corner store."

His strong, smooth forehead wrinkled with doubt. "Sugar?"

I pointed to the left. "It's just two doors down."

Clearly, he wasn't buying it, but I knew he'd borrow the excuse if it gave him a chance to check out my place without a warrant. I didn't care what he'd find. Well, except for Lola. But she could handle this guy with her hands tied behind her back.

As soon as Marco climbed the stairway to my living quarters, I shut the door and raced down the street, stopping at the corner of the blond-brick apartment building that bordered the west side of the green lot. Drummond was sitting on a bench reading a magazine.

I scoped out the rest of the lot, which was an abandoned area with a few trees and a jungle gym. Empty as usual. It was time to move. For a split sec-

ond fear chilled me and the contrasting Chicago
summer heat suffocated my skin. Beads of sweat
slid down my back. I was aware of my muscles—
strong biceps, small but rock-solid thighs, sinewy
shoulders—especially at times like this when adrenaline pumped them to the max. I was also aware that
retribution specialist was a role I played and Detective Marco's arrival had thrown off my rhythm.

I took a deep, calming breath and walked down
the gravel path to the middle of the tiny park. I
stopped twenty feet away. "Drummond," I called.

He looked up and put the magazine aside. "You
da one who called?" he said in a typical Chicago
dems-and-doze accent.

"Yeah, I called."

"What's dis all about? You got some kinda job
for me?"

"It's about Janet."

He stood and rubbed his palms on his thigh-clad
jeans. He towered a foot and a half above me and
looked like an overstuffed bear—one that bench-
pressed about two hundred and fifty pounds. He had
a scruff of blond hair, a drinker's nose and mean,
bloodshot eyes. I'd been briefed on Drummond by
the director of the abuse shelter and had hired a private investigator to fill in the gaps. I'd done my research and knew what to expect, but the prospect of
fighting a guy who weighed three times as much as
I did was always daunting, no matter how much I
tried to psych myself up for the fight.

"You a cop?" he said, his eyes glazed with
confusion.

"Don't you wish." I moved in closer.

"A lawyer? I ain't givin' her a divorce."

I barked out a laugh. "When's the last time you saw a lawyer dressed like this?" I tipped up my chin so he could get a good look at my tattoo.

His sausage fingers clamped into his fists. "You callin' me stupid?"

"Yeah, but not for the reasons you think. You're stupid because you think you can control your loved ones with violence. I don't like men like you, Drummond."

Confusion cleared from his eyes like fog in a wind. "Damn! You're an avenger."

"That's right, Einstein. A Certified Retribution Specialist."

He looked totally flummoxed. I'd seen this reaction from ROVORs before. He couldn't believe there was a CRS contract out on him. Then his disbelief turned on a dime. He rushed forward like a Chicago Bears' defensive lineman. I hadn't expected this, but I was ready for him.

I ran forward and squatted at the last minute, pushing up when his shins hit my shoulder. Down he went with a thud. This was going to be too easy, I thought. Then he surprised me by shooting his hand out and clamping hold of my ankle as I leaped away, pulling my leg out from under me.

My face hit the grass, and I twisted hard like a writhing snake, but he crawled on top of me and gripped my neck before I could slither away. He moved his bulky frame faster than most thugs I'd encountered.

I couldn't remember the last time I'd been downed so fast, I thought as he tightened his grip. I'd been distracted by the cop. Hell, I could use another distraction about now.

I clawed at his arms, drawing blood, but it only made him angrier. He tightened the grip on my throat as he cursed and spat at me. Soon I couldn't breathe, and my lungs silently screamed for air. I kicked up at his fat, muscled back but couldn't reach his head. Blood pounded in my head. *My God,* I thought, *I'm going to die here.*

"Hey, Mommy, look at that man." It was the voice of an angel—or a kid. Either way, it was divine intervention.

Drummond looked over his shoulder and, at the sight of the kid and his mother, he loosened his grip. I saw my chance and took it, somehow managing to wrangle out from under his three-hundred-plus pounds.

As soon as I was on my feet I gave him a furious uppercut to the jaw. The jolt of it ricocheted through my body. He groaned, wide-eyed, but he remained upright on his knees. Damn, I hadn't meant to fight this guy—especially one built like a tank. He looked at me with astonishment.

"That's right, asshole, you're messing with the wrong girl." To make sure he didn't come after me again, I gave him a roundhouse kick to the side of the head and he toppled over like a bowling pin. He raised his head, too stupid to give up.

I took one last whack at him—a full frontal kick

to the groin. As my kung fu master had taught me, I employed *fei mai qiao*. My leg flew like a feather, but the *chi* behind it walloped his crotch like a hammer. My ankle burned from the impact.

Finally, Drummond groaned in defeat and rolled into a fetal position. Only slightly winded, I knelt beside him and grabbed him by his lapels, pulling his face close to mine.

"You're gonna die, asshole." I pulled out my counterfeit Gibson Warrant—what I should have done from the very start—and waved it in front of his face. "See this? This is a court order from Judge Gibson himself with your name on it, Drummond. If you try to talk to Janet one more time, I have permission to shoot you on sight, no questions asked."

His eyes narrowed on the folded paper, then he went pale. Thank God he had enough brains to keep up with the news and understood what I was talking about.

"This is your last warning. If you violate your restraining order one more time, you're a dead man, Drummond."

He set his jaw tight and for a minute I was afraid he was too mean and stubborn to know what was good for him. I smelled his fear, though.

"Understand?" I let go of him and stood, dusting myself off. "You have to leave town. Tonight. Any CRS who catches you harassing Janet can kill you. Legally. You understand?"

He closed his eyes and licked sweat from his upper lip. Then he nodded in surrender. "Yeah."

"Good." This would be the last time I saw this poor excuse for a human being. Maybe Judge Gibson had done this town some good after all.

Chapter 3

Blast from the Past

I grabbed my daily newspaper, which had been tossed into the boxwood outside my front door. Then I hurried upstairs and found Detective Marco flipping through my index of music. I had a big collection of classical files, as well as contemporary artists. He seemed fascinated by my choices. His thoughtful concentration surprised me.

I glanced around. Lola was gone. She'd probably slipped out the back door, which was just as well. I didn't need her complicating matters. I took a moment to study the cop. He'd taken off his coat—a retro double-breasted linen sport coat dating back to the turn of the century. He even had on suspenders. They pinched his starched-white shirt and clung to a waistband that tightly fit his narrow waist. His olive skin above the collar attested to what I could assume, given his name, was an Italian heritage.

"So you like Morbun Four," he said without turning.

"It's a good group. What of it?"

He glanced over his shoulder. "Ms. Baker, this isn't an interrogation. Relax."

I forced myself to take a breath. I didn't let any man close enough to find out what kind of music I liked, much less what perfume I wore. Which was none. I'd rather be down at headquarters asking for a lawyer.

"I thought you went to the store for sugar?" There was a smug gleam in his eyes.

"The sugar shelf was empty. I got a newspaper instead." I tossed it onto the coffee table, headlines faceup. "It looks like Chicago's finest still haven't found the twelve Chinese orphans who were stolen from the Mongolian Mob. People think they can sell kids like cattle."

He glanced at the newspaper and back at the music files. "Is that the paper I saw outside your front door?"

"I thought you said this wasn't an interrogation. What do you want, Marco? Ask your questions and get out. On second thought, just get out now."

His intense focus shifted from the files to me and he cracked a smile. "Having a bad day?"

"Not particularly. All my days are bad. I like them that way. I know what to expect when I wake up in the morning."

He studied me a moment with a perceptiveness that confirmed my original suspicion. This was no ordinary cop. Finally he turned from my music collection and faced me. "If I told you Mayor Alvarez sent me, would that make you feel better?"

My stomach hit the floor. "No, but it would convince me to let you stay and—what did you call it?—chat."

"That's right."

"You thirsty?"

He nodded. "Sure. The mayor told me you weren't as scary as you tried to appear. Guess he was right."

"Isn't he sweet. Did Alvarez really send you?"

Detective Marco shrugged strong shoulders he'd probably been born with. I resented him more by the minute. I didn't need some prissy-dick, Brooks-Brothers-police-academy graduate in here pulling rank. What concerned me the most was how he'd found out about my connection to Mayor Ramon Alvarez. I'd done a top-secret retribution job for the mayor, which had been set up by my foster father. I didn't think anyone but the three of us knew about it.

I went to the sideboard. "What do you want, Detective?"

"Alcohol straight up."

I poured him a neat glass of classic Vivante—a tasteless liquor that took on any flavor that the imbiber thought about. If you couldn't make up your mind, the taste would change with every swallow—rum one sip, brandy the next. And you never had a hangover from mixing drinks. I put the glass on the edge of the sideboard.

"So let me guess. Did I rough up an informant of yours?"

He retrieved his drink as I poured one for myself. When he was just inches away, I inhaled, expecting nauseating cologne. I smelled nothing, but felt a twinge of closeness. He was one of those men who used his personal skills to conduct his professional duty. A dangerous habit.

As he retreated with his glass, I realized we were having a four-way conversation. There were words. And then there was the unspoken energy between us. It had been a long time since that had happened to me. I'd spent so much time with AutoMates I'd nearly forgotten how to handle subtext with a human male.

"I heard you were direct," he said at last.

"Thank you."

"I'm not sure it was meant as a compliment."

"Really?" I shrugged. "Imagine that. Have a seat."

I motioned to the brown leather couch and over-stuffed chair by the empty marble fireplace. I'd never spent one iota of time worrying about decor. My apartment was furnished with a collection of hand-me-downs. Seeing it through Marco's eyes, it struck me as terribly masculine and not very fitting for a woman. Marco would probably be more comfortable in my foster sister's apartment. It was feminine, like her, with colors like peach and lilac. She had silky hair, high heels for every occasion and seductive reticence. In other words, she was my antithesis.

He settled at one end of the couch and I sank into the nearby armchair. As he leisurely sipped his Vivante, he took in every detail of my apartment and not in the surly, suspicious way of an everyday patrolman. Not even in the cool, jaded way of a seasoned detective. He was more like an art appraiser—scanning ancient plaster walls, my black-and-white framed photographs, the white-brick fireplace that had been painted over a million times, the hardwood floor scuffed by my myriad boots.

Suddenly, I wanted him out of here. "You're not a regular detective, are you?"

"No, I'm not. I worked in psy-ops for five years."

Psychological operations. He was a frickin' shrink. No wonder he gave me the heebie-jeebies.

"Two years ago I went back to the academy to enter a new program designed to streamline the training of solo detectives to replace those killed by the mobs. I graduated yesterday."

And today he was at my door. This was getting worse by the minute. "Why did you decide to switch from being a shrink to a gumshoe?"

He looked at me with those dark-lashed eyes of his. "You don't want to know."

Goose bumps spread over my arms. He was gunning for me. But why? I didn't think it had anything to do with Alvarez. The mayor's nine-year-old niece had been molested. The guy got off because he'd been smart enough to leave no DNA. After the trial, I'd found him and brought him to the mayor's brother for a little justice. That was the end of my involvement. I had a feeling Detective Marco had done some research on me and mentioned the Alvarez case simply to get in the door.

"Let's cut to the chase, Marco. Is this about the Gibson Warrants?"

His mouth twisted with irony and he took a drink, watching me as he sipped, then said, "No, that's not why I came. But, since you mentioned it, I'm head of the Fraternal Order of City Police committee working to outlaw your profession. I was actually happy about the Gibson Warrants. They've shown the world what I've known all along—that you're nothing more than a bunch of outlaws. This isn't the Wild West, Ms. Baker."

"Oh, but it is." I moved to the edge of my chair. "That's precisely the point. I don't approve of what Judge Gibson has done, but I understand it. How many hundreds of thousands of restraining orders have judges given out over the last hundred and fifty years? How many of them have actually stopped an enraged husband from killing his wife? Everyone knows restraining orders are a joke."

"But if you commit murder to prevent murder, is society any better off?"

"I haven't decided that yet." I wasn't about to tell him that I thought the warrants went too far. For some reason, I didn't want to give him the satisfaction.

"So you want to play God. Are you saying that you—or Gibson—have the power to determine who lives and dies?"

"People are going to live and die no matter what we do."

"You can't be that cynical, Baker."

I gave him an exaggerated scowl. "Don't be such a Boy Scout. You know as well as I do that rich people almost never pay for their crimes because they can afford great lawyers. And anybody, rich or poor, who is smart enough to keep DNA out of a crime scene will be back on the street, even with a conviction, after only two years. That's a slap on the wrist. You've got to hate that, Detective. All your hard work trying to catch the perps goes to waste."

"The system sucks, I agree. So why don't you try to change it instead of compromising it?"

"Because the system is controlled by giant corporations and international crime syndicates who don't give a damn about life, liberty or the pursuit of happiness, thank you very much. But if I can protect one woman from an abusive husband, or help a victim at least get an apology from his assailant, then at the end of the day I've done something worthwhile."

"An apology?" A sardonic half smile tugged his lips. "Is that all your clients want from their perps after you hand them over? Some of the ex-cons you people haul in wind up at the bottom of Lake Michigan."

Heat burned my cheeks. "That's not my fault."

"Isn't it?"

"I don't take any clients who would do that sort of thing. Nor does any other retribution specialist who is certified. We have a professional code and contracts that specify that no perpetrator can be killed or tortured. Surely you know that."

"What I know is that you're playing with fire. You can't take the law into your own hands, no matter what criminals do. Even if what you do is legal, it's not right. You have to leave law and order to trained officers. We'll do our job."

I snorted in derision. "And who are you? Elliott Ness? You think you're going to clean up this town like Ness cleared out Capone and his gang back in the early 1900s?" I shook my head. "Cops. You're all either corrupt or egomaniacs who think you're going to save the world."

He blinked slowly. "Why do you have such a low opinion of legitimate law enforcement?"

I took in a deep breath. *Because the cops who arrested my mother and put her in jail for bookkeeping had been placing bets at her apartment the night before. Because the social workers who put me in foster care the next day knew my foster father had a history of abuse. Because I don't trust anyone.*

"Because," I said in a rough voice, "even if you do your job perfectly, the bad guys are going to go free. Judge Gibson wants to change all that. While you can argue with his method, I can't imagine anyone who would argue with the result."

"So you've used Gibson Warrants?"

I leaned back as I thought about my encounter with Drummond. "You might say that."

His chestnut-colored eyes darkened. "How many people have you executed?"

"In the past two months?" I shrugged. "I've lost count."

For some reason he wanted to hate me, but he knew I was yanking his chain. He sighed and leaned back, taking another sip.

"What are you drinking?" I asked.

He licked the clear liquor from his lips. "Chianti."

"Chianti." I smiled. He was Italian. "I should have known. But I might have taken you for a Scotch man." I hated Scotch.

In the pause that followed, the old-time elevated train roared by not two hundred yards away. It was the only original el-track still functioning in the entire country and a real tourist attraction. In the mid-twenty-first century, all of Chicago's elevated trains and subways had been replaced by aboveground superconductor lines, which were virtually noiseless. I had the dubious privilege of living near the only remaining electric track capable of making my two-flat rattle from its vibration.

"So, Detective," I said when the rumble died, "let's cut to the chase. I'm not a bloodthirsty ogre and we both know it. What really brought you here?"

"Danny Black," he said.

Two words. They may as well have been two fists pounding into my solar plexus. For a moment I couldn't breathe. I tried to keep my cool, but my eyes closed of their own will while unwanted images flashed in my mind. I saw Officer Daniel Black's body lying in a pool of blood in a rat-infested alley in the Loop. A minute before there had been seven of us—me and Darelle Jones, a drug dealer I'd been contracted to bring in, Officer Danny Black and four dealers—connected with the neo-Russian mob.

Darelle opened fire, killing everyone but me. I was close enough to witness the massacre, but just out of sight around the corner of a nearby building. When the smoke cleared, I was the only witness. The fact that I was the lone survivor and had prior connections to the assailant made me doubly suspicious. But a thorough investigation cleared me of any collusion.

I put the unpleasant memories aside and opened my eyes. I found Detective Marco heading toward the door, readjusting his sport coat. He wasn't even going to hear me out.

"If you've bothered to look at the record, Marco," I said as I stood and crossed my arms, unwilling to chase after him, "you know that I was found completely innocent in that tragedy. The chief even held a press conference announcing that conclusion. The case is closed."

He opened the door, adjusted his collar and seared me from the distance with a laser-beam glare. "I've read the record, Baker. And you're right, you were cleared of wrongdoing. But you couldn't be more wrong on another count. The case isn't closed. It's now officially reopened."

He slammed the door behind him. I didn't move for a long time. I couldn't have been more stunned if he'd said, "Frankly, Scarlet, I don't give a damn." And in a way, that's exactly what he did say.

Chapter 4

Black Coffee, Blue Dragon

As soon as Marco left, I called the private eye whom I'd hired to watch the abuse shelter where Drummond's wife and kid were staying. Some retributionists who make good money have a whole staff of private investigators who do everything from watching over victims to tracking the whereabouts of ex-cons. I kept my operation simple by using a freelance P.I. when needed.

My guy was an old pro from Skokie. I told him about my fight with Drummond and told him to call the cops and me, in that order, if my threats failed to cower Drummond and he showed up at the shelter. The police could legally shoot the sonofabitch if he attacked his family. I could only do it with a bogus Gibson Warrant and wind up in jail for fraud.

I had just hung up when someone knocked on the door again.

"Now what?" I muttered as I flung it open. And there, standing before me with a rakish smirk and a tilted fedora, was none other than Humphrey Bogart.

"Bogie," I said on a long sigh of relief. "I forgot you were coming. Man, am I glad you're here."

He passed me with a wink and a whiff of tobacco trailed behind him. There was something so simply and confidently masculine about him that just watching him climb the stairs and saunter into my flat made my wire-tight shoulders unfurl. Okay, fine. I'd given in to Chicago's uniquely primal summer heat. I was here. He was here. My libido was definitely here.

Though Bogie wore a trench coat, he wasn't sweating. I was. He shrugged out of the coat and tossed it onto my couch, then poured himself a glass of Vivante. Bourbon. You never had to ask with a man like Bogie. He took a long sip, then looked at me long and hard. His upper lip twitched once—one of his rare signs of emotion.

"You look tired, Angel."

I nodded. "More than you could ever know." Between Drummond and Detective Marco, I felt as if the whole world was against me. I needed someone who would accept me as I was, ask no questions and leave no doubts that I was a woman. Lucky for me, that someone was standing in arm's reach.

When Bogie put down his glass on the serving bar and came my way, hands tucked into his suit pocket, my skin tingled all over. He kissed me lightly. I smelled tobacco on his breath, and it was so real I melted in his arms.

"Make love to me, Bogie."

"Is that an order?"

I nodded. He took me to my bedroom and undressed me. His jaded eyes lit with hunger.

"Here's lookin' at you, kid."

And I knew from experience he would do much more than that.

The next morning I arose, as usual, to the soft sound of Mike's Chinese gong and the smell of incense. Both were di rigeur for his meditations. Sound and scent floated up from the garden through the open French windows in my bedroom. I flopped my arm across my double bed, not expecting to find Bogie there. And I didn't.

I'd only contracted with AutoMates to have Humphrey Bogart until 3:00 a.m. With his internal clock fully engaged, quite literally, Bogie always rose promptly, no matter how deliciously exhausting our lovemaking was. He'd light a cigarette, which Auto-Mates were permitted to do. After all, tar and nicotine can't hurt a robot. Granted, second-hand smoke was still a problem, but the stinking rich AutoMates corporation lobbyists had convinced Congress that a few smoking movie star robots couldn't produce all that much smoke.

After lighting up, Bogie would dress in darkness, his rugged features illuminated only by the red glow of his cigarette, and depart.

His zombielike obedience to time always reminded me a little of those blond people in *The Time Machine* who went off in a trance whenever the Morlocks called. The 1960s movie, starring Rod Taylor and Yvette Mimieux, was a classic. It was in color, but I still liked it.

The fact that Bogie had been programmed to send me to the moon diminished the afterglow, but not by much. With a compubot produced by AutoMates, the premiere manufacturer, satisfaction was always guaranteed. And I was lucky enough to get exclusive dibs on the star attraction of Rick's Café Americain, the reality bar down the street.

Yet I'll admit the physical satisfaction did little to relieve my loneliness. That's why I always sent Bogie home before morning. The emptiness of our so-called relationship always glared in early daylight. The problem was I just wasn't sure if I could handle a real man again. I wasn't exactly lucky in love. While on the outside I looked fearless, my heart was about as tough as a bowl of cherry Jell-O.

I made coffee, and when I had a steaming cup in hand, I went into the garden, thinking my martial arts trainer would give me a break from training today. Mike's savage attack cry promptly disabused me of the notion.

"Haieeeeyaaaa!" he screamed.

My every muscle tensed. I knew what was coming next. Nevertheless, as the stimulant-dependant occidental that I was, I managed to take a slurp of my treasured caffeine before going into defense mode. Not only because my sluggish brain desperately needed it, but because it made Mike mad.

As a former Buddhist monk, he'd prefer I ate no meat, drank no caffeine, engaged in no sex and slept on a straw mat. He wanted me to live like a...well, a monk. It was my lifelong determination to prove to him that I could be every bit the fighter he was even while maintaining my status on the top of the carnivorous, lecherous and indulgent food chain.

I saw a tornado of sienna-colored robes rounding a bank of blooming pink azaleas.

"Aaiiiyeeee!" he cried again, every tendon straining as he squatted and assumed a pose of steel.

"Oh, hell." He was opening with *the iron buffalo ploughs the field.* That classic Shaolin kung fu move was enough to make me want to dig a foxhole. I took one last slurp of coffee and tossed my mug into the grass. "Hey, Mike, can we talk about this?"

His typically enigmatic Oriental expression, boyish for his thirty years of age, was distorted into a mask of savagery. Boy, he wasn't kidding around. My dalliances with Bogie always pissed him off. Mike believed compubots could suck the *chi* out of you for days. He was trying to teach me a lesson. But while I was sporting the just-laid look, I had more energy than he suspected. The question was, what move?

I cleared all thoughts as Mike had taught me, making way for instinct. He blazed toward me—jumping, squatting, rolling on the ground and flailing. But just before he downed me with a blue dragon tail-wag move, I leaped and grabbed the twisted tree branch that was shading a bed of hostas and pulled myself up with catlike grace. Squatting barefoot on the branch, and wearing nothing more than a tank top and boy-short briefs, I pounced down on him—now the tiger—and flattened him.

"Ha!" I cried out when he sank back in defeat. I stood on my adrenaline-pumped legs. "I told you never to do that before I've had at least two cups of coffee."

He sat up, not the least the worse for wear, and smoothed a hand over his shaved head. "I make sure you are awake."

"Well, it worked. But I lost a perfectly good cup of coffee. And I'm going to have more," I said emphatically as I combed through my sprigs of platinum hair and headed back to the kitchen.

"Wait, Baker."

His somber request stopped me cold. It was more his tone than the words that worried me. He always called me Baker. Ever since I'd rescued him from a prison camp in Joliet, Illinois, he'd called me by my last name, thinking it was my first. The Chinese put their last names first. His was Pu Yun. Yun would be his first name, except he'd taken a classic American nickname.

"What is it, Mike? Can't it wait for another cup of java?"

His long pause worried me. But finally he nodded. Reluctantly.

With a steaming cup of joe, I joined him in his shed at the end of the long, fenced-in garden. I always called it a shed, but it was much more than that.

Mike lived in a cozy twenty-by-fifteen-foot reno-
vated coach house. With a bare wooden floor, it was
insulated but not well heated, so we had put in a
potbellied stove.

In accordance with the principles of feng shui, a
water pond coated with green lilies and stocked with
white and red carp sat serenely outside his door. Inside, colorful painted images of a dragon, a red bird
and a tortoise adorned differing walls.

I glanced around and noticed the place was un-
usually cluttered—Taoist amulets and talismans
scrawled on red and yellow strips of paper were
pinned here and there, his bag of *I Ching* tablets lay
in the corner, incense burned before a small statue
of the Buddha, and he'd been working at his suit-
case-size desk on a purple astrology chart. Fact was,
Mike was superstitious, as were most Chinese
who'd grown up in the old country.

"I have very bad luck," he'd said when I first
brought him here five years ago. His wrists had been
scarred from being chained after numerous attempts
to escape from the work camp. He was skinny and
looked like a concentration camp victim. "My father...his grave is in a bad place near Shanghai.
Pointing east. We are all cursed, my family, because
of this."

Not if you're one of the elite Shaolin monks, I'd
thought at the time, which he was. The monks and
their kung fu style of martial arts had first come to
the attention of Westerners in the 1970s because of
a television show. When the Chinese communist
government realized they could make money off of

the monks, the Shaolin Temple north of the Shaoshi Mountain opened to tourists. While Mike had made a name for himself at the Shaolin temple, he had come to America in search of social freedom.

Whether it was because of bad luck or naiveté, he had arranged his trip through a crafty travel agency sponsored by the Mongolian mafia. Mike unwittingly ended up in a prison work camp operated by the mafia on the outskirts of Chicago. He'd slaved in Illinois's legalized opium fields for two years before I'd rescued him while taking a tour of the camp, a spontaneous act of mercy on my part.

After his escape, Mike could have returned to the Shaolin temple, but he'd felt that his imprisonment was such a bad omen that he had brought dishonor to his fellow monks. So he stayed with me, employing his fighting skills on my behalf, teaching me the kung fu style of martial arts. I'd been studying tae kwon do, the Korean style, since I was a kid.

So while Mike was a fighter, he still had the heart of a monk and often spat out cryptic sayings and insightful diatribes that had vaguely ominous, spiritual overtones.

"I had a dream," he said darkly.

I swallowed. "Oh?"

"While you slept with that *thing*, I dreamed your fate."

"Look, Mike, I didn't ask you to do that, and he is not a *thing*. Bogie is a…a…" My voice trailed away. I rubbed my forehead. I didn't even know what to call him. Truth was, I should be making love with a real man. Maybe Lola was right. I heaved a sigh. "So what happened in the dream?"

"A blue dragon...she rose out of water and..."

"Yeah?" I prodded when he frowned down at the astrology chart. "So?"

"You are so impatient, Baker!" he snapped.

I was stunned into silence. I'd never heard Mike lose his temper before. I slowly put my cup down on the table. "I'm sorry."

He frowned and nodded, not looking at me. "Blue dragon must fight two-headed eagle."

I waited, afraid to interrupt.

"Something has happened, Baker. A storm gathers. Our time together may be at an end."

He looked at me as if for the last time. I shivered with foreboding. A sudden wind blew up, rare in the north side of the city. The skies opened and warm rain descended unannounced. Big, fat dollops hit the roof, the sidewalk, cleansing them, leaving behind a humid, silver scent. Mike and I exchanged looks. He'd once told me blue dragons had power over rain.

Jeez. I was getting downright superstitious myself. I took my coffee cup and left without saying another word. I didn't need to. Superstition aside, I had a funny feeling the Chinese gods were about to fling some ox pies our way.

Chapter 5

To Lola with Love

Irony sucks.

At least it did when I went to see Lola on Howard Street in the Rogers Park neighborhood to make sure she was okay. I arrived thinking I understood the extent of my mother's shenanigans and left realizing I didn't know the half of it.

Two blocks east of the public transportation station, Lake Michigan lapped on the sandy shore in the glare of the moonlight. I couldn't hear the waves, but I remembered them from my childhood—remembered intrepidly diving into water that was cold even in July.

Back then I'd wanted to be a mermaid when I grew up. I used to practice holding my breath under water so that one day I could live in the lake, but I always had to come up for air. That was my first clue that I might be destined for something else.

I was six, and the lake was an oasis from Lola's parlor, where mobsters of every ethnic origin came to have their fortunes told or, more likely, bets placed. One year later, when Lola went to prison for bookmaking, I was yanked out of there by the Department of Children and Family Services. Since I didn't even know who my father was, D.C.F.S. plunked me into foster care, if you could call it that, in one of the sprawling suburbs, a concrete oasis known as Schaumburg. I didn't see the lake again for two years. By the time I returned I didn't believe in mermaids anymore.

I brushed the memories aside as I exited the superconductor platform onto the grimy street. I turned left and walked one block until I saw the red neon Fortunes Told sign blinking outside Lola's second-floor window. The *T* had shorted out so it read Fortunes old. That was for sure.

More childhood memories came flying at me, and not all of them bad—Lola and I holding hands as we walked to the corner ice-cream shop, trying not to step on cracks; laughing together when she tried to curl my hair and it ended up looking like she'd put my finger in an electric socket; lying in my lumpy bed at night, listening to the sounds of traffic and gunfire, so grateful I had my mother to keep me safe.

Even then I must have known it wasn't going to last. I'd cherished the chaotic and neglectful life I had, not knowing it could be better. And later, when I knew it could have been, I yearned for it still. You never stop missing a mother when she's gone, even when you can't stand to be near her.

I picked up my pace. I'd been worried about my mother ever since her visit and Mike's ominous dream. I felt guilty about blowing her off. Why I worried about a woman who could outsmart the devil himself, I didn't know. That is, not until I drew close enough and saw that the police had cordoned off the sidewalk in front of her brick apartment building. The cops had used old-fashioned yellow police tape. They didn't waste decent laser barriers in a neighborhood like this. Not when they'd probably be stolen. There were a couple police aerocars hovering on the street outside.

I ran the last few feet and ducked under the police tape, fully intending to dash up the crumbling concrete steps to the second-floor apartment.

"Hey!" shouted a patrolman from his car. He turned off the engine and the squad car sank a foot to the pavement with a hiss. He climbed out. "You can't go in there!"

"I'm a relative!" I shouted over my shoulder.

Just then an older cop came out of the door. By the time I met him on the small porch, he had drawn his taser. "Stop right there. Who are you?"

I looked up into his deeply lined face and my mind sizzled with a long-forgotten memory. It came like the flash of a July Fourth sparkler. I recalled the night the police had arrested Lola for bookmaking twenty-one years ago. The officers who handcuffed her had been placing bets in her parlor for years. I hated the hypocrites. For a long time I loathed the sight of a police uniform.

"Who are you?" the big, square-framed cop demanded as he hoisted up his sagging pants.

I no longer felt like explaining. I pulled a trick Mike had taught me.

"Follow the bouncing ball." I put two fingers like a fake gun to his forehead, arm extended, and threw every ounce of *chi* I had into his third eye. I don't mean that literally, of course. In eastern religions, the place in the middle of the forehead is considered a portal to the soul—a third eye. The cop in front of me didn't know that. Nevertheless, he froze and closed his eyes. I turned and jogged up the stairs three at a time until I reached the apartment.

The first room I saw was the kitchen. An overturned table lay in the middle. There was blood everywhere. There were times when I had been ready to murder Lola with my own bare hands, but I wasn't prepared for this. I hesitated just long enough for the patrolman to break out of his trance and come barreling up the stairs after me.

"Hold it right there!" he ordered.

Just then a detective stepped in my line of sight.

"It's okay, Officer. She's family."

It was Detective Marco. He guided me in with a soft touch to the elbow. When the older cop left, I stopped and pulled my arm away and glared at Marco. "What are you doing here?"

"I'll explain later."

"Is she dead?"

"As far as we know, your mother is alive. The lady in there wasn't so lucky." He spoke low and calmly. It was an intimate, soothing sound, and I was grateful, even though I knew it was the voice he doubtless used with his psych patients.

I looked in the family room area, where a couple of detectives were collecting evidence, and saw a body covered by a sheet.

He followed my gaze. "We're identifying her now. A neighbor says the victim came here regularly for readings. The neighbor also says she saw two men taking your mother away out the back entrance of the building. It was an apparent kidnapping."

"Don't call her my mother." My eyelids fluttered at the hard sound in my voice, but I wouldn't give an inch on this. I'd learned to accept her, but only on my own terms. "Call her a suspect. A perp. A victim. Lola. Whatever you want."

Curiosity had replaced his suspicion. He still didn't like me, but now he was trying to understand me. "Okay. Lola, then."

"I only lived here until I was six. Then I went into foster care. I hardly remember my childhood." My voice was the same monotone I'd adopted during the two years I'd spent in an abusive foster home right after Lola went to jail. The numbness faded when I'd landed with a nice, suburban couple who raised me as if I were their own.

Marco had been staring at the bloody mess but turned his focus back to me. God, I had to put an end to this blubbering. The last thing I wanted was for him to have insight into my psyche.

"So what are you doing here?" Marco asked. "Do you know anything about this?"

"No. I came because I was worried about her. Right before you came to see me, she said she was in some kind of trouble. But she didn't get a chance to elaborate." *I didn't let her,* I thought with a sigh. "What I want to know is why *you're* here. Don't tell me it's a coincidence you're handling my mother's kidnapping case at the same time that you're investigating me."

He slipped his hands into his pants' pockets and briefed me like the cool professional he was. "Two undercover detectives were in a car outside. They saw the assailants enter and heard a commotion, but by the time they got up here she was gone. I had assigned the men to keep an eye on Lola."

"As part of your investigation of me?"

He nodded.

I should have been angry, but the truth was, I didn't feel much of anything. I was too good at numbing myself. "I'll look at the body. Maybe I can identify her."

"I doubt it," he said but didn't stop me.

I understood what he meant when he led me to the body and pulled back the bloodstained cover. All that remained was a trunk and limbs—no head, hands or feet. The victim wore one of those nebulous, sleeveless paisley frocks women wear when they give up all hopes of being glamorous.

"The R.M.O.," I whispered. The Russian Mafiya Organizatsia was notorious for ruthlessly dismembering victims. No wonder the apartment looked like someone had put blood in a blender without a lid. "I see what you mean."

"We're running a quick DNA test now. We should know who she is later this evening."

I nodded. My stomach twisted with regret. Lola had come to me for help. Said she was in big trouble. Now this. I should have listened. "Do you mind if I go into Lola's parlor and look around?"

"Fine. That area has already been scanned and logged."

While Marco and the death scene investigators finished up with the bloodbath, I wandered to the front room where Lola did her scrying. That was the fancy word she liked to use for reading her crystal ball. She claimed she could see scenes from the future reflected in the glass. What a crock. All she could really see was the money she was conning out of her unsuspecting victims. My guilt morphed into anger. She wouldn't be in this trouble—whatever it was—if she didn't hang out with lowlifes and thieves. That wasn't my fault.

The perfectly round grapefruit-sized crystal sat on a small pedestal in the center of the table. I eyed it warily. I hated that thing. To me it represented all the painful lies my mother had told to me, to clients, and to D.C.F.S. when she was trying to get me back after her four-year stint in prison. I tore my gaze away and strolled around the room. With flocked wallpaper that was antique three times over and beaded fringe lamps, it looked like a Victorian whorehouse. Like the madam of a bawdy house, she had pictures of her most famous clients on one peeling wall.

Photos displayed the smarmy grins of a few lounge lizards who played in northside synthesizer bars. There was also Juan Villas, the Cubs' star pitcher. I was impressed. When I saw a signed photograph of the mayor, I paused. She had to have bought that one on the Internet. I looked closer. It looked like the real thing. Or was that a forgery? Knowing Lola, it was forged.

The last baffling photograph was of Vladimir Gorky. I'd seen him in the news. He was head of the R.M.O. here in Chicago and a top lieutenant in the national neo-Russian mob. While he was a known mobster, he was so high up on the food chain that the cops could never tie him to the crimes committed by his underlings. And since he had been smart enough to launder his money in legitimate businesses, he was somewhat of a society celebrity. He was like a white-collar criminal who never does time in a luxury prison and just happens to have invisible blood on his hands.

Wow. Lola was either knee-deep in syndicate crime or she'd really improved her fortune-telling act.

I looked closer and saw scribbled in ink, *To Lola, the best fortune-teller outside of Chechnya. With love, Vlad.* I nearly stopped breathing. Lola had been scrying for Gorky himself. She'd done a lot of book-making for low-level mob types when I was young. But this was big-time. Unless this whole wall of fame was just another one of her scams.

I glanced at the crystal ball, then did a double take. Before it had been dark. Now it glowed orange.

I snorted at my own superstition. Of course it couldn't glow. It was just the reflection from the neon light outside the window. To reassure myself, I looked out the sullied window at the "Fortunes old" sign. It was set to blink on and off, on and off. I looked back at the ball. The glow was steady, clearly not a reflection.

I walked toward it, stopping at the edge of the round, velvet tablecloth where it sat in a black stand. Curious as hell, I reached out and touched the glass globe.

"Ouch!" I yanked my hand back. It was hot. Not enough to burn, but enough to surprise me. Hell, did Lola have this thing hot-wired to impress her clients?

I reached out again, this time letting my hand smooth over the ball. It was definitely warm. I sat down and pulled the ball and its small black tripod stand closer. No wires. I put both hands on the globe. Suddenly I heard her voice. *Help me. I didn't mean it.* Her voice was in my head. The glass burned hotter in my palms. I looked down and saw Lola's face in the ball. She was crying. Then someone hit her. I heard words I couldn't quite understand. English, Russian, French, Chinese? All or none of these? Or just words played in reverse, comprehensible in a different direction.

I recoiled and pulled my hands away just as Marco entered the room. He drew back the curtain with a whoosh. Light from the living room flooded the parlor.

He looked damningly from me to the ball. "Does fortune-telling run in the family, Baker?"

Short of a snappy comeback, I was momentarily speechless. What if it did? *No,* I thought as I wearily rubbed both hands over my face, collecting myself, *no it couldn't, because Lola was a fake.*

"What if I did inherit psychic abilities?" I finally managed to reply sarcastically as I stood. "You're a shrink. Aren't you supposed to appreciate the powers of the mind?"

"I'm also a cop. I appreciate the ingenuity of grifting in all its forms." He cocked his head over his shoulder. "Let's get out of here. The body has gone to the morgue. The evidence has been bagged. We're the last ones out."

"Look, uh, Marco, would you mind if I took this home with me?" I motioned nonchalantly to the crystal ball. "You know it…well, it has sentimental value."

His mouth tugged in a cynical line. "Yeah, sure, what the hell. It's against the rules, but you bend them all the time, don't you?"

That stung, but I smiled sweetly. "Think whatever makes you happy."

"Go ahead. Maybe you'll actually be able to see your mother in that thing and tell us where she is."

"Ha, ha," I said, forcing a laugh. That would be a hot one. As hot as a crystal ball burning beneath my hands. I had no idea what just happened to me, and I might never know. But one thing was sure. I was going to find out who had kidnapped Lola and murdered this poor innocent victim. If I didn't take a stand, who would?

Chapter 6

Wicked Witch of the East

Let me tell you something about the Russian Mafiya Organizatsia. The foot soldiers in the R.M.O. are some bad, bad asses. While they call themselves Sgarristas, an Italian word for foot soldier borrowed from the Cosa Nostra, they make other Chicago mobs look like wimps.

Capone had his tommy guns, John Gotti had cement shoes, but these guys had unrivaled ruthlessness born of relentless suffering in a failed communist economy.

Efforts by U.S. politicians to rein in the R.M.O. largely failed because no campaign finance reform laws were strong enough to keep mob money out of the democratic system. Not that the police are eager to go after the R.M.O. Not only are such encounters usually fatal for Chicago's finest, but the arrests made rarely end in convictions, at least not for the mob kingpins, because the Mafiya maintains a careful balance of legitimate businesses and criminal activities.

I'll never forget seeing the R.M.O. slaughter four Chicago police officers who'd thought they were invincible with their SMART uniforms. Sgarristas torched the officers. The flames danced right through the cops' invisible bulletproof shields. They had all died of burns. And that was old technology. The Sgarristas were said to have new weapons not even the military had yet.

I was thinking about the Sgarristas when Marco and I left Lola's building. In fact, I was doing more than thinking. I knew someone was out there.

"Hold it," I told Marco just before he opened the foyer door to the sidewalk. A weird feeling made my shoulders quiver with a chill.

He looked at me. "What?"

I swallowed hard before I said what I couldn't possibly know but knew nevertheless. "Someone's out there waiting to nail us."

Marco's eyes glittered unkindly. "Is that what Angel the Soothsayer says?"

I was too spooked by the hair standing on my nape to be irritated by his sarcasm. My heart banged like a drum pulled too tight. I could almost feel death waiting for us beyond the door. What was going on here? I'd always been the intuitive type, but this is ridiculous. *Someone is out there.*

Where could we go? The inside door that opened to the tenants' mailboxes had already closed and locked behind us. Marco didn't have a key. The only place for us to go was outside this ten-by-ten-foot outer foyer.

"What's the matter?" he said impatiently. "You have nothing to worry about. There's a patrolman waiting for us outside."

"He's gone. He left." I propped an arm on the door and leaned heavily against it. I had to think.

"You're not a suspect in this murder case. You don't have to create a scene here to impress me, or throw me off the scent."

"Pardon me for saying so, but I don't think you have a scent. And this isn't about you or me. Someone is out there. If you're so sure I'm wrong, then go ahead. When they run out of bullets, I'll follow. Gentlemen first."

He narrowed his eyelids as he studied me with a curious mix of amazement and amusement. "I can't believe you're serious. Fine, I'll call ahead." He pulled his cell radio clip off his belt and called to the car. Silence. "Crappy equipment," he muttered, staring at the black device in his hand.

I nodded and gave him a gloating smile. "Your line has been jammed. Typical R.M.O. tactic."

He glared at me, for a moment considering my case. Then he shook his head. "No, this thing has been on the fritz all day. Department budget cuts."

Nevertheless, he reached into his suit coat, tucked away the radio and pulled out a Mortal Taser, setting it to Kill.

"Now we're talking the same language," I said, glad that he was armed. I'd left my Glock at home.

"That's a first," he muttered.

In spite of the danger I was sure awaited us, I couldn't help but notice how gracefully his hands cradled the weapon.

"Hey, Baker."

I looked up and almost gave a start when I saw how penetratingly he was staring at me. "Yes?"

"When we get outside and you see you were wrong, you'll have to buy me a beer."

I grinned. "And if I'm right, *you're* buying."

He moved toward the door, then halted, letting out a breath of relief. "Look. I told you."

I followed his gaze, which focused on a pulsing red light that throbbed through the cloudy etched glass embedded in the upper half of the old-style oak door.

"So what?"

"Those are called lights," he replied, sarcasm fully restored. "They put them on squad cars. My backup is there. You're good, Baker. Very good. You almost had me convinced."

He walked out of the door like Gary Cooper in *High Noon*. What a jerk, I thought. Then irritation turned to absolute panic. The vague danger I'd sensed turned into a sharp, sizzling sound in my head that made me nauseous. I saw bricks just inches from my face. They looked like they were burning. I didn't know what it all meant but I just knew something very bad was about to happen.

"Don't!" I shouted, but he was already outside.

Like a tornado, I flew out the door and smashed into his legs, tackling him. He crashed into the cracked concrete sidewalk. His taser flew from his hand, skittered into a street drain and vanished down through the iron slats.

"Damn it, Baker," Marco cursed.

At the same time a company of bullets sprayed the glass and brick wall where Marco had been a second before. By the sizzling that followed in the eerie silence, I knew the bullets were acid eaters—a favorite of the Mafiya. It wasn't enough to roto rooter your insides with SMART bullets. The R.M.O. wanted to burn away your internal organs with chemicals, just to make sure you were *really* dead. With a chill, I realized I'd heard the same sound a moment before in my mind. I looked up from the ground and saw acid fumes curling up from the bullet holes in the redbrick wall. That must have been the smoke I'd envisioned.

"What the—?" Marco growled as he yanked his legs from my embrace and twisted up from the trash-littered sidewalk. He stopped as soon as he saw the bullet holes. In unison we glanced hopefully to the flashing red light.

Unfortunately it topped a street cleaner parked across the street, not a squad car. I had been right. The patrolman was long gone. The street looked like a ghost town.

"Let's go!" He reached for my hand and together we scrabbled to safety around the side of the building. Panting, we both stood and flattened ourselves against the wall. "My taser—"

"Forget it," I rasped, still clutching his hand. "It's gone. Useless anyway." From my experience, the hard-core mobs would outgun you every time. Hand-to-hand combat was the only useful weapon against mobsters, if you were lucky enough to get close. Sgarristas didn't usually train in martial arts. They didn't need to. So it was the only weapon that worked against them when your back was up against a wall, so to speak.

"Guess I'm not buying that drink," I said. I pulled my hand from his tight grip and clutched the rough wall. "Don't worry, Marco, I'll handle this."

"Like hell you will. I'm not going to let you get killed."

I gave him an incredulous look. "For your information, Marco, you're not letting me do squat. I'm going to save my butt and yours in the process."

"Do you always have to be in control, Baker?"

"Don't psychoanalyze me, Marco. You should have stuck to head-shrinking back at headquarters. You'd be dead by now if I hadn't—"

I heard a rustling noise and the squeak of a rusty wheel, and fell silent. We both looked at ourselves mirrored in the plate-glass windows of the storefront across the alley. In a distorted reflection created by a bright rainbow-colored billboard on the brick wall over our heads, we saw a stooped figure pushing a rickety grocery cart.

"A free-ranger," he whispered, his face visibly relaxing. "An old lady."

Free-ranger. I hated that term. It was a euphemism for any homeless person who hadn't gone underground to live in Emerald City, which was a euphemism for the abandoned subway tunnels that had become a city for the poor.

A number of homeless Chicagoans who preferred to brave the elements in order to enjoy the light of day remained above ground. Calling them "free-rangers" sounded like something happy, like free-range chickens.

The reflection of the homeless lady approaching with her rusty grocery cart full of bags, empty cans and trash became clearer. Her dirty gray hair looked like a Brillo pad, her nose looked borrowed from the Wicked Witch of the East from the classic *The Wizard of Oz,* and her teeth were MIA. Maybe a methop junkie whose brain had turned to mush. They were usually harmless.

She pushed her cart past the edge of the building and smiled at us as she passed. I was just about to relax when I saw something round and hard poking out of the many tattered layers of her clothing.

No time to curse. I shot my leg out at a ninety-degree arc, ramming the toe of my boot into the soft part of her temple with a sickening thud. The free ranger-who-was-not flew backward and landed in an awkward, still heap. Knocked out cold. Mike would be proud.

"Damn I'm good." I straightened my collar and glanced at Marco, who looked down at the unconscious body in horror.

"I ought to book you for that." He ground the words through clenched teeth and bent to help the prone figure, until I grabbed his upper arm.

"Don't be such a patsy," I whispered. "This is a setup."

He glanced around and saw what I had—an ominously deserted street. It was as if someone had shut down traffic for a parade. The Sgarristas probably had. But for just one assassination? They must have really wanted us dead.

"Let's get out of here," I said. "I don't know why the R.M.O. sent this guy to kill us, but this isn't the place to debate the issue."

I quickly squatted and pulled out the weapon I'd seen, which was still hidden in the assassin's clothes, and held it up for him to see.

His face sobered. "You were right. I didn't see the gun."

"Hell, yes, I was right. Don't worry about it. You have to spend some time on the streets before you notice these things." I handed him the Uzi-size weapon and felt for a pulse in the assassin's neck, which was partially covered with his latex mask. "This guy will be coming to soon."

"How do you know it's a guy?"

I grinned at him over my shoulder. "There's only one sure way to find out."

I tucked my fingers under the edge of the latex and pulled the mask off, revealing the sweating, unconscious face of a dark-haired, twenty-something guy whose ancestors definitely once vacationed on the Baltic Sea.

"You were right again," Marco acknowledged.

"I usually am. Don't ask me why."

"How did you know this guy was waiting for us?"

"I really don't know. I've always had great intuition but this was...this was too weird."

He nodded, but hardly looked convinced. He turned his professional scrutiny to the contraption in his hands. "What do you think this is?"

"I don't know, but I feel a lot safer knowing it's in our hands and not his."

I stood and he handed it over for my examination. It was surprisingly light. There was a trigger, but that was the only conventional technology on the foot-and-a-half-long contraption. The nose ballooned like a flamethrower, but I was sure it shot out something far more subtle and dangerous. Something inside of it glowed unnaturally. All ruminations came to a screeching halt when Marco stiffened and pointed down the empty street.

"Baker."

"I see her." A figure stood staring at us five hundred yards down the road. This time it really was a woman. I could tell by the natural flow of her long black hair, the knockout body in black tights, the cocky, somehow sexy stance. "If this is Tweedle Dee, there's Tweedle *Dumb*. Though I have a feeling she's anything but."

My supposition proved all too true. While she distracted us, the Sgarrista on the ground grabbed a knife and lunged toward me. Damn. I had been so entranced with the first weapon I hadn't searched for another. Marco turned and socked the guy hard in the jaw. I was impressed. But the Sgarrista barely moved. Oh, great! Jaws of steel.

The assassin kicked his leg out and rammed me

against the brick wall. I groaned, half expecting to hear the crack of bones. He grabbed Marco by the collar and had the knife to his throat so fast I couldn't react in any other way. I aimed the mysterious weapon and pulled the trigger. I didn't even hesitate.

What happened next was amazing. I've never killed anyone, but in this case, I had no choice but to use the assassin's own weapon against him.

Some sort of glowing laser beam soundlessly emitted from the snout. The Sgarrista watched with intense horror as it apparently penetrated his bullet-proof vest. He scrambled backward as if it were a giant, creepy spider crawling up his chest. Then he dropped his knife and his shoulders slumped in complete defeat. I turned the weapon to the James Bond chick who watched the whole thing from down the street. She took one look at it, turned and ran.

The assassin then got up from the sidewalk. He wasn't hurt. But somehow his face already looked dead. Despair welled in his black eyes. Even though there was no visible penetration of his flesh, he looked as if I'd just dealt him a mortal blow. He held out his hands. "Arrest me."

Marco and I exchanged looks. What did he know about this weapon that we didn't? As Marco pulled a pair of cuffs out of his back pocket, he said, "Why are you making this so easy?"

The sweating, bruised young man replied, "Because I'm dead already. You have a gun? Shoot me, please. It will be faster."

"I'd shoot if I had my weapon," Marco muttered

out of the side of his mouth. Then he marched forward, spun the assassin around and cuffed him. "Killing you would be too compassionate. You're going to have to endure overnight lodging courtesy of the county of Cook."

"*Govno*," the gunman cursed in Russian.

"Just think of the jail as a bed-and-breakfast on a budget."

I chuckled in spite of the circumstances. Marco shot me a smile, which I returned, then I frowned. It was time to start figuring out why the R.M.O. had tried to kill us. More important, I needed to know when the next attempt on our lives would be since they weren't easily discouraged.

Chapter 7

The Long, Hot Night

Marco called into headquarters on his lapel phone. He got no answers as to why his backup had disappeared, but a squad car arrived quickly and took the R.M.O. assassin downtown. The APB on Lola had turned up nothing. And DNA results indicated the headless body was a Polish cleaning lady who took care of Lola's apartment in exchange for future predictions. By the looks of the apartment, Lola and her cleaning lady had ripped each other off.

When Marco offered to give me a lift home, I made no attempt to decline. Granted, a niggling voice inside my head warned me that his insidious masculinity and good looks were a lethal combination. Therefore, I definitely should have returned the way I'd arrived, via public transportation. But I was dog-tired and didn't want to fight a crowd. Besides, when you almost bite the bullet with someone, you want to talk about it over a couple of beers.

Marco took me back to my place in his old hydrogen-powered SUV. Because my back was sore from our scuffle outside Lola's apartment, he took Lake Shore Drive. The land lanes on LSD were well paved, unlike the grid of neglected city streets. Just before we arrived in front of my two-flat, Marco received bad news. The backup he'd been counting on had gone missing under suspicious circumstances.

In the brooding silence, as cars whizzed by on the curved ribbons of pavement, I felt his sense of betrayal in my own gut. Not good. I could not afford to empathize with this man. I glanced at his profile—the strong, straight nose, the rugged jaw, the lush yet firm-set lips. My mouth almost watered.

Nope, there would be no beers tonight. We could commiserate about our brush with death another time. Right now I needed distance from him. When he pulled up in front of my two-flat and turned off his engine, I reached for the car door.

"Hey." He grabbed my left arm. "I owe you a beer, remember? I can run to a store and come back."

"No." I was quick to answer and forced a bright smile. "No, it's okay. I won't hold you to that. I have to go."

"But I want to."

He still held my arm. His strong fingers felt like kindling catching fire on my skin. Amazed, I looked at his hand, then into his eyes, not even pretending to be tough. "Detective, I know that when you face danger with someone, there is a sense of…closeness. But it's a false sense of comfort. You don't like me, remember? Besides, I'm bad luck. Someone wants to kill me and they almost took you down in the attempt. So let's just call it a night."

I whisked out of the car and shut the door before he could protest. I waved through the passenger window and almost changed my mind when he simply stared back, disappointment unabashedly simmering beneath his thick, dark lashes. *Turn and walk away, Angel,* I ordered myself. *You know the routine.* Yes, I certainly did. So I did just that.

I took a long, soothing bath and stretched out on my couch. It was too hot in my bedroom to sleep. Like Marco's radio, my air conditioning was an off-and-on proposition at best. Right now it was off. So I opted for the ceiling fan in the living room.

Though I was exhausted, sleep eluded me. I watched the fan rotate around and around, my head spinning with the crazy turn of events. I kept thinking about that poor woman in Lola's apartment. And when I finally succeeded in pushing aside those gruesome images, I thought about my visions of Lola in the crystal ball.

Is that really what they were? Please, God, let it be anything but that. Perhaps I just had a wild imagination. That would explain everything. But the lame notion died before I could even begin to convince myself. Marco was right. I'd known exactly what was going to happen tonight.

Had this ability, or curse, always existed? I thought back to the many times I'd escaped danger—always dodging bullets at the last minute, always changing plans when my instincts told me I was in too deep. Was intuition the same as psychic ability? I refused to even think of myself in those terms. I was not a quack or a fraud like Lola. I was just lucky.

Yeah, right.

I rolled to my other side and tried to think of something else. Someone wanted me dead. But who and why? Who in the R.M.O. syndicate could benefit from my death? Maybe somebody wanted to kidnap Lola without having to worry that a pesky daughter might come in search of her. I could think of no other explanation. But why kidnap Lola in the first place?

And then there was Marco. He really believed he could change the world. It had to be killing him that he was wrong. One of Chicago's finest, a member of his own force, had betrayed him tonight. It almost made me sorry I was right. Almost.

I rolled onto my back and sweat pooled between my breasts. Tonight, just before I got out of his car, he wasn't looking at me like a professional. For a moment, under his dark gaze, I felt like a real woman in the presence of a real man. And for a brief moment, it had been exciting. Just before excitement had turned to panic. *Circle the wagons, Angel. Don't let him in.*

I sat up, tired of pretending things were normal. Tired of pretending I was satisfied with this cleverly crafted life of mine. I rose up on my knees, leaned against the back of the couch and craned my head out the window for a breath of fresh air.

I saw a couple walking by after a night at Rick's Café Americain. Perfect timing. They giggled and smooched, obviously in love. Then my gaze wandered until I found something that floored me— Marco's SUV. *He was still here?*

It looked like he was sleeping in his car. He was leaning his head against the headrest and his forearm hung out the window.

I listened to distant traffic noise, and the sound of someone's music blaring from an apartment a block away, and wondered why. Why the hell had he stayed?

As if he heard my silent question, Marco raised his head and caught me staring. He got out of his car, and crossed the deserted street, heading toward my door. I walked down the stairs ready to tell him I could take care of myself. I reached the ground level entrance and paused when my hand grasped the doorknob. I pushed back the short sprigs of hair that clung to my moist forehead, then smoothed over my loose, long cotton pajama pants and spaghetti-string top. How silly to worry about how I looked.

I opened the door and found Marco standing in midnight's shadow. He exuded masculinity like an aura, and I wondered how taught his muscles were beneath his crisp and fashionable linen shirt. I could reach out and find out myself, if I had the guts.

He thrust his hands into his pants' pockets and squinted at me through a sliver of moonlight. "You change your mind about that beer?"

"No, I need you to get the hell—"

He closed the distance and the words died in my throat as one of his strong, tanned hands moved around my narrow waist, massaging the tight muscles in my back. He pressed me against him.

"Marco," I whispered, stunned by his gentleness, "you're very good at this."

"Shut up, Baker, and try to relax for two seconds." He pulled me closer against him in a bear hug. For one pure second I felt at peace.

And just like that, the moment passed. We slowly parted. At least he had the decency to look as disturbed as I felt. It was time for that beer.

We sat out on my second-floor garden balcony, silent for a long time. The embrace notwithstanding, I felt amazingly comfortable in his presence and began to relax. For some reason I couldn't explain, I trusted Marco. Besides, we'd almost died together.

Part of the multilayered wooden deck nestled like a big tree house in the giant elm shooting up past my roof. Now and then the leaves around us rustled in a desultory breeze. Marco rested against the railing and drank from the bottle of beer gripped in his big fist. I sat in a wicker chair, occasionally pressing my cold, brown-glass bottle to my temples, occasionally sipping. When you're really wiped out, nothing beats a beer in an old-style glass bottle.

"So…" he said.

Instead of looking at him, I gazed at the stars glimmering in the blue-black sky. He would want to know about my apparent foresight at Lola's apartment, and I dreaded the topic. But he surprised me by grilling me on a subject I hadn't thought about all day.

"So tell me about that night," Marco said. "The night Officer Danny Black died."

I took a swig of beer. It was cold and delicious. I licked my lips. "Can't you just read the file, Marco? I've been through this a million times."

"I have read the file…a million times. I want to hear about that night from you. You were the only witness."

I leaned back in my chair, balancing my feet next to him on the rail. "It was a lot like tonight. Muggy as hell. I'd been hired to drag Darelle Jones's sorry butt in for a little retribution. Actually, what my clients wanted was to save his soul."

Marco let out a huff of surprise. "His soul?"

I shrugged and grinned. "Darelle had gotten involved in the African Methodist Episcopal church down on Balboa. Darelle was a flimflam man. He'd promised to raise enough money to build a dining hall next to the sanctuary. But he'd used the money to pay for a drug delivery. The witnesses hadn't shown up in court and the case was dismissed. So Reverend Samuel Williams and the sweet little old matriarchs who ran the church decided they wanted to save Darelle's soul, even if they couldn't get their money back."

"Intriguing case," Marco said.

"To say the least. I probably should have turned the contract down, but I let my curiosity and the last remains of my cockeyed optimism cloud my judgment."

He tipped up his bottle and finished off the suds. I had two more bottles in a cooler and tossed one to him.

"Thanks," he said.

"I did a little investigating and found out that Darelle was hip-deep in methop."

Methop had been big for years. It was a time-released combination of methamphetamines and opium. Users went sky-high then landed on clouds. The drug never induced crash landings. With a regular supply, the euphoric roller coaster never ended. At least not until you gave up the ghost. It was the perfect drug. Too perfect.

Even though the recent U.S. government had decided it was okay if opium really *was* the opiate of the masses, Chicago cops had been ordered to crack down on methop. It was eating into the profits of the big drug companies who had legal substances that created the same effect. The street drug dealers charged less, which siphoned off the profits from the pharmaceutical companies, who didn't like giving up so much as a dime.

"I followed Darelle one night, hoping to corner him alone in the Loop. I didn't know he was about to make a big trade. I was just about to step out and confront him, but something held me back."

"What was it?" Marco asked.

I briefly shut my eyes. "A feeling maybe. I suppose that's too nah-nah-noo-noo for you. What's your working theory?"

"Any thinking man could only assume you had set Danny up. That's twice that I'm aware of that you've survived an R.M.O.-related bloodbath. Nobody can be as lucky as you are, Baker. How is it you always walk away when the dust settles?"

I smiled grimly. I had no answer for him. He wanted to blame me for Officer Black's death, that much was clear.

"What happened just before you decided to hang back—that night and tonight?"

I wiped a rivulet of perspiration that trickled down my neck. "This is going nowhere, Marco."

"Tell me," he demanded.

I shook my head. "I don't know. The night Black died I—I remember being sick to my stomach, even before the arguments began. Maybe I saw something in my mind—blood maybe—but I don't remember. Tonight I actually heard the sizzling of those acid eaters before it happened. I wasn't quite sure what I was hearing, but I knew it was trouble."

Marco crossed his arms and planted his chin in an upturned palm, staring hard. "Could you have saved Danny?"

Guilt washed over me and I looked down at the dead leaves on the deck. I had wondered that same thing, until I was finally able to put it behind me.

"Marco, I was around the corner. Darelle huddled with these guys, then Black burst out from nowhere and told everyone to drop their guns. He took a big chance coming out like that, all alone. He looked like such a rookie."

"He was a rookie," Marco said, his deep voice gravelly.

"Darelle pulled out an annihilator. It happened so fast. I was horrified. I didn't think Darelle was capable of that kind of violence. I learned that night that anyone is capable of anything under the right circumstances." I wiped a hand over my face. "Needless to say, the A.M.E. church gave up on plans to save his soul."

"You left the scene."

"I didn't leave right away. I went after Darelle but he got away too fast. I quickly returned to help the victims, but they all were dead. When I heard a siren's wail, I knew help was on the way. I left then, but turned up to make a report at headquarters the next day."

"Why risk being blamed?"

"I knew my information was critical to the investigation. Like I've told you, I follow the law."

He nodded and for once he seemed to believe me. He gave me a melancholy smile. "You saved my life tonight. Why couldn't you…?"

His voice faded and he shook his head.

"You wanted to know why I didn't save Black's life, too."

When he gave me a half-accusing glare, I swallowed hard. "I didn't plan any of this, Marco. We got lucky tonight."

"Did we?"

"Yes! I'm not a superhero. I couldn't have saved Dan Black's life if I'd tried." When he said nothing, I pressed on. "Why is his death so important to you?"

"Because his life meant even more to me." He

looked away, then looked back at me without emotion. "He was my brother."

"What?"

"From my mother's second marriage. I talked him into joining the force. Told him together we'd clean up this city. Guess I was wrong. Dead wrong."

I realized I was holding my breath. When I grew light-headed, I let it out. For one fleeting moment I'd felt comfort in a living, breathing man's arms. Unfortunately, it had been in the arms of a man who thought he had reason to hate me.

Irony sucks. Big-time.

Chapter 8

Thieves in Law

I woke up the next morning determined not to think about Marco-and his brother, considering I'd had nightmares about them all night. And considering I had a host of other problems to solve, not the least of which was rescuing Lola. I decided to start by seeking help from Henry Bassett, my foster father, who had ties to the news business and knew a little something about everything.

The Bassetts lived in Evanston, a university town on the lake that touches the northern border of Chicago. Ironically, Evanston is spitting distance from the Rogers Park neighborhood, where Lola lives.

My two childhood homes had been so close and

yet so far apart. Lola's flat was a mere ten-minute drive from the warm and loving mansion I'd shared with the Bassetts. I chose to forget entirely the two years I'd spent in foster hell between the ages of seven and nine in the Chicago suburbs with a dysfunctional family who shall remain nameless.

Not that my life in serene and wealthy Evanston had been without problems. I was reminded of that when I walked up the stone sidewalk of the Tudor mansion on the lake and found my foster sister gazing at me through the open door.

"Well, if it isn't my darling little sister, Angel. Mother! Look what the cat dragged in!"

"Hello, Gigi," I said, and mentally patted myself on the back for not gagging as I said it.

"What brings you up to Evanston, sweetie?" She stood in the doorway, making no move to let me in.

I contemplated my reply. As I did, I stared almost disbelievingly at my foster sister. I hadn't seen her in months and had almost forgotten how surreal she was.

Picture, if you will, a thirty-year-old woman with a bouncy, feminine figure who dressed in the sleek, simple twenty-second-century style, but wore odd little touches that advertised her own manipulated ultraperky personality. Like the thick turquoise headband over platinum hair that flipped at the middle of her neck and bounced when she walked. I wanted to cut all that sunshine from her scheming little head. Yeah, she looked like Doris Day, but she manipulated like Joan Crawford. And she hated me. Like me, Gigi loved old-time movies, but she preferred the cheesy color films that were popular in the 1960s. She was all flash and no class.

"Mom and Dad have missed you. You worry them so. What's kept you away so long, hon?"

"I was here last week, Gigi," I said and pushed past her.

"Really? Mom didn't tell me. You haven't returned my calls in ages."

"Is Henry here?"

"Daddy's working in his study. Mother is—"

"Georgia, did you call?" Sydney Bassett came into the well-appointed marble foyer and looked up with a beaming smile. "Angel! I'm so glad to see you."

"Hi, Sydney." She gave me a warm hug and I basked momentarily in the only selfless love I had ever encountered, besides from Henry.

My foster mother was the quintessential college dean's wife. She had salt-and-pepper hair pulled back in a loose bun, expensive bifocals that perched on her matrician nose, flawless skin, understated perfume, and she could always be found kneeling in her garden or curled up on the floral chintz love seat in the sunroom reading.

Sydney and Henry had taken me in at the age of nine after rescuing me from my first abusive foster home. For that I worshiped them. Still, I had never called them "mom" or "dad," though I think they'd wanted me to.

I withdrew from Sydney's tender embrace and from over her shoulder caught Gigi's crossed-armed, jutting-hip sulk. If invisible daggers were real, I'd be dead.

"I didn't expect you, sweetie," Sydney asked. "What's up?"

"She probably needs money," Gigi murmured.

Sydney didn't even bother to chastise her. She just gave me a "you know Gigi" look. My eyes warmed in return. I certainly did.

My foster parents had taken me in when Gigi was eleven and hopelessly spoiled. She had a younger brother, Henry Jr., but his birth had done little to dethrone Her Royal Highness. I was supposed to be the companion and the competition that would even out her rough edges. It didn't work out that way. Gigi never missed an opportunity to remind me that she was adopted while I was only a foster child. It didn't matter to her that the Bassetts couldn't adopt me because Lola wouldn't give up parental rights. Meanwhile, Hank Jr. and I had become the best of friends.

"Come in and say hi to Henry," Sydney said, leading me by the elbow.

"I've got to go." Gigi slipped the handle of her handbag to her shoulder. "Say, sis, let's do lunch."

"Sure, Gigi," I replied, confident it would never happen.

I found Henry in his book-lined study. No surprise there. He was the recently retired Dean of the Medill School of Journalism at Northwestern University. He finally had time to catch up on all the pleasure-reading that his role as head of one of the most prestigious journalism schools in the country had prevented.

We chatted about family stuff. It seemed Gigi

was considering a third stab at marriage, no pun intended. Husband number two had fallen off the face of the planet. I half expected him to be found stuffed in one of Gigi's suitcases.

Sydney and Henry no longer asked if I was dating seriously. They knew it was a touchy subject. When I was twenty-four, I'd fallen for Peter Brandt, a hot-shot investigative reporter who was vying for a job at WFYY, the network TV station where Henry still wielded clout. As soon as Peter got the job, I got the cold shoulder. Six months later he married some rich chick from the north shore. Talk about humiliating. What a fool I was to think a con artist's kid stuck in the foster care system would grow up to belong anywhere. But I've never let myself be used again.

Sydney went off to make tea, leaving me to get down to business with Henry. I told him what had happened in the past twenty-four hours and that I thought Marco was too distracted by his own agenda to be of much help in finding Lola. Henry stroked his neatly trimmed, silver vandyked goatee as he listened, leaning back in his burgundy-leather manor desk chair.

Then he pushed a button under his desk and a transparent screen lowered from the ceiling. His veined hands caressed the touch screen keyboard imbedded in his desktop and words splashed up on the screen, changing too quickly for me to follow.

At lightning speed images from International News Database appeared, one after another, warping into a new map, article or photograph. Henry could read at lightning speed, which was pretty much a requirement for journalists these days. With the ever-increasing capabilities of computers, information overload had practically turned into information fusion. He scanned the most recent IND articles and archives.

Henry leaned forward, his concerned expression intensifying. "I have no idea why the Mafiya would be interested in Lola. But I can give you a quickie course in history and geography so you can make your own deductions."

"Thanks, Henry. I don't need to tell you I nearly failed both subjects in school."

He smiled as he grabbed a chair and pulled it next to his. More than anyone, Henry had always appreciated my special talents, even though they were the exact opposite of his own. He'd offered to give me a full ride to Northwestern University, but I was too proud and tried to pay my own way. At the same time I was spending too much time in the tae kwon do studio and flunked out of college.

Still, I'd used my natural talents to support myself even without a degree, and I think Henry was proud of that. While he wished I'd chosen a more cerebral and safer career, he admired my courage and skill and said it was important to pursue my own goals instead of borrowing them from somebody else.

"Have a seat, honey," he said.

I did, and prepared myself to listen and learn as a map of Chicago flashed in the screen.

"As you know," he began, "Russian immigrants

flocked to the north side of Chicago in the 1980s before the fall of the Berlin Wall." He tapped his desktop touch screen and the map swirled into a close-up of the Rogers Park neighborhood nestled against Lake Michigan. "Before long, the shops on West Devon stopped selling donuts and hot dogs and started offering beluga and borscht."

"And that process intensified after the breakup of the Soviet Union," I said.

"That's right."

Sydney quietly slipped in with a tea tray, then hurried off to answer the door. I poured tea for us and handed a mug to Henry.

He caressed the touch screen and a photograph of Russian determination and pride appeared in a swarthy face. "That's when Ivan Petrov came to Chicago and established the powerful Chicago arm of the Russian Mafiya. Back then Russian mobsters were called *Vor y Zakone*."

"Thieves in law," I said. "I do know a little about that from my encounters with the Sgarristas on the street."

Henry gave me one of those measured looks of his that reflected both admiration and fear. "Have I ever told you that you should consider a safer line of work, Angel?"

I didn't bother to reply to his ironic query. He knew I never would. He just said that to make himself feel like he was fulfilling his fatherly duties. When I'd decided to become a retribution specialist, he had argued loudly against the idea until I had reminded him that his job had once put him in harm's way, as well. He'd been shot as a foreign war correspondent. He'd realized then that I was just as passionate about my work as he had been about his. When Mayor Alvarez, a family friend, needed retribution, Henry had confidently and confidentially recommended me.

"A Sgarrista tried to assassinate me today," I said quietly.

Henry nearly dropped his mug and some tea splashed on his pants. "Damnation." He put the mug on his desk and glared at me. "Angel, do you know what you're dealing with?"

"Some real assholes."

"The Sgarristas are ruthless."

"Tell me about it."

"They cut off the heads, legs and arms of their victims."

"Oh, really?" I inquired innocently. I wouldn't mention what I'd seen in Lola's apartment.

"Before the era of quick DNA tests, they dismembered victims to wipe away their identity and erase evidence of the crime. Now they do it simply because it's a tradition."

"What about the R.M.O.'s business dealings here in America?"

"They're pervasive. It started with the usual vices—gambling, prostitution, drugs. Then came child sex rings and slave trade. Petrov's descendants have managed to buy their way into legitimate operations on virtually every level of society. Their dirty money is so deftly laundered, the government simply can't track it. Even if U.S. agencies could shut them down, the R.M.O. dons, or *vors* as they're called, would simply launder their money back in the motherland."

"So where does Lola fit in? She's small potatoes. I wouldn't think the R.M.O. would consider her worth kidnapping. Maybe she was just a victim of random violence."

"I doubt it," Henry replied. He pushed the button again and the screen silently retreated into the ceiling. "She was probably a victim of extortion. Maybe she didn't pay her monthly business fee to the Mafiya and paid the price. She lived on Howard Street, didn't she? That's not far from the R.M.O.'s stomping grounds. Maybe the syndicate was shaking her down for so-called protection."

"I think she would have mentioned that to me." I shook my head. "I just still can't believe Lola would catch the interest of a big league mob. She had an autographed picture of Vladimir Gorky in her parlor."

Henry whistled in amazement. "Gorky is Petrov's modern-day counterpart. He's a powerful figure."

"He would place bets with his own organization, but I find it hard to believe he came to her for readings."

"Stranger things have happened. She was good at what she did."

We shared a look. He was gracious enough not to call my birth mother a con artist, but that's what he meant.

I sighed, leaning forward. "What if Lola was reading Gorky's fortune and made up something that intrigued him?"

"If he believed in her talents, he could have hired her to be his personal psychic. The Russian culture is steeped in superstition."

"Do you suppose she might have blurted out something that made him think she'd actually had a psychic vision of something he wanted to keep secret? He didn't know she was a scam artist or he wouldn't have paid her for a reading."

Henry sipped his tea then wiped his silver mustache. "I don't know, Angel. If he was worried that she had unearthed something important, he would have simply had her assassinated. Maybe she said something that made him think she could help him."

"So, how do I contact someone in the R.M.O.?"

Henry raised a silver brow. "You'd better call Hank. If anyone would know what Gorky's mob is up to, it would be Mr. Producer. If your little brother doesn't know, he can hook you up with someone who does. They have researchers down at the TV station who do nothing but keep tabs on the mobs."

I smiled. "Yes, Hank does love to dig into corruption. Just like his dad. Thanks, Henry." I stood and kissed his forehead, adding before he could, "And I promise I'll be careful."

Just before I closed the oak-paneled door to Henry's study, he called, "Angel?"

"Yes?"

"What if Lola really does have psychic powers? That might explain Gorky and the R.M.O.'s interest in her. Have you ever considered that possibility?"

"No." I willed my features to remain impassive. It would explain much more than Henry had even considered. Like why I always knew what was coming around the pike. I was, after all, my mother's daughter. "No, Henry, that's not possible."

Chapter 9

What's Wrong With This Picture?

When I exited the bullet train station on Southport in Wrigleyville, I was assaulted by the odors of my neighborhood—whiffs of trash that tumbled on the broken pavement, stale beer wafting from dingy taverns and the pleasant aroma of plump and juicy beef hot dogs from corner vendors. The hot dog was practically a city mascot. Needless to say, the pleasant atmosphere of elite Evanston evaporated from my mind by the time I reached my block.

I studied the intricate cracks in the sidewalk with my hands stuffed in my pockets, mulling over my conversation with Henry. I'd taken his advice and called Hank on my lapel phone on the ride back.

Hank was going to look into the R.M.O. on the newsroom database and get back to me.

Just before I reached the trees growing out of the pavement in front of my two-flat, something made me look up sharply. I saw Detective Marco leaning against a lamppost with his hands in his pockets. He was poised and graceful, yet solid and masculine. Defiantly so in a way I couldn't quite get my hands around it. Something in his demeanor made a chill run up my spine. He was the kind of a man who would who never be happy just going to bed with you. He wouldn't be happy until he'd crawled under your skin. Or inside your head.

My chest tightened and I couldn't get a full breath. I continued on and stopped when I was just close enough to inhale his pheromones. If he could bottle the stuff he'd make a million bucks.

"What is it? Did they find Lola?"

He shook his head. "No, but they're looking. I've handed your case over to Detective Hoskins," he said.

I frowned. "What?"

"I don't think I can be objective about your mo— about Lola's case. Hoskins is a good man. He'll be contacting you today."

He handed me Hoskins's card. I glanced at it, but refused to process the information. I didn't want a stranger coming in at this point. It would be like starting from scratch. Besides, Marco and I had come to an understanding...I thought.

I forced a bright smile. "I understand. You got what you wanted out of me last night and now you're history. If you can't quite pin fault for your brother's murder on me, then I'm no fun to hate anymore."

His tanned face, which one day would be handsomely craggy, creased with a regretful smile. "Angel, about last night—"

"Stop!" When he looked up sharply, I took a step in, staring him down. "Who said you could call me Angel? Look, Riccuccio Marco, I'm sick of your Captain Planet routine. You're a phony, you know that? You don't care what happens to Lola. And while you prattle on about law and order, all you really care about is revenge. You think what you do is somehow more noble than *my* work? I'm sorry as hell your brother is dead. But my crazy mother may still be alive and I'm going to find her, so don't get in my way and don't waste any more of my time."

I whirled around and jammed my hand against the security pad on my front door. After a quick scan of my prints, the device unlocked the door and it swung open. I was about to slam it in a self-righteous finale when I realized he hadn't moved. I spun around and found him still watching me, hands in his pockets, a patronizing smile plastered on his whiskered jaw.

"What?" I shouted. "Why are you still here?"

His piercing gaze didn't waver. "Because you're still under investigation in connection with the shooting death of Officer Dan Black."

I was flummoxed. "I don't understand."

"After we talked last night, I went back to headquarters and looked over Dan's file. What you told me was very valuable, and I plan to pursue the

R.M.O. connection further. But then I decided to pull your name up on the Master Comp."

I let my hand drop off the doorknob and looked down at the broken concrete stoop. Great. He'd just read my entire history. There were no limits to what the justice department could put on your Master Comp portfolio. He'd seen the long list of Lola's arrests, the details of my short stint in juvie when Lola had made me grift with her on the street, the photographs of the cigarette burns on my back from my first foster father, and my arrest record after I'd run away and got caught shoplifting before I'd moved in with the Bassetts.

"So what?" I said, which was my ready-made answer for times like these.

"So I noticed that you were involved in several different altercations over the last four years involving your efforts to track down criminals for your clients. A couple of accidents, some shootouts and, fortunately, only one incidental fatality, my brother's. But in every case you escaped injury. Hospital records show you've never once been seriously injured. That's rare, don't you think, considering your line of work?"

"What's your point? I thought we hashed this out last night."

"I've come to realize there's a bigger picture here. It's not just what happened with Dan and you and me. Your ability to escape danger is a striking pattern that I need to investigate."

When I merely crossed my arms and shifted weight, he continued.

"Look at it this way, Baker. If I don't find out what's going on here, some other cop will, and chances are he won't like you half as much as I do."

"Gee, thanks."

"Don't mention it."

"So what exactly do you hope to find out about me?"

"You're either incredibly corrupt or you have some special psychic talent that could be used for the betterment of mankind."

"I don't like either of those options, Marco. How about this—you go away and leave me alone and spend your time trying to find real criminals."

I went inside, slammed the door and leaned my head against it for a long minute. Detective Marco was intent on playing the sheriff in a game of cowboys and Indians and he had already determined that I was no better than the town charlatan.

When I came out a half hour later, Marco was gone, but there was a guy in jeans with a ponytail and dark sunglasses reading the paper on the bench across the street. He had that—oh, *je ne sais quois?*—scruffy undercover cop look.

I'd changed into tan cargo pants and a tailored white blouse. I looked almost respectable and had recovered my cool. I wanted to visit Drummond's kid and wife at the shelter and didn't want to scare anybody. Retribution specialists weren't exactly considered Girl Scout Troop Leader material. So there would be no whips or chains today.

The undercover cop followed me, but I managed

to hop onto a train just as the doors closed. He could tail me if he wanted, but he'd have to wait for the next train.

I reached the shelter twenty minutes later and chatted briefly with my P.I., who was reading a newspaper on a bench across the street. The building he was staking out was nondescript brick. No "You Are Here" arrows pointing the way for abusive husbands who just can't take no for an answer. The only visible sign in the soaped-up plate-glass window was Storefront For Rent.

At my knock, the door opened a crack and a pale young woman poked her head out. "Can I help you?"

"I'm looking for a place to rent."

"I'm sorry, we just let the place. I haven't taken the sign down."

"Myrtle sent me."

She blinked at that and nodded, then opened the door. "She's in the back." As soon I cleared the door, the young woman shut it and flipped two sets of dead bolts.

Myrtle Lancaster ran the shelter. I went back to her office and she greeted me warmly. As well she should. I'd taken on a few pro bono cases for her out of the goodness of my heart. In fact, she'd made all the arrangements for the Drummond case. I hadn't even talked to Janet Drummond face-to-face, only over the phone.

"Hello, Angel! What brings you here?" Myrtle, an abuse survivor herself, stood immediately and came around to embrace me. Nearly sixty, she had graying strawberry-blond hair pulled up in a frizzy bun, a softly freckled face and a few visible scars on her cheeks—tokens from her marriage.

"I took care of Drummond." I withdrew from her plump embrace and came away smelling like old lady powder.

She eyed me warily. "So he won't be back?"

"I doubt it."

"Angel, I don't know what we'd do without you."

"May I meet his wife?"

Myrtle nodded and took me through a private door to the common area of the shelter. There was a television blaring and some children working on crafts at a table. She pointed in the corner where a thin woman in her late thirties sat reading a gossip magazine, the kind that contains articles about two-hundred-pound babies and proof that Madonna is still alive. She nervously fingered the pages and smacked gum as she read. Next to her sat a thin, beautiful, black-haired girl who gazed sullenly out the window. Mother and daughter seemed completely unaware of each other.

"The girl's Chinese?" I asked incredulously.

"Yes, odd, isn't it? Recently adopted. She doesn't speak English."

"That's incredible."

Full-blooded Chinese girls were revered in China. A long time ago, during China's one-child birth control program, girls were given up freely for adoption while parents clung ferociously to their boys. But after a generation or two of this policy, there was a deficit of marriage-aged native women and young Chinese men had been forced to marry foreigners. The worm finally turned. These days a pure-blooded Chinese woman could write her own ticket.

"I can't believe Drummond had the money or inclination to adopt a Chinese girl. When did it happen?"

"Why don't you ask Janet? The girl's name is Lin." Myrtle led me toward Drummond's wife and introduced us. Just then the red warning lights posted in a half dozen spots around the room began to flash. Immediately the room fell silent as all the women and children went into rehearsed emergency mode. Someone flipped a master switch and the lights went out, except for the exit signs. I'd been here before when this had happened. It always reminded me of movies about air raids in World War II.

"Is it Drummond?" I asked Myrtle sotto voce, hair raising on my arms. If I hadn't done a good enough job scaring that scumbag away, he might have come back mean and ornery.

Myrtle pressed her earpiece with two fingers so she could better hear the briefing from the security guard who kept watch on the premises. Then she shook her head and answered my question. "No, it's Mr. Jackson. His wife and kids are upstairs in the sleeping quarters. I've got to go and warn them."

"Myrtle, I was being tailed by a cop. He might be out there."

"Good to know, Angel, dear. Thanks. Got to go." She'd been through this routine many times before. Myrtle wasn't rich, and her security wasn't exactly high-tech. But she'd only lost one woman to an abusive husband on her premises in twenty years. Better odds than any other shelter in the city.

As she hustled off, I instructed Drummond's wife to follow me and to get the girl. We snuck out the back door into an empty playground area surrounded by a fifteen-foot brick wall.

"We're safe here," I said, motioning to a wrought-iron bench. Janet Drummond sat warily beside me while Lin went obediently but unenthusiastically to a swing. She sat and twisted the seat around and back again, digging her shoes into the gravel, warily glancing our way now and then.

"She doesn't look very happy," I said by way of breaking the ice.

The corners of Janet's thin mouth tugged with bitterness. Her pale blue eyes hardened. "Would you be?"

"No. I just want you to know, Janet, that I took care of your husband."

Her head snapped my way. Her eyes flew open. I couldn't tell in that brief moment of stunned silence if she was horrified or relieved.

"I didn't kill him," I hurried to add. "I'm a retribution specialist, not an assassin."

It bothered the hell out of me that people sometimes didn't know the difference between the two, all public relations efforts notwithstanding. But what was I thinking? Judge Gibson had complicated everything.

"Is he coming back?" This time the emotion that

whitened Janet's already pale cheeks was clear. She was terrified.

"No. At least I hope not. I tried to scare him. I think it worked."

Relief shivered through her brittle body. I'd seen lots of women who looked like Janet Drummond. She came from good Polish stock. But there was little trace of her robust ancestors evident in her thinning blond hair and her rounding shoulders. Too many generations spent in the shadows of city buildings without a tree in sight had taken their toll. Add to that her husband's apparent abuse and what resulted was one unhappy, prematurely aging woman.

"Thank you," she muttered, wiping a tear with thin fingers. "Now we can get out of here."

"I wouldn't do that too quickly if I were you. Let's just make sure he's going to stay away. You're safe as long as you're within these walls."

"I'll be okay. I've got plans."

I instinctively doubted that any of Janet's plans would be good for Lin. My stomach began to feel nauseous. I clamped my eyes closed, trying to remain objective. Unwanted images shoved their way into my mind's eye, stinking of rot. I clinched my teeth and tried not to breathe.

You stupid little bitch! I'm going to kill you. See this cigarette? It's burning, Angel, honey. You don't believe me? Come 'ere. Take off your shirt. Come 'ere, I said! I'll teach you to disobey me.

I forced my eyes open before I could smell what came next—burning flesh and the sour hint of urine.

It was only a memory. But some memories never faded. This one would. Someday. If I tried hard enough. If I—

"Are you all right?"

Janet's voice caught me off guard. I was embarrassed to see her worried about me. It wasn't supposed to be like that. I was here to save her.

"Yeah. I'm okay." I leaned forward and rested my elbows on my knees, rubbing my hands together as I frowned. "Let me ask you something, Janet. China shut down female adoptions fifty years ago. You can adopt a Chinese boy easily enough. But you can't get a girl for less than half a mil, and only on the black market. I don't want to be nosey—well, actually, I do. Myrtle says your husband is a carpenter and you're a waitress. How did you come up with that kind of dough?"

Her listless eyes warmed with pride. She raised a penciled eyebrow. "We've got *connections.*"

That sounded ominous. "What kind of connections?"

"Tommy did some rehab work in North Chinatown."

South Chinatown was older and more mainstream. That's where the locals went for moo goo gai pan and egg rolls. The newer Southeast Asian enclave on the north side was called Small Saigon. The newest variation on that theme was Little Beijing on Clark Street just around the corner. Little Beijing was run by the Mongolian mob. There the restaurant signs saying Take Out referred to the Uzis, poison gas and garottes sold out the back doors in the alley. Personally, I preferred egg rolls.

I sat back and crossed my legs, scowling. "That must have been some rehab job if you could afford a Chinese adoption."

"Tommy worked for Corleone Capone. He remodeled Capone's bathroom."

My jaw dropped. My eyes nearly popped out of my head. "What? *Capone*?"

She nodded with a triumphant little smile. Every dog has her day.

"Holy shit." I ran both hands over my soft, upright hair, then rubbed my arms.

Corleone Capone was *the* head of the Mongolian mob. I couldn't pronounce his Chinese name, but it didn't matter. He had been considerate enough to take on a ludicrous Italian *nom de guerre*. He was apparently fascinated by the legendary Italian Cosa Nostra that once was the reining mob in America.

"Uh, Janet—" I stopped to clear my throat. "Are you sure that all Tommy was doing for Capone was construction work?"

Fear returned to her eyes and she nodded tersely. I didn't believe her. "I had to get Lin away. He was going to hurt her."

"Who?"

"Tommy. I didn't want her hurt like I'd been hurt. You know?"

I know more than you realize, I thought. Lin seemed to be aware that we were talking about her. If she was afraid, she didn't show it. She was aloof. Enduring. I wished I could set her spirit free. But she was stuck with adults who didn't know the first thing about how to nurture a young girl with a bruised heart.

I'd actually gone through training to be a foster parent, but after completing the program I was too chicken to assume the role of motherhood. I knew too well what a responsibility it was. So while I didn't have the guts to mother a motherless child like Lin, I could protect her. That's really why I'd chosen my profession. Because there were always more victims than protectors in this world.

"When was the adoption finalized?" I asked Janet.

The pause that followed was so long, I turned to make sure she'd heard me.

"Last week," she muttered.

They hadn't known each other long. That would explain the emotional distance between mother and daughter. But there was more to it than that. I said my farewells, promising to return soon, and made a mental note to check with whatever agency it was that handled Illinois adoptions. I'd be willing to bet my next date with Bogie there was no official trace of this dysfunctional little family.

Chapter 10

A Kiss is Still a Kiss

By the time I exited Lancaster's Shelter, the sun had reemerged from behind the clouds. It felt good on my cheeks. I paused and inhaled the lemony scent of sunshine, squinting in an effort to see in the glorious summer glare. I spotted Marco with the undercover cop across the street. The intruder, Paul Jackson, was handcuffed in the undercover cop's unmarked sedan.

Marco looked up and spotted me. Just before he assumed the cocky air of a detective who had just bagged a criminal in the act, I saw relief flash across his rugged features. He'd been worried about me, I realized. Myrtle told me Marco had wrestled Paul Jackson, the intruder, to the ground. Now we were even, as far as saving the day went. But not for long.

I didn't think it was possible, but the sun grew brighter. It was as if someone was squeezing it and it was about to pop. I saw Marco shove off his hydrodrive, hips first, and swing into a leisurely stroll across the street to meet me. I had to shut my eyes against the brightness. When I did, I saw something very different.

A rusty, yellow Humvee rounds the corner. Marco freezes in the street. The driver floors it. Metal thuds into muscle and bone. Marco's body flips through the air, his twisted body landing on the sidewalk.

"No!" I shouted. Marco froze, staring at me as if I were mad. "Go back!"

Then everything went into slo mo. I raced across the street as Marco slowly turned to see the Humvee barreling his way. I tackled him, ignoring the pain that shot down my already sore back.

We fell together just as the Humvee roared past, spitting gravel from under skidding tires. I hit first, smashing into the fender of the unmarked aerocar. Then all went black.

I heard the soft, rhythmic whoosh of a blood pressure machine, the steady beep of a heart monitor, and the drone of nurses and doctors walking down a long metallic corridor. I tried to open my eyes, but was blinded by a great white light. Not *the* white light, I prayed.

Wherever I was, it was warm and safe and I fell back into sleep, or unconsciousness, or denial, wishing it could last forever. I felt peaceful for the first time in a long time. I'd been working so hard. I'd driven myself, trying to bring justice to an unjust world.

I was tired. Would it be okay just to stop awhile? I wondered. Would I still exist in one piece if, for once, I didn't try to save the world? What was I trying to prove? All my good deeds—my dark, good deeds—wouldn't wipe away what had happened to me. I could never have that pair of rose-colored glasses other people wore. If someone didn't give them to you when you were young, you were shut out of the club.

I tried to open my eyes again and in that blurry space between my blond lashes, I saw a dark figure standing over my bed. Ah, so the devil had come for me at last. I was afraid of this. And I thought I'd earned my way to the other place. Guess I shouldn't have slept in all those Sunday mornings.

He sat down and leaned over me. I tried to talk, but no words would come. If he wanted me, he could just take me. I couldn't fight like this.

"Angel," he whispered. His voice was muffled, otherworldly. "I'm so sorry."

He leaned down and kissed my forehead. *Isn't that sweet?* I thought. This guy had really gotten a bad rap.

"I understand you now, Angel. Maybe more than you understand yourself."

He leaned over and with exquisite tenderness put his lips to mine. Oh, that felt soo-oo good. He smelled just like Marco—musky and tempting.

"Get better, Angel." He kissed my forehead again. "Don't give up."

The devil placed his warm, strong hand on my

chest between my breasts. It took me a blurry minute to realize he had covered my heart. It seemed to leap up into his palm. The heart monitor went faster.

"Yes, she's doing much better," said a woman in white who leaned over the devil's shoulder. "She's going to be fine."

Om mani padme hum. Om mani padme hum.

I awoke the next day to the sound of recorded Buddhist chanting coming from a handheld sound system. Sweet sandalwood incense filled my nostrils. Water trickled nearby. A soft breeze floated over my prone body. Maybe I'd made it to heaven after all. Except Buddhists don't believe in heaven. Even if they did, I probably wouldn't make it any farther than purgatory, since I was raised Catholic.

I creaked open one eye and found Mike kneeling in his orangish-red robe at my feet. I was in his shed. He was meditating, amber dharma beads in hand. He looked up, though I'd made no sound. He was always supremely aware of changes in his surroundings.

"Baker," he said in greeting. His voice was monotone, but I knew him well enough to know he was hugely relieved.

"Hello, Mike."

"You live." A tiny smile curled his lips. His eyes remained expressionless.

"Yeah. Lucky again."

"No. It was unlucky."

It hurt too much to smile, so I frowned. "Does that mean you sent that Humvee to kill us?"

"I mean, luck has no place in this."

I glanced at the beads in his lean fingers. "Okay, I have good karma."

"No."

"Okay, I have lousy karma. I also have a splitting headache. Look, Mike, I appreciate your tender loving care, but I'm a little confused. Last thing I remember was diving headfirst into— Marco! Is he alive?" My head sprang up. "Ouch!"

"Marco lives, thanks to you," Mike said. "You were in hospital overnight. Concussion. Doctors give you submersion therapy. Keep you in deep sleep. Send you home. Say you will be better when you wake."

"I don't feel better." I propped myself up gingerly on the pillows. There was no bandage on my head, but it was tender. I looked around and blinked. "I had the strangest dream last night."

"What?"

"I don't remember, except…were you at the hospital last night?"

"Yes. I stay by your side all night."

"Huh. Was Marco there, too?"

"Yes."

I licked my dry lips. "Did he…did you see him…what I mean is, did anything…weird happen last night?"

Mike shrugged. "No." He frowned and tilted his head as he studied me. "Baker, Detective Marco is a good man."

I shut my eyes and smiled. "I see he's got you fooled."

"You take a shower now. Eat. He will come for you this afternoon."

My eyes flew open. "What? Why?"

"He take you downtown. Show you something important."

"Wait a minute, have you two been conspiring against me?"

"No. We conspire *for* you."

He poured a cup of oolong tea from a delicate red-enamel Chinese teapot. He handed it to me and I drank with relish. Hmm. Caffeine. I missed you, baby. Yes, I was getting back to normal.

"Mike, need I remind you that you are uncomfortable around the police?"

As an illegal immigrant, Mike had studiously avoided anyone official. After I'd rescued him and helped him get his green card, he'd still cross the street whenever he saw a policeman heading his way. "Do you really think you should be hanging with a cop? And what's this sudden interest in Officer Un-friendly?"

Mike moved from his knees to a lotus position, getting comfortable. His face darkened with memories. "When you save me from chain gang," he quietly began, "I tell you my brother is dead."

I looked at him, curious. "Yes, you saw him being gunned down by Mongolian guards when he escaped from Red Fields in Joliet."

Mike nodded. "But last year, at Chinese festival, I think I see him in a crowd. He was speaking Russian to someone."

I frowned. "He's alive? How would he know Russian?"

"I saw him only a moment. Now I think Mafiya has him."

"But why? When I met you, you were being held by the Mongolian Mob. What does the R.M.O. have to do with your brother?"

I remembered that fateful day in living color—the leaden sky over the endless Illinois plains, snow-dusted fallow poppy fields, concentration-camp-style wire fences containing hundreds of Chinese workers, each dressed in a neon-blue uniform, and the chiseled black headquarters in the distance that looked like Mordor. Technically, the operation was legal. The inmates and imported workers harvested hybrid opium plants for legalized drugs. Ethically, however, the setup was bogus.

I'd gotten in for a tour of the so-called Cultural Training Camp. "Here at Red Fields we pride ourselves on the training each of our happy campers receives while working in opium production. We train our Chinese immigrants to read and write English, to learn American customs, and to be productive members of society." I'd yanked off the tour headphones and slipped through a door with a Do Not Enter sign into the factory, where the opium grown the previous summer was being processed. I'd been hired to find a camp guard who hadn't yet properly expressed his remorse over a fatal drunk driving accident.

Before I'd found him, though, a factory supervisor had found me. He'd accused me of being a journalist and raised a rifle to shoot, but Mike had appeared out of nowhere, a whirling dervish of Shaolin moves. He'd downed the supervisor and turned to me.

He'd said in broken English, "Take with you."

I had nodded and we'd escaped out the back. He'd stripped out of his condemning blue jumpsuit down to his skivvies and I'd given him my coat. Fortunately, we'd been with a crowd of Buddhist monks from Augusta, Missouri. He had fit right in. We'd rejoined the tour and waltzed out the front gate owing each other our lives.

"Mike, how do the Sgarristas fit in with Red Fields?"

"I ask Detective Marco about my brother."

"When, this morning?"

Mike nodded. "He say R.M.O. trains Mongolian guards in Russian tactics. I think my brother is kidnapped, or he come to me. He was shot by Mongolians but taken in by R.M.O. fighters who were there that day."

I considered this. "So how do you plan to find him?"

"Marco will help me."

I groaned. "Oh, Mike, do you really think Detective Marco cares a rat's ass about your brother?"

"Yes," Mike replied firmly. "The Buddha say, 'man who grabs tail of big snake and dies…dies at his own hand, for he fails to grasp snake properly.'"

I nodded, pretending I understood the profound message. "Uh-huh."

"Detective Marco understand," Mike said in conclusion.

"Uh…okay, I think I get it."

He eyed me dubiously, then nodded.

I frowned at my tea. If Marco had persuaded Mike to trust him, it was two against one. Not good betting odds, Lola would say. Not good at all.

I wasn't seriously hurt. But between the bruise on my back and the knot on my head, I walked like Quasimodo. After eating some soup and taking a nap on the back balcony, I decided I'd had enough of feeling sorry for myself and changed into a decent pair of slacks and a blouse that was almost feminine. I resented dressing for an event about which I was clueless. Where could I possibly be going that both Mike and Marco felt was important enough to take away time that I should be using to find Lola? But I trusted Mike, and he apparently trusted Marco.

I went back out on the second-story deck and tried to relax the muscles in my body that were still traumatized by my crash landing outside the shelter.

I took a deep breath and shut my eyes, concentrating on the cinnabar field. That was the Shaolin term for the abdomen, the source of all *chi* and power. In and out, I breathed.

Chicago's notorious wind, which locals called the hawk, had flown the coop and moisture beaded between my breasts. When I felt myself regaining my center, I slowly stretched through a series of moves.

When I had released just about all of my kinks, I went on automatic pilot and retrieved a pack of cigarettes Lola had apparently dropped during her hasty exit from my apartment. The contraband had been preying on my mind ever since I'd first glimpsed it.

I returned to the deck and studied the package of death sticks. I'd started smoking when I'd just turned seven. I'd wanted to be a grown-up like my mom. When a neighbor told me I was killing myself, I quit. Lola never would. That was the difference between us. One of many.

Where the hell was Marco? He'd told Mike he would be here at two. I pulled a cigarette and put it between my lips, watching as Mike bowed repeatedly in front of a statue of the Buddha at the end of the garden. We were so different. He would meditate and work out and be the better for it. I'd work out and then return to my evil ways. So American of me, I thought as I lit up. I took a long drag and pulled my hand away gracefully, like Ingrid Bergman in *Casablanca*. I held the smoke deep in my lungs. Then I puked out a graceless cough.

"That's against the law," Marco said from the doorway. "I'm placing you under arrest."

Still coughing, green-faced, I turned to him, my lungs burning like Georgia. "Like hell you will," I rasped. I so wanted to flush the cigarette down the toilet, but wouldn't give Marco the satisfaction.

He broke into a satisfied smirk and sauntered forward, grabbing the pack from the wooden railing. "May I?"

Slowly recovering, I nodded, saying, "Sure," as I watched him light up. He didn't cough. He'd done it before. "You smoke?"

"Used to. When I was a kid working at a pool

hall." He took an artful drag, pooling the smoke in
his mouth. He almost let it out, but masterfully
sucked in at the last moment, and the ball of smoke
vanished down his throat. He turned his penetrating
eyes my way and gloated as he exhaled.

I took another puff, forcing myself to inhale. "I
don't smoke, either." I coughed again.

"No foolin'?" When he grinned, I flicked the
damned thing over the rail. He took one more puff
and did likewise. "At least you're up on your feet and
getting into trouble. That must mean you're okay."

In sync, we leaned over the railing and gazed
down at the garden. It was green and crisp and lush.
Sirens wailed far away. This was as private as it got
in Chi Town. Downright cozy.

There were times that I loved what I did for a living. The pain reminded me that it wasn't easy. The
sacrifice made my work more meaningful. It wasn't
easy trying to do good in this world. But it was the
only thing worth doing. I sensed Marco felt the same
way. Perhaps we weren't so different after all.

Our arms—ten inches apart—weren't touching,
but they felt connected. It was as if a magnetic force
field bonded us. I resisted the urge to look over at
him, but I could see his profile from the corner of
my eye. God, those lips. I wanted to devour them.
Kiss me, Rick. Kiss me like it's the last time. Okay,
I had to get that movie out of my mind. This was real
life. There were no happily-ever-afters. There wasn't
even one in *Casablanca*.

Suddenly I felt flushed and hot all over. I didn't
like it. Not one bit. Sex with Bogie was safe, almost

athletic. This was something very different. I needed to maintain control. Somehow I had to douse the flames burning me up.

"I started smoking when I was seven."

He whistled low. "Wow. Must have been a hard habit to break."

"Not really. I stopped when I realized it was wrong, which was a lesson I obviously didn't learn from Lola."

"Sounds like Lola didn't exactly have good parenting skills."

I let out a sputtering laugh. "Understatement of the century."

"So who were your role models?"

"Later, Henry and Sydney Bassett. My good foster family."

"Tell me more."

I took in a long breath. The air felt thick in my throat and I wondered how much of it was the intimacy that always seemed to creep up around me when I was with Marco. Why was I telling him this personal crud? It was my business, not his. And yet the words poured effortlessly from my mouth as if they'd been waiting for this opportunity.

"After Lola went to jail, I went to Schaumburg to live with a bill collector and his wife. Jack was his name. He weighed about three hundred and fifty pounds, ate copious amounts of junk food, yelled a lot and told me I was worthless."

"Great guy," Marco said with just the right amount of sarcasm.

If he had sounded too empathetic, I would have

clammed up and he was smart enough to know that. I didn't like to think of myself as someone who needed sympathy.

"In a way, I owe my good health to Jack. I started tae kwon do to deal with my frustrations that accrued during our time together. And he's the one who really convinced me cigarettes were bad."

"How did he do that?" Marco turned to face me. His expression was impassive, but I felt his caring. It lapped gently over me.

Lulled, I said, "He used to burn my back with lit cigarettes. I guess you read that in my Master Comp files. But Jack only did that when I was bad, which, according to him, was about every other day."

I laughed, but it sounded weird. I didn't dare open my mouth again. The silence drew out. He stared at my profile. I didn't want him to. I didn't want anyone to see me like this. But before I started talking about something inane like the weather, I simply had to ask him about last night.

"Marco, when I was in the hospital, I had the strangest dream."

After a long pause, he said, "Yes?"

"I dreamed…someone…well, the devil, actually…kissed me when I was unconscious."

"The devil, huh? Lucky guy."

I turned sharply to read his expression. For the second time in as many days, I compared him to Clark Gable in *Gone With the Wind*. His eyes held devilment and he barely contained a smile that dimpled one cheek, but he still kept his cocky distance. His expression admitted nothing.

"Baker," he said, "I want to take you someplace that I think you'll find very enlightening. Mike will stay here in case there is a ransom call. The phones are tapped. Hoskins is working full time on Lola's case. You can spare a couple hours to do something that might, in the end, help break the case."

"Okay," I said. It felt good to have someone else make decisions for a while. Maybe, just maybe, I'd finally found a man I could trust.

Chapter 11

The 13th Floor

I grew queasy on the ride downtown—all five minutes of it. Marco had taken a police cruiser, so we hovered a few feet off the ground in one of the aerolanes on Lake Shore Drive. They're faster than the land lanes, which were typically bumper to bumper with hydrocars and cabs. Only the rich could afford aero vehicles, so I felt hoity-toity.

In spite of the smooth ride, my stomach pitched as if I were riding the *Titanic*, and I didn't have to be a shrink to know it was caused by anxiety. I had put myself entirely in Marco's hands. In the past, just the thought of losing control was enough to make me break out in hives.

You could have stamped my trepidations "justified" when we arrived at the Lincoln Federal Center and got out on the thirteenth floor, I kid you not. Because thirteen wasn't listed on the elevator touch pad, Marco had to get a special code from the first-floor security station to get the elevator to stop at that level. It wasn't unusual for buildings to omit the thirteenth floor out of silly abeyance to medieval superstition. What was unusual was to have a thirteenth floor and keep it a secret from the general public.

"Here we are," Marco said when the doors whisked open with a ding. We stepped out into a plush foyer and found ourselves in front of spotless glass doors etched with the acronym IPAC. Below that, etched in smaller letters, was: Investigative and Psychic Alternatives Consortium.

I froze on the spot, then looked at Marco as Caesar must have glared at Brutus. "What is this?"

"IPAC," he said, casually putting his hands in his pockets and regarding me innocently. He'd pronounced it *eye-pack.* "It's a quasi-governmental agency that works closely with university researchers and the Teaching Institute of Parapsychology to develop practical uses for ESP and other mental phenomenon. Some of the telepaths trained here work with police on cases that are hard to crack."

I rubbed the back of my neck, which had broken out in a nervous sweat. "Marco, I don't know what you had in mind bringing me here, but I already know that Lola is a crackpot. I don't need a flash bulletin from an official source to convince me she's a fake. Her faults notwithstanding, I'm still going to find her."

"This isn't about Lola." His gaze softened as they roved over my face, then settled, twinkling, on my eyes. "This is about you."

"Me?" I looked back at the cloudy letters etched in glass, my narrowed eyes focusing on one word. Psychic. "Uh-uh. No way."

"Angel, be reasonable."

I scowled. "What did I tell you about using that name?"

"Baker, stop being a stubborn brat. You are in complete denial, do you know that?"

"This is a bunch of crap, Marco. Taxpayer-funded C.R.A.P. Figure out *that* acronym in your spare time."

"Think about it. This is a place where you can find out once and for all if you have psychic abilities. If you do, then you can use your skills to find Lola. If you don't, then the subject will be closed."

I opened my mouth to argue, but couldn't. He was right. I wasn't one to hide from the truth. And this subject bugged me just enough to want answers. "All right. But let's it make it quick. I already know how this is going to turn out, and I don't want to waste any more time than I already have."

After waiting only a moment in the lobby, we were greeted by a fast-walking, meticulously dressed man named Robert Steele. He had a pencil-thin black mustache, thinning hair and precise enunciation. He introduced himself as the site manager, shook hands briskly, and gave us a quick tour.

I was astonished to see how many people and apparent resources were dedicated to exploring the use of what Steele called "alternative intelligence." This was a double entendre, he explained, since the government considered psychic powers and telepathy a form of mental capability, for want of any better explanation.

"So human intelligence," Steele said in his clipped manner, "is being exploited to assist human intelligence, the latter, of course, referring to criminal investigative and international information-gathering work."

"Spying, you mean," I bluntly observed.

His sharp eyes turned my way and he gave me a crisp smile. "Precisely. Our purpose here at IPAC is to find ways to help law enforcement agencies—federal, local and international—do a better job fighting crime. Our goal is not to prove that extrasensory capabilities exist. If you spend more than a day here you'll know they do. We simply want to strengthen our trainees' natural capacities to help the FBI, the CIA, Homeland Security and local police."

"If you're so certain alternative intelligence exists, Mr. Steele, then why isn't this floor labeled?" I asked. "Why haven't I heard about IPAC before?"

He smiled patiently. It was obviously a question he'd received before. "There are many reasons, Ms. Baker. Until the genetic and biological source of alternative intelligence is pinpointed, the public will not consider this consortium an appropriate recipient of tax dollars. But the agencies we assist consider our work crucial, and we can't continue without funding. So we work quietly, trying to bring little notice to our efforts.

"Another consideration is safety. Ethnic mob leaders tend to come from mystogogic cultures, rife with religion, myths and superstitions. They are less inclined to doubt our crime-fighting capabilities than the average citizen. If they knew where we were, this building would doubtless be blown to bits."

Steele continued around the circular pattern of labs, rooms and cubicles. He showed us a testing area, where potential psychic operatives were tested at partitioned cubicles with picture cards and other devices. We then passed a comfortable room where someone who looked like a Gypsy was giving a lecture on séances. She didn't look all that different from Lola and I fought the urge to scoff.

We passed another large room, labeled the Psychometry Lab, filled with rocks and artifacts that trainees practiced touching in order to see scenes from the past. It reminded me of a former acquaintance who used to tap into her so-called past lives with hypnosis. When I asked her why, in her previous lives, she was always a queen or a princess and never a servant, she stopped talking to me.

"Don't tell me they're getting paid for this," I muttered to Marco as we continued on and ignored his look of warning.

Steele spoke and walked so rapidly that I could hardly take it all in. Finally we found ourselves back at the testing area.

"So," Steele said, finally getting a good look at us. "Why don't we begin testing, Ms. Baker? Unless you have questions..."

Again, I gave Marco my "Et tu, Brute?" look. "Marco, is there something you need to tell me?"

"Excuse us, Mr. Steele. This will take only a moment," he said with irritating confidence. Then he pulled me aside. "What's the problem?"

"The problem is that I didn't agree to take any tests."

"You agreed to find out whether you have psychic abilities. How else can you find out?"

"I've taken a look around," I spat. "I saw those people touching rocks and imaging the past. I see evidence of a lot of money being spent. These people have too much invested in this project to be objective."

"They're scientists, Baker. They have to be objective."

I thrust my hands into my pockets and looked away. I didn't want to hear this. I didn't want to put my fate in someone else's hands. What if these tests proved I was psychic? Granted, we could stop debating the topic, but then what? Life as I knew it would be over. I'd be at the mercy of a talent I not only didn't understand but didn't want.

"The only reason you want me to take this test," I hissed at him, "is so you can find out whether or not I let your brother down."

For once, he was speechless.

"That's right, Marco. If I'm psychic, then you can prove that I could have saved Danny but didn't. And if it's all my fault, then you can stop feeling guilty about his death."

"That's absurd."

"Is it?"

He raked his fingers through the loose strands of his dark hair and appeared to be counting to ten. "Suppose you're right, which you aren't. What do you care? Last time I noticed you didn't give a damn what I thought about you."

I sucked up my shoulders, content that my facade had fooled him. "You're right. You're absolutely right. I don't give a damn what you think."

"Then take the test! Lola needs you, Baker."

I turned to him as if he'd just spoken in a Martian language. "What did you say?"

"She needs you. That's what family is all about."

I swallowed hard as my chest deflated. He was right. She did need me. And that, more than anything, was why I didn't want to take the test. Because if I was psychic, then that meant she probably was, too. And I'd have to forgive her.

"What are you so afraid of?"

I looked at his penetrating frown and knew he had me cornered, though I would never admit defeat. "Fine. I'll do it. And when the test shows you that you're wrong, I don't want you to ever bring up this topic again. And then I never want to see you again. And I don't want you to ever see Mike again, because he conspired with you, and—"

"Save it, Baker."

And I did. I shook my head lightly to clear it and

walked over to the site director. "I'm sorry to keep you waiting, Mr. Steele. What do I need to do?"

I started out by looking at the backs of a series of cards portraying various objects. The woman who tested me would look at the card, think about it, and then slide it toward me facedown. I had to guess what the object was without turning the card over. The tests began quite simply with four different colors, then moved on to more complicated objects such as dogs and cats, then numbers.

I had trouble concentrating at first. Just before the lights surrounding our testing booth went dark, I could see Marco and Robert Steele watching me through the glass observatory window. I felt a little self-conscious and realized I was feeling testing anxiety. Pretty silly since I suspected most people failed this test. But something else was bothering me. I kept thinking about the woman on the other side of the partition.

Dr. Roz Hunter was an attractive brunette who looked to be in her thirties. It was hard to tell because her long hair was pulled back in a braid and she had big glasses that distanced her periwinkle-blue eyes. Steele said she was a parapsychology expert, so I assumed she was a Ph.D. and not an M.D. In any event, I couldn't help but feel we had met before.

Finally I tuned out all distractions and completed the tests, which concluded with a series of questions I had to answer on a computer. My answers, I knew, were being projected on a monitor in the observatory booth, just as my verbal responses to the cards had been piped in earlier. Very high-tech. I could understand why Steele was afraid of losing taxpayer funding.

When I finished the last test, Dr. Hunter came to the computer table where I'd been working and touched my shoulder. "That's it, Ms. Baker. You can go out to the observatory room now."

I stood and squeezed the bridge of my nose. My eyes were burning. I felt like a fool and wished that somehow I hadn't gotten roped into this. "How did I do?"

"Fine." She smiled reassuringly. "Mr. Steele will tell you about your results."

When she walked away, I had the feeling I'd been a disappointment to her. Even though I always found it hard to fail at things, doing so in this case would be good. It would mean I wasn't psychic and I could get Marco off my back.

Dr. Hunter hit a switch and the track lights in the ceiling slowly brightened. I could once again see outside of the testing lab. I looked for Marco, eager to gloat over my "failure." Then I did a double take. Where once there had been just Marco and Mr. Steele, now there were perhaps fifteen others crowded in front of the glass panel. They all stared at me with dumbfounded expressions.

What had I done wrong? Then I focused on Marco. He broke into a smug grin and arched one brow in a look I would have recognized a mile away. *I told you so.*

Steele, uncharacteristically at a loss for words, leaned toward a microphone and broke the silence.

"Ms. Baker, your score is off the charts. We're, uh, we're going to want to do further testing on you."

On the ride home, I didn't say anything and Marco wisely focused on driving. I'd politely turned down Steele's offer of further testing but gave him my name and number and said I'd be in touch. I was so shaken by the test results that I didn't even think to ask if there was anyone at IPAC who could help me find Lola. Then again, if the test results were accurate, I wouldn't need any help.

I watched the high-rise apartment buildings lining Lake Shore Drive zoom by as we sped north out of the city. The further we went, the more downtown looked like one of the tourist snow globes you could buy at O'Hare Airport—compact and dazzling.

The Chicago area, or Chicagoland as it's called, is a sprawling grid of endless suburbs. Downtown, though, is a majestic cluster of looming skyscrapers that cast long shadows on a lake so big it might as well be an ocean. It was all an architect's dream. In spite of its problems, Chicago truly was one of the great cities of the world—and one of the most expensive.

Thinking about my town always brought me out of myself, and right now I wanted to be anywhere but trapped inside of me. I barely noticed when Marco took a detour at the Lincoln Park exit and tooled down to the sandy public beach. He parked the cruiser and went around to my side of the vehicle, opened the door and offered a hand. I released it as soon as I was on solid footing.

"Come on," he said, "let's take a walk."

We strolled near the shoreline, which lapped gently with water that I always found surprisingly cold. Sunbathers dotted the beach, kids rollicked with beach balls and Frisbees, and bicyclists cruised by on the nearby bike path. When we fell into an easy rhythm, Marco began his pitch.

"The way I see it, Baker, is this. Regardless of Lola's occupation as a fake psychic, it just so happens that you are genuinely gifted in that area."

"Maybe the test was wrong," I said in a monotone.

"Steele explained the statistics to me. It's simply not possible. You are a true, blue telepath."

"I don't want to be a telepath," I practically snarled. "Don't you get it? This is like telling a prosecuting attorney that when the moon is full he turns into a serial killer with long, pointy claws."

"That's not a good comparison. Think about how much good you can do."

I heaved a sigh. "Maybe."

"I was in psy-ops for years. That's an umbrella term for a large department that covers everything from propaganda to psychological evaluations to parapsychological investigations. We have a whole team of psychics who work with detectives, and most of them were trained at IPAC."

"What do you mean, trained? According to Steele, you're either gifted or not."

"We all have some extrasensory perceptions. I think most people have had the experience of thinking about someone and a second later that person calls on the phone. Haven't you heard stories about a person who gets a bad feeling about a ride on the train and takes the bus only to find out later that the train crashed that afternoon?"

"I thought those were urban legends," I said, crossing my arms over my chest as we strolled.

"Perhaps, but there's often a core of truth in urban legends. A hundred years ago the only people who could help police investigations were the genuinely gifted telepaths. They were few and far between. IPAC helps people like that strengthen their skills. But for the last twenty years or so they've been using a telepathic enhancing computer chip designed by Clear Sight Technologies. It's implanted in the brain. The program captures ESP images in the carrier and magnifies them, freezing the images in still shots."

I stopped walking and looked up at him, amazed as always by how far technology was changing our world. "These people can actually see the future?"

"Whatever natural capabilities they have are enhanced. Some people see scenes from the future, some from the past, some can locate people and items by touching objects associated with them. The people who choose this profession and accept the implant are called Clear Sighters. It comes from the word 'clairvoyance,' which is French for clear sight."

I was more inclined to trust implanted technology than any so-called natural ability. Increasingly it seemed like the machines would be the ones left standing victorious over humans at the end of time...along with the cockroaches.

"Sounds like those tests were a waste of time,

then," I said belligerently. "You don't need natural psychics if you can create them. Let's call Detective Hoskins and get a Clear Sighter on Lola's case right now."

Light-headed, I stopped and dabbed perspiration beading on my temples. The sun blazed down on us.

Marco stopped a second later and turned back. "Are you okay?"

I nodded. "Just hot."

He reached out to support my elbow, then pulled his hand back at the last second. I glanced up and caught his frown just before he smoothed it over.

"You're afraid of me," I said.

"No, Baker, I'm not."

"You think I'm a freak because of those tests."

He rolled his eyes. "You are not a freak."

"Then why did you stop yourself from touching me."

"I didn't want you to think I was patronizing you?"

I looked hard at him, waiting for him to admit that he now considered me as bizarre as my mother, but he held his ground. Shrinks were good at that. I turned and started back toward the car. "Let's go before I melt."

We started back toward the cruiser. "Clear Sighters have one big drawback," he continued.

"Just one?"

"The transmission from the computer chip to cognitive pathways in the brain can be short-circuited under certain circumstances."

"Like what?"

"Sometimes a simple electrical anomaly in the environment can interfere, though that's rare. The greatest threat comes from R.M.O. operatives. They have technology that can short out computer-enhanced telepathy entirely."

I took this in, then stopped. I felt like I was playing the obtuse Watson to his clever Sherlock Holmes. He'd laid out all the clues, but I still couldn't quite put together why he cared about my talents in this area. "So you think that I'm the only one who can find Lola because the R.M.O. will short-circuit any other computer-enhanced operative called in to work on this case."

"Yes."

I stuffed my hands into my jeans and felt my hip-bones. I couldn't remember the last time I'd eaten a decent meal. "Did it ever occur to you that if I had the ability to envision Lola's whereabouts I would have done so already?"

"Yes, it has. But using psychic ability is like driving a car. You can't even turn on the engine until somebody gives you the key. In this case, the key is confirmation of your ability. You just need confidence, and a little practice."

He sounded perfectly reasonable, but that hard nut inside my chest that my doctor called a heart tightened with suspicion. He had to get something out of this, too, or he wouldn't be going to so much trouble.

"So what do you want?" I said bluntly.

He raised his brows. "What do you mean?"

"What do you get out of this? You want the credit if I find her? Is that it?"

He gave me a dimpled grin. "You're damned cynical, Angel Baker."

"Damned right I am. And hot, too."

"Come on. I'll turn on the air." He motioned toward the car. It was only a hundred yards away.

We continued on and stopped when we reached the front passenger door. He electronically unlocked the door, but when I tried to open it, he shut it again and leaned against it, crossing his arms.

"Okay, you're right," he said. "I do want something from you."

"I knew it."

"But it's not recognition or glory. I don't give a damn about that."

My eyes narrowed. "What then?"

"I do have interest in your telepathy regarding my brother's case, but not in the way you think. I want you to use your skills to help me find out what happened just before Danny was gunned down. I don't think traditional methods of detection are going to work. There's some kind of cover-up going on."

"What do you mean, cover-up?"

"After I looked at your file on Master Comp the other night, I looked up Dan's partner. The next day he skipped town. Someone tipped him off that I'd been snooping into his record. I know I'm on to something. And since Dan was killed during a drug deal with the R.M.O., I need someone to help me investigate the mob, someone whose brain can't be short-circuited at the crucial moment."

I considered his proposition carefully. It would feel good to bring closure to Danny Black's case.

But could I work with his brother and keep my emotional distance? For some reason that I couldn't understand, I trusted Marco. If I trusted him too much, I might let down my guard. And I knew all too well how that would turn out.

I crossed my arms again, which seemed the safest pose when his pheromones were igniting electrical fires in the most indecent parts of my body.

"I might consider your proposition, Detective Marco, if you offer to help me in return."

He held out his open hands. "I'm all yours."

If only that were true, I thought as I eyed the dark, silky chest hair peeking out of his open collar. "Great, then we have a deal."

"But on one condition," he said.

Here it came. "Oh?"

"When we've closed both cases—and together I believe we will—you give up your work as a CRS."

I laughed and tilted my head in exaggerated confusion. "Excuse me, are you my father?"

"It's wrong, Baker. What you do is wrong."

"Oh, so now you're my priest."

The set of his square jaw hardened and his nostrils flared. I was getting under his skin. Now this was fun.

"If I told you the real reason I'm asking this of you," he said, "I doubt you'd believe me."

"Try me."

"I'm worried about you."

"You're right. I don't believe you."

He nodded and looked into the distance. Then he pushed off the car and went around to the driver's side. We got in and drove awhile in silence, which he broke, saying, "I shouldn't tell you this, but my committee believes the state legislature is going to outlaw the retribution profession in the next session. I don't want them to make an example out of you. With the brouhaha over the Gibson Warrants, things are going to get ugly. If the mayor's political enemies find out you did a job for him, you'll be the poster child for the anti-CRS movement."

"I'll take my chances. If the law is passed, I'll start zapping burgers for a living. Meanwhile, we don't have to let that stop us from working together."

He looked at me with a bittersweet smile. I braced myself for what was coming next. "I'm sorry, Baker. I can't work with you until you swear off your profession. I'm the head of the committee who has been lobbying for the new law."

"So you're worried what others will think if you hang with me."

He didn't nod. He didn't need to. I blinked hard and looked out the window. We were now on Addison, passing Wrigley Field. I shut my eyes and saw a vision of my former fiancé, Peter Brandt. Handsome, brilliant Peter. I was going to be his partner, help him achieve his potential in investigative journalism. But I wasn't quite good enough for Peter. While he could and did use my connection to Henry Bassett to forward his career, in the long run he needed someone with cachet, with class.

I didn't say any more until we arrived back at my two-flat. "No need to get out. I can see myself in."

I opened the door and stepped onto the sidewalk,

bending to look at him in the car for my parting shot. "News flash, Marco. I guess you were right about this whole psychic thing. I just had a vision of the future. And it doesn't include you."

With that I slammed the door.

Chapter 12

Wizard of Oz

I went upstairs and checked in with Mike. He'd taken a couple of messages—one from the P.I. I had hired to watch Lancaster's Shelter. All was quiet on the western side of Chicago. No sign of Drummond.

Detective Hoskins called to say he'd placed a surveillance crew at Lola's apartment. So far there had been no return of the R.M.O., according to undercover police operatives. Hoskins said it was surprising, but that Lola's kidnapping and the assassination attempt on me and Marco might have been an anomaly. In other words, Lola had probably pissed somebody off, was now dead in an alley and her nosy daughter was long forgotten.

I refused to believe that Lola was dead, but was happy to hear that the Sgarristas were otherwise occupied. Meanwhile, Hoskins was going to pay Vladimir Gorky a visit and canvas some of the Russian stores on West Devon. I doubted Hoskins would get anywhere near Gorky. He didn't have the clout.

Mike didn't ask any questions about my visit to IPAC. As usual, he would wait until I was ready to talk about it, even though I knew he wanted me to use this so-called ability of mine to help him find his brother. Unlike Marco, Mike would never pressure me. That made me feel all the more responsible to help him. Meanwhile, he excused himself to work out in the garden.

Without consciously deciding to, I retrieved Lola's crystal ball and tripod and placed them in the middle of the kitchen table. Just curious, I told myself. I poured a glass of water and sipped while I stared at the ball.

Don't go there, a voice inside my head warned me. *Don't go anywhere near there.* But I did.

I put my empty water glass in the sink and sat at the table, then cracked knuckles in preparation for a laying on of the hands, and changed my mind. I quickly rose and poured a cup of coffee. I sipped from my mug while I leaned against the sink and watched the afternoon light play off the crystal. Mike's workout noises floated in through the screen door—*Aaaaaiiiieeee. Heeeeyaaaaa. Hawuuuu!*

Finally, I sat and placed my hands on the ball. It was room temperature. No surprise there. Instinctively, I knew the room should be dark. It would be hard to see any images with the sun glaring in. So what? If this crap was going to work, it would have to be without any help from me. I listened to the old-fashioned clock tick in the hallway. It dated from the reign of Elizabeth II. I'd picked it up at the great little antique shop on Halsted. What a deal. I remember—

"Holy shit!" I stared in amazement as a face appeared in the ball. No, make that an eye. A big, bloodshot, creepy eyeball. It was as if the scrying crystal was a monocle and someone was trying to focus through it at me. I jumped back and the image disappeared.

My heart pounded three times for every second the clock ticked. I gripped the edge of the table. *I had to see more.* It was like paying to see a scary movie. You can't leave until the end, even if you watch the whole thing through a crack between your fingers.

Swallowing hard, I forced myself to breathe and placed my hands back on the ball. This time it was warm. *Something was really happening here.* I couldn't deny it. Images flowed herky-jerky. It reminded me of one of those little pads of paper with sequential drawings that you get in party bags when you're a kid—you flip through the pages and the character moves. The faster you flip, the smoother the motion appears.

The first image was in black and white. A thin, big-eyed man was spitting out orders I couldn't hear. I could see the images in the crystal ball and in my head at the same time. It was a strange sort of depth perception. Then the ball went black.

"No!" I cried. "Come back."

I willed my energy through my fingers, trying to warm things up. If the heat of my touch triggered images, the warmer the better. Or was it the images that triggered the heat? Suddenly sound added into the mix. I heard crying, but it wasn't Lola. It was a young girl, or several young girls. Then I heard water dripping. Each drop echoed as it hit a pool, slow and undisturbed like water that coagulates in a cave. Did that explain the darkness?

The ball brightened suddenly. Actually, the image simply vanished and what I now stared at was the sun reflecting off the glass. The vision was gone. I felt robbed. It was like listening to music on a super digital system, then switching to an antique hi-fi whose needle has reached the scratchy end of a vinyl record.

"Damn it!" I pulled my hands away, still staring at the dark globe. Already I was addicted to the images I'd seen. I wanted more. It was like magic, a different world I never knew existed. Except it was this world, and whatever I'd seen either had happened, was happening now or was about to happen.

I sank back in my chair, dumbfounded. Marco had compared this to learning to drive a car. If only I could sign up for lessons. What was I supposed to do with this information?

Mike came up the back stairs from the garden. He opened the door and focused on the ball, then eagerly looked at me. "What?"

"What what?" My lips thinned. "You knew I'd do it, didn't you?"

He padded silently across the ceramic tile floor

in bare feet and sat across from me at the table. "What you see?"

I explained the brief, seemingly disconnected visions. After recounting the weird eyeball that focused on me, I shivered.

"Mike, it was like a scene out of *The Wizard of Oz*, when the witch looks back at Dorothy through the crystal ball."

"Oz Wizard?" he asked.

"*The Wizard of Oz*. It's a classic movie all American kids see at least once. The little girl named Dorothy gets lost in a tornado and ends up in the land of little people." His frown deepened. "She has to get to the Emerald City so the wizard can magically transport her back to Kansas, though God knows why she wants to do that. Anyway, when she gets there she discovers the wizard is a fraud, but she catches a ride in a hot-air balloon—actually she never quite gets in, but then—"

I stopped, not only because I was tired of hearing myself talk, but because it hit me. "Emerald City," I whispered.

Mike's sable eyes finally lit. "That is the city under Chicago. People with no homes live there."

"Yes." Our gazes locked. A chill of premonition and excitement spread over my flesh. Downtown Chicago. Years ago Lower Wacker Drive, which wound under the Loop just south of the Chicago River, was lit with fluorescent green bulbs and dubbed the Emerald City. Lots of homeless found havens and hideouts in the nooks and crannies of the subterranean street. Even though the green lights were eventually replaced with sodium vapor lights, the name stuck.

A century later when the homeless took over the abandoned underground subway rails on the north side of the river to create a more permanent home, they carried the name Emerald City with them. I didn't know much about the inhabitants, except that they were called moles, for obvious reasons. Many of them never see the light of day.

I shut my eyes and recalled my vision—so much darkness and moisture, like a cave. Then I recalled the brief vision I'd had of Lola when I'd first touched the crystal ball in her apartment. She'd been crying for help, a vision of tatty red hair and dripping mascara against a sea of black. A bolt of certainty seared through me. Lola was there. Underground.

"Mike, Lola is somewhere in Emerald City, I just know it."

"Then we go there," Mike said simply.

"Yes."

There was no question about it. I'd been great at avoiding business with the moles. I wasn't prejudiced against them, but I'd heard some creepy stories. Some of the more primitive clans bred and harvested rats to supplement their foraging. I'd have to talk to Hank first and get the facts straight.

"We'll go as soon as I talk to my foster brother, the kid wonder. If anyone can prepare me for this, it's Henry Bassett Junior."

One of the things I love most about this crazy day and age is the eclectic clothing you see on the commuter trains. I watched the free fashion show in the crush of passengers who loaded and unloaded at every stop on the old elevated Red Line during the ride downtown.

There was a Hasidic Jew who wore a timeless black suit, braids and Coke-bottle glasses, a young girl dressed like Queen Elizabeth I in a six-inch-deep white ruff collar and a farthingale petticoat that stuck out a foot all around. There was a businessman in a tailored suit and a middle-aged woman who wore only a thong and a paste-on bra. It was a regular circus.

Every day in this town is a masquerade. Clothes aren't just expressions of individuality, they're cultural markers. These days you get to choose your identity, unless you're in one of the ultra subnational mobs. If you're in the Cosa Nostra, the R.M.O., the IRA, the Mongolian Mob or any number of other national syndicates, you touted your pure bloodlines and tried to marry within your own ethnic enclave. Otherwise, over the last century, America had become amazingly integrated.

I credited the rise of computers. If people spend all their time on the Internet—shopping, chatting, playing games—then their world becomes almost medieval in its social simplicity and isolation. Think about it. If you socialize on the World Wide Web instead of the town square, who is going to ostracize you for marrying "one of those people"? No one. You're in a world of your own making and, *voilà!* Tolerance sneaks in the back door.

Over the course of a hundred years, technology

allowed America to finally achieve the impossible dream: racial and ethnic tolerance. While there were still definable ethnic neighborhoods in the city, these days most people's genealogy charts look like the ingredient list on a bottle of ketchup.

The chick in the Elizabethan costume probably couldn't tell you if she had more African, Swedish or Irish blood in her veins. But she could tell you all about who belongs to the Elizabethan Society she visits nightly on the Internet.

The only groups that adamantly polarize around their ethnicity are the mobs and gangs, and that's because their culture is what sets them apart and enables them to remain a unique money-making entity. Dirty money, but money nonetheless. And this is America, after all. We may have achieved racial integration, but we'll never stop worshiping the almighty dollar.

The politics of fashion often led to comical results. After watching my fill of jiggling cellulite on the middle-aged woman's butt, I concluded that thongs shouldn't be sold without a license. Of course, I had no right to remark on unusual styles. Mike wore a dark yellow monk's robe and I literally wore a suit of armor, albeit one that looked like silk.

The problem with millifine steel is that while it deflects bullets and blades, it's hot as blazes and not entirely flexible, like a long-sleeved denim shirt left out to dry in the sun. I felt a little like the Tin Man, which was appropriate considering our mission, but I promised Henry I'd be careful of the Sgarristas, although I hoped we wouldn't run into any downtown.

We spilled out of the train station into the river of rush-hour traffic flowing down the sidewalk and made our way past Water Tower Place. I went into hypervigilant mode. A retribution specialist never knows when she'll run into someone she's bagged in the past. Mike was tense, too. He hated downtown. He hurried ahead of me until we reached the TV station.

We met my brother Hank on the management level. He took one look at my outfit and frowned. "You in trouble?"

"Nah," I said, giving him a hug. "Just wanted to make your pop happy."

Hugging Hank was always heaven. I loved him unconditionally. He was taller than me and strong enough, but somehow he hugged like pudding. I let him go and gave him a sisterly once-over. "Look at you! Handsome as usual."

I shoved a lock of his tousled cinnamon hair behind his ear and waited for that "Aw, shucks, leave me alone" look that made a mess of his softly freckled face. It was a game we played. While he looked like Jimmy White from *Superman,* he was brilliant and already a relentless journalist. I resisted the urge to gush "I'm so *proud* of you!" Lola had said that to me recently, and I had vowed I would never turn into my mother.

"Let's go to my office." Hank led us to the newsroom, which was reassuringly chaotic as producers and on-air talent prepared for the five-o'clock news. Police alerts sounded in the assignment room, where stories flashed in red on the assignment board. Interns who would sell their souls for a chance to go on camera tensely dashed around while the seasoned journalists who'd already supervised the editing of their reports joked at the water cooler about the six floaters dragged yesterday from Lake Michigan. Apparent suicides.

I never got used to reporters' lackadaisical attitudes toward death, even though I knew it was necessary for those who had to deal with tragedy every day. Here, everyone except for the top reporters dressed like they were in a war zone—bulletproof flak jackets and boots—and with the snipers that frequented downtown, it was necessary.

Mike and I followed Hank like ducklings into his small office where he'd been researching his latest undercover segment on the effects of hydrogen emissions on the environment. He told us the hole in the ozone layer created by outmoded carbon dioxide was closing back up. But the new energy source was creating problems of its own, a new kind of pollution whose effects were still not understood. Cause and effect, Henry used to lecture us. Everything in the universe has a cause and effect. It was a lot like karma.

Henry Jr. poured two cups of coffee and handed me one.

"I won't even bother to offer you coffee, Mike, but help yourself to the water," he said as he sank into his chair and propped his soft-soled shoes on the desk. He grabbed a pencil and twirled it in his fingers. "What's up, sis?"

"I told you already about Lola's problems with the R.M.O."

"I assume that's why you're wearing that sexy armor." His brown eyes sparkled with humor and journalistic curiosity.

"You'll have to admit, it does accent my best and hide my worst features," I said, shrugging out of the jacket and hanging it over the back of my chair. Then seriously, I said, "The police believe the Mafiya took her. So do I. But I have reason to believe she's being held underground."

"Emerald City?" he said. He physically recoiled as he whispered the words. That shook me up. Hank had seen it all at the ripe age of twenty-five, as does anyone who works in the news business.

"What's the matter?" I asked with an uneasy chuckle. "You act as if I just said she was being held by ghouls and trolls."

"That's not far from the truth from what I hear," he said, shaking his head. "We had a reporter go down there one time and never return. It's like a bog. People get swallowed up and are never seen again."

I stared hard at him, then exchanged a look with Mike. A jolt of fear crisscrossed between us and I swallowed hard. As I held Mike's steady gaze, I remembered one of his many platitudes that always put things in perspective. *The Buddha once said, Birth and death are like sunrise and sunset. Now come. Now go.* Easy come, easy go. Even I could understand that. I was, if nothing else, a fatalist.

I let go of my captive breath and looked at my brother calmly. "I'm going to go after Lola, Hank. I know the dangers. I accept them. Mike feels the same way. He's looking for his brother. We're in this together. You don't have to worry about me."

"Thanks, but if it's all the same to you, I will worry. Only in my spare time, mind you." He twirled the pencil. "Let me ask you this. How do you know Lola's there?"

From the corner of my eye, I saw Mike shift his weight. I did so, as well. "I can't say." Actually, I wouldn't say. *It's the whole vision thing, Hank. Psychic nah-nah-noo-noo. Like mother like daughter.* "I can't reveal my sources."

He chuckled and leaned back in his chair. "I can relate. Well, I know I won't change your mind. Did you tell Mom and Dad you're doing this?"

I bit my lower lip. "Not exactly."

"Gotcha. Mum's the word."

"Thanks."

"The least I can do is tell you what I know about that hellhole so you can go in with eyes wide open. And they will be, literally. It's pitch-black down there."

"But I thought it was fully lit, like the station at Chicago and State."

"That's just a tourist trap. The tourists come down and look around, listen to a lecture about Emerald City's founding fathers, buy primitive art painted by moles, take a few pictures and leave. It's the underground's version of an interpretative center. But if you go far enough through the rail tunnels you'll find nothing but inky fingers of abandoned railways lit by the occasional gas outlet. Now and then there's a gas explosion. There's one pocket of moles who survived a bad blast about ten years ago. They were badly scarred. Jon Moore, one of our researchers, tells me the burn survivors are treated like a leper colony by the other moles."

"How does anybody know what goes on there if no one comes back?"

"Some do, but they're mostly N.G.O. types and ministers who go there to help the homeless. The moles don't like writers and reporters snooping around. And like most subcultures on the edge of society, the moles's leaders want to control everything. They don't want to be mainstreamed because that means they'll lose power. So on behalf of their captive followers, the Emerald City council members have spurned all efforts to integrate their people back into normal society."

"How do you know all this?" I still didn't quite understand how reporters did what they did.

"Jon told me. He pulled a groundhog." He took a long sip of coffee, clearly thinking an explanation was unnecessary.

"Okay, I'll bite. What's a groundhog?"

He frowned in exaggerated dismay. "I thought you retribution specialists heard it all on the streets."

"We don't listen," I deadpanned. "We do the talking."

"So true," Mike muttered without cracking a smile as he gave me a long-suffering glare.

Hank laughed out loud. "You've got her number, Mike. Okay, let me explain. A groundhog is someone who abandons Emerald City and comes back up above ground to live. Most people don't know the

difference between a free-ranger and a groundhog.
Moles think of free-rangers as wayward souls who
foolishly choose to live aboveground. But ground-
hogs are considered traitors. Jon could write a book
about his experiences, let me tell you. There he is
now talking to another reporter." Hank motioned to
a young man leaning against a desk in the newsroom
across from his office and gestured for him to step
inside.

"Hey, Jon, this is my sister, Angel, and her friend
Mike. They want to wander around Emerald City.
Can she call you if she needs anything?"

"Sure."

Jon was older than Hank by about five years, I'd
guess. He was five-foot-seven, thin and very pale.
Ghost pale. He wore dark sunglasses, which he lowered down his nose to pierce me with pupils that had
forgotten how to contract. They were like marbles,
hard and permanent. My skin prickled beneath that
eerie gaze. The glasses went back up and the moment passed.

Catching Jon's look, Hank said, "Yeah, I know,
she's nuts, but you won't talk her out of it, believe
me. She wants to find somebody down there who's
been kidnapped. Go over the map in the newsroom
with her, will you, and show her all the working tunnels?"

"Sure."

Man of few words, I thought. I guess he still had
a lot to learn about social graces aboveground.

Hank turned to me. "Jon lived down under, as it
were, until he was eighteen. He came up for an edu-

cation and has been here ever since. Some members of his extended family consider him a traitor, but his parents wanted him to have a better life. After college, he was hired here at the station as a consultant and researcher. He gives us all the background we need when stories break from down below."

We chatted awhile, made arrangements, then Jon left. "His eyes are…penetrating," I remarked.

"Even though he's been a groundhog for nearly a decade, he still can't handle the light. His eyes never really adjusted. Hence, the sunglasses." Hank reached for a file on his desk. "By the way, I did some digging on the north side R.M.O. hierarchy. It may come in handy. I also did a run on Lola's background. She has quite a history."

My skin burned down to the roots of my hair. After all these years, her criminal background still embarrassed me. Especially when the subject came up with members of my foster family, who had as much integrity as Lola had scams.

Hank pursed his lips as he reviewed the information. "I think it's very possible she did a reading for Vladimir Gorky. I'm not sure you know, Angel, just how well connected your mom is."

"With the bad guys, you mean."

"Yeah, well, those lines get blurrier every day, don't they?"

"Not if you're a decent person."

He closed the folder. "That's what I've always loved best about you, Angel. You expect a lot from others. And yourself. Too much, sometimes."

"Let's cut with the Freudian analysis, little bro." I crossed my legs with some effort. My steel pants shimmered from the overhead lighting. "Why did the Mafiya take her? And if they did, why is she being held underground? The Sgarristas don't usually associate with moles, do they?"

"No. I dunno what gives here, but I'll keep digging." He leaned forward and slumped a cheek in his upraised hand, looking at me as if I were an impossible puzzle. "Angel, I've always looked up to you."

My face softened with a wary half smile. "Uh-oh, here comes the lecture."

"I've never questioned your judgment." He frowned and wiped his supporting hand over his face, leaning back with a loud sigh. "I don't know how to say this without hurting you but…is she really worth it?"

My smile faded. What was Lola worth to me? My own life? She would never have risked hers for me. So what was I trying to prove by rescuing my mother? That I could go one better than her? Was I trying to rub in her face that blood ties really mattered? I wasn't so sure myself. Maybe I was the one I was trying to convince.

"I don't know, Hank," I said at last. "I just know I'm going to do this. Trust me. I'll come back alive."

He looked at me like someone waving goodbye to a loved one for the last time. Then he laughed. "Sure, sis. I know you will. You always do."

Chapter 13

Rick's Café Americain

Mike and I talked at length with Jon about where we should go once we entered the black labyrinth underground. After picking his brain, we decided to head north to the old Wrigleyville station. Jon's clan squatted there and he said his family would give us advice on where to look for Lola. He assured us most moles were friendly and just trying to get by like anybody above ground. The problem was the Rogues and the Shadowmen.

The Rogues were descendants of the mentally ill who'd sought shelter in the abandoned subway system during the healthcare crisis in the early 2000s. They were usually loners and erratic at best.

The Shadowmen were members of a vicious gang

that sometimes went aboveground to fight as mercenaries for other gangs. They spent most of their hours weight lifting and ate lots of meat. I liked to think they raised rabbits in underground warrens, but more likely they hunted plentiful rats. According to Jon, the Shadowmen were monstrous, unconscionable thugs who should be avoided at all costs.

A lone Rogue I was confident I could handle, but the Shadowmen weighed heavily on my mind as we traveled home. Mike and I decided it would be best to leave in complete darkness. There was a little time to kill. I listened to my messages as I dressed for our late-night mission.

When I heard Marco's recorded voice, I froze and felt a strange quiver inside. It had been a long time since I'd both dreaded and eagerly awaited contact from the same man. I couldn't concentrate on his words. It was pathetic. Get a grip, Baker! I hit Replay and listened closer.

I know what you're up to, Baker. You've decided to go it alone. But you need my help.

"Like hell I do," I said to the answering disk.

I'm coming over.

"Shit."

I'll be there no later than eight.

I looked at the clock. It was seven forty-five. "I've got to get out of here."

Don't be stupid, Baker. We're in this together.

I bristled at that. He didn't know anything about me. I would succeed or fail on my own just as I had since I was seven. I quickly dressed in my black cat-burglar-style outfit, strapped my organizer on my leg and headed down to Rick's Café. I'd wait there until Mike came for me. Marco would never think to look for me there.

The sidewalk outside the AutoMates Reality Bar at the corner of Southport and Roscoe was crowded with locals and tourists who mingled with second-beer buzzes, deep in sometimes-slurred conversation. Above them a neon sign declared that this was Rick's Café Americain.

I strolled in through the side entrance and immediately walked into a haze of unfiltered French cigarette smoke and a soft breeze from the giant overhead fans. The place smelled like 1942 Morocco.

Obviously I'd never been there, but I'd seen the movie *Casablanca* a million times. I thought I could detect the scents of the north African city where so many had gone to escape Nazi-occupied Europe. I stood a moment, taking it all in—the bristly worsted wool of double-breasted suits on men seated at the crowd of round tables. Even though they were compubots, they somehow managed to sweat in their crisp white shirts from the Mediterranean heat pumped in through the vents, giving the place a vividly accurate air.

The men chatted with small-waisted compubot women dressed in vintage World War II–era suits and dresses that carried heady whiffs of classic perfumes like Coco Chanel No. 5 and a vanilla hint of Shalimar. Automates, Inc. left no detail to chance.

There were several of these classic movie fran-

The Silhouette Reader Service™ — Here's how it works:

Accepting your 2 free books and gift places you under no obligation to buy anything. You may keep the books and gift and return the shipping statement marked "cancel." If you do not cancel, about a month later we'll send you 4 additional books and bill you just $4.69 each in the U.S., or $5.24 in Canada, plus 25¢ shipping & handling per book and applicable taxes if any.* That's the complete price and — compared to cover prices of $5.50 each in the U.S. and $6.50 each in Canada — it's quite a bargain! You may cancel at any time, but if you choose to continue, every month we'll send you 4 more books, which you may either purchase at the discount price or return to us and cancel your subscription.

*Terms and prices subject to change without notice. Sales tax applicable in N.Y. Canadian residents will be charged applicable provincial taxes and GST. Credit or debit balances in a customer's account(s) may be offset by any other outstanding balance owed by or to the customer.

NO POSTAGE
NECESSARY
IF MAILED
IN THE
UNITED STATES

BUSINESS REPLY MAIL

FIRST-CLASS MAIL   PERMIT NO. 717-003   BUFFALO, NY

POSTAGE WILL BE PAID BY ADDRESSEE

SILHOUETTE READER SERVICE
3010 WALDEN AVE
PO BOX 1867
BUFFALO NY 14240-9952

GET FREE BOOKS and a FREE GIFT WHEN YOU PLAY THE...

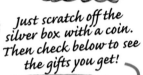

SLOT MACHINE GAME!

Just scratch off the silver box with a coin. Then check below to see the gifts you get!

YES! I have scratched off the silver box. Please send me the 2 free Silhouette Bombshell® books and gift for which I qualify. I understand I am under no obligation to purchase any books, as explained on the back of this card.

300 SDL D34A   **200 SDL D34C**

| |
| |
FIRST NAME   LAST NAME

ADDRESS

APT.#   CITY

STATE/PROV.   ZIP/POSTAL CODE

7	7	7
🍒	🍒	🍒
♣	♣	♣
🔔	🔔	🍒

Worth TWO FREE BOOKS plus a **BONUS** Mystery Gift!

Worth TWO FREE BOOKS!

Worth ONE FREE BOOK!

TRY AGAIN!

www.eHarlequin.com

(S-B-08/04)

DETACH AND MAIL CARD TODAY!

chise bars in the Chicago area. Tiffany's was downtown, featuring an Audrey Hepburn compubot, and a place in Cicero featured James Cagney. Of all the gin joints in town, though, I walked into this one. Because it was in my own neighborhood. The only reason I was the lucky customer who always got to go home with the star was because I'd done a retribution job for one of the AutoMates executives a couple years ago.

I said hello to the Moroccan host at the door who wore a fez. Sam played the piano and sang with his usual bright smile gleaming in the smoky spotlight. He winked when he saw me enter through the oversize doors, never missing a note. The tourists at tables scattered around the large room were enraptured by his routine. Ingrid Bergman sat at a table alone, looking so damned classy I sighed. She took one look at me and her eyes narrowed.

I know AutoMates aren't programmed to feel on their own, but I swear she was jealous of me. Maybe I flattered myself. And maybe I took this whole reality entertainment thing too far. But it was a nice escape. I could use some of that before going to my possible death in the bowels of Chicago.

When Carl, the plump, white-haired waiter with the Austro-Hungarian accent, passed by in his bulging tuxedo, bearing a tray of martinis, I followed him to a table to catch his ear.

"Where's Rick?" I inquired after Carl deposited his drinks. Whenever I was here, I always called Bogie by the name of his character in *Casablanca*.

It lessened the chance of confusing the supporting cast and shorting out their programs.

"Rick?" he sniffed as he headed back to the bar, with me following. "Madam, he's probably in the back, having a private party."

"Tell him I want to have a drink with him."

"Rick never drinks with customers."

Yeah, yeah, yeah. I'd heard it all before. It was one of the great moments in the movie, when Rick suddenly agrees to drink with Ingrid—I mean, Ilsa, and her husband, Victor Laszlo. Rick was the classic cynic with the heart of gold.

Across the room he came out of the private room, where guests entered only at his invitation, and went to the bar. He struck a match, lighting a cigarette, and found me through the veil of smoke. Talk about smoldering looks. I was definitely going to have that drink. Unfortunately, it was going to be seltzer. I never imbibed before a job.

I meandered my way toward the bar, with one eye over my shoulder looking for Mike. The place was filling up fast. I stopped briefly to chat with a retributionist I'd met on the south side. But Bogie was waiting, and I moved on.

"Hello, Angel," he said when I reached the bar. He never cracked a smile, but I could tell by the glint in his eyes he was glad to see me. He was the master of understatement. "What brings you here?"

"I'm going out on a surveillance op and may not come back."

He took a drink from his bourbon glass. "You always come back, Angel."

"That's nice of you to say, Rick, but you never know when—" I glanced at the door and stopped cold. There was Mike standing out like a sore thumb in his martial arts garb, and beside him stood Detective Marco, looking dashing, as always, in his well-tailored suit with its knee-length coat. I made a mental note to kill Mike the next time we were alone for bringing Marco here.

The good detective was being obnoxiously persistent in his pursuit of me. I was almost flattered, but I didn't want him to know I'd resorted to robot and instead felt embarrassed, then indignant. What I did in my private life was none of his business. It was because of arrogant men like him that I'd turned to Bogie in the first place. I glared defiantly at Marco from the distance until he spotted me through the smoky room. When he saw me standing next to Bogie, his strong jaw turned to stone and he frowned. He was pissed. Good. I'd give him even more to stew over.

I turned back to Bogie and ran my hands up his flawless, sharply tailored white tuxedo. "Kiss me, Rick. Kiss me like it's the last time."

It was as if Pavlov had just rung his bell. Bogie heard that line from the movie and lunged for my lips. I half expected music to swell in the background. Instead, Sam and his orchestra finished a number and the place fell silent.

"Look!" a lady in red polka dots shouted to her husband, pointing at us. "Is that Rick and Ilsa? No, who is that woman? Was she in the movie?"

I reddened as it seemed the whole room was focused on our corner.

"Come on, Ms. Baker," Bogie said, "Let's go in the back."

I didn't argue when he took my arm and firmly led me to his private party room. I felt Ilsa's mental daggers in my back and gave her an immature grin of triumph as I departed. She strolled to Sam's piano, and I knew what song she would request.

No sooner had we reached the relative privacy of Rick's gaming room than Marco marched in. He shut the door behind him and slowly walked toward me, hands in his pockets, an ironic smile on his face. He stopped too close.

I put my hands on my hips and turned to him. "What do you want?"

"What the hell is this all about?"

"What is *what* all about?"

"This!" He motioned to Bogie, ignoring him completely. He obviously hadn't seen any of the "Compubots are people, too" ad campaign commercials. AutoMates had feelings, albeit preprogrammed feelings, and I felt indignant on Bogie's behalf.

"Don't be rude, Marco. This is Rick Blaine. He owns this place."

"Yeah, right."

Bogie stepped between us. "That's enough, Mr…?"

"Marco," I said, filling in the blank. "Detective Marco. He's a big shot, Rick. Educated out the wazoo, bent on revenge with a Superman complex. He'll use you up and spit you out and take no prisoners and make you feel the whole time like he really understands your feelings."

Bogie processed this smoothly. "I see. I'm sure Captain Renault can answer whatever questions you have, Detective Marco. He's the local authority here in Casablanca."

"Captain Renault?" Marco looked at me with labored patience, still ignoring Bogie.

"You know," I whispered, "the little French guy who's always running interference with the Nazis. He and Rick go off together at the end of the movie. It's one of the classic lines of all time. Rick says to Renault, 'Louie, I think this is the beginning of a beautiful friendship.' Don't tell me you haven't even seen *Casablanca*. Men like you kill me, Marco, you really do. Get some culture, for God's sake."

Marco finally turned his look of disbelief from me to Bogie. "I can't believe you'd resort to this…this *thing*. What are you doing with your life, Baker? Are you absolutely determined to throw it away?"

"Will you shut *up?*" My face positively burned. "You have no right to come in here and mock him, or anyone else. This is none of your business."

"It's time for you to go, Detective Marco," Bogie said, stepping forward.

When Bogie grabbed Marco's arm, he jerked it away. "Get your hands off me, you damned compu-bot."

"Marco, stop!" I hissed.

Suddenly the sounds of Sam playing "As Time Goes By" drifted in from the other room.

"I knew it!" I muttered. Ilsa *was* jealous. She had Sam play that song knowing Rick couldn't resist.

"If you'll excuse me." Bogie headed out of the room like a man walking to his destiny. My knight in shining armor had hung up his lance to trot after his beloved damsel, and Ingrid Bergman didn't even have to whistle.

I growled under my breath. "Boy, that was really mature, Marco. You almost got in a fight with a compubot, you know that?"

"You should talk. You almost got laid by one."

I bit my tongue. He didn't know the half of it.

"Look," he said, running his hand over his frown, "Mike told me you think you know where Lola is."

"Did he tell you where?"

"No. But I don't think now is the time to go off on a wild-goose chase. I just found out that the R.M.O. and the Mongolians are about to go to war over those missing Chinese orphans that have been in the news. The R.M.O. apparently stole the girls before the Mongolians could sell them on the black market."

"Maybe that's why the R.M.O. lost interest in us. They had bigger fish to fry." And maybe, I thought, that's where Lin came from. Janet Drummond said her husband had done work for Corleone Capone. "This sounds serious."

"It is," Marco said. "So promise me you won't go to Little Beijing and mess with Capone."

"I promise."

"And promise me you won't go to West Devon and get involved with Gorky's gang."

"No problem."

He looked at me so thoroughly goose bumps rose

on my arms. Suddenly it dawned on me—duh—he was jealous of Bogie. The air between us thickened and I swallowed.

"You're not going to tell me where you're going, are you?" he said in husky voice, now looking at my lips.

His gaze was like a laser beam, burning me up. "No."

He nodded. "I didn't think so."

He stepped even closer. I felt chilled, then flushed, then chilled again. God, what was he doing to me?

"So," he murmured, "use your talents, okay? Stay one step ahead of trouble."

"Okay." My voice was breathy. I couldn't get enough air. "I'm good at that."

"And wear this." He pulled a minuscule tracking device out of his jacket pocket and held it out between his thumb and forefinger. "This will tell headquarters where you are. If you get into trouble, turn it on. I've got a buddy at HQ who is going to keep an eye on the monitor for me. I'll be able to reach you at a moment's notice. Just pinch the little button in the middle and a silent alarm will go off."

"Sure, Marco. Thanks," I said, though I had no intention of turning it on. I held out my hand, and he dropped the silver button into my palm. I dropped the tracker into my pocket and gave him a dubious look. "So why are you giving up so easily? You're ridiculously tenacious. I thought you might pull my fingernails out one at a time until I told you what's up."

He shifted weight to one foot and slipped his hands into his pockets as he grinned. "Now why would I do that? If I try to play the hero, you'll just end up having to rescue me again. I have no doubt you'll succeed at whatever it is you're planning. Just be careful, Baker."

He whispered this last word in a tone so intimate I felt liked I'd been slammed up against a wall.

"Yeah," I brayed, "don't want to lose your free psychic, huh? Ha, ha."

He didn't even hear me. He was moving in for the kill—I mean, the kiss. His lips touched mine and my head literally swooned. Shit. *Shit, shit, shit.* Get a grip, Baker.

I pulled back, feigning boredom, but not fast enough. Bogie slipped back in the room and caught the tail end of our lip lock.

Marco grinned. "Uh-oh. Here comes your leading man." He looked down and winked at me, then gently chucked my chin with a fist. "Here's looking at you, kid."

I smiled, then shook my head as I watched him spin around and leave. So he *had* seen the movie. Damn, that man was playing me like a fiddle.

Marco nodded to Bogie on his way out. The dapper AutoMate sauntered my way. "So who was that?"

"That was trouble," I said. "Big trouble. With a capital T."

Chapter 14

Cosmo the Magnificent

By the time Mike and I left the bar, it was dark outside. As we walked toward the Southport station, I gave him a good tongue-lashing for taking Marco into his confidence. Mike took it with his usual serene expression. I had absolutely no idea what he was thinking, but I didn't think he was listening.

He clearly trusted Marco. Part of me felt betrayed and part of me was relieved. His confidence in Marco made me feel like I wasn't being a total idiot. As for swooning in Marco's arms, what was *that* all about? I couldn't think about that now.

Just before we reached the station, my lapel phone buzzed. I popped it in my ear.

"Baker here. You've got thirty seconds and it better be good."

"Angel, it's Hank. Whatever you're doing, stop and listen."

I stopped in the middle of the sidewalk and pressed the button more firmly in my ear. "Shoot."

"Jon called. He was able to make contact with his family. They'll be looking out for you just north of the Addison station."

Jon gave us directions to a secret entrance that fed into the underground. That meant we wouldn't have to start all the way downtown and work our way north. It beat the heck out of meandering through miles of abandoned subway tunnels hoping we wouldn't run into a band of Shadowmen trotting by in their jack boots. Best of all, the entrance was within walking distance of my apartment.

I thanked Hank profusely and turned to Mike as I pulled the button out of my ear and hung up. "Things are looking up, Mikey. Who would have thunk it? The moles' secret north side entrance is in the old Cubs stadium. Right under our noses."

The original home of the Cubs was built in 1914. It was a cozy, natural grass park with low seating close to the diamond and had retained its old-world charm to the end. Now it was a deteriorating relic etching the skyline, a fond memento like the Coliseum in Rome, minus the cats.

The Chicago Cubs baseball team abandoned the site in 2095, moving to TerraForma stadium that floated on Lake Michigan. The team owners said, in essence, build a new stadium and we will come—

or we move to Bali. Mayor Richard J. Daley VI cried uncle and the city financed the project.

Personally, I don't think the city should have subsidized billionaire players, especially since the team hasn't won a pennant since 1908. You can only hold your breath so long. But no one asked me. Naturally, the new stadium cost a fortune. The only people who can afford tickets are rich, which is convenient since most of them have yachts they can ride out to the stadium.

So the old bleacher bums who used to get drunk in the outfield and Wrigleyville locals who used to catch a game in the afternoon now come here to reminisce. For the cost of a beer, you can sit in what remains of the stadium and listen to a play-by-play of the division playoffs when the Cubbies had a real shot at victory.

We entered what remained of the oval concrete perimeter on the west side. Baseball fans filed in and out as if a real night game was going on. My heart tripped with excitement when I saw the floodlights filling the great, green oval space that contained the diamond.

I couldn't resist going up the ramp to get a good look at the action. There was a big crowd, except along the east side, where the seating had crumbled beyond repair. Hundreds of fans ate hot dogs and pretzels, drank beer and soda. They all stared at the empty, brightly lit field as if a game were going on. In their minds' eyes it was. When the announcer— a Harry Caray hologram—exuberantly shouted "And it's out of the park!" the crowd jumped to its feet, whooping and hollering in victory.

Mike came up beside me, tucking his entwined hands neatly in the folds of his monk's robe. He regarded the imaginary game and shook his head, muttering, "Only in America."

I grinned at him. "You love it and you know it. Come on, let's go get some cotton candy."

We wandered back down to the area where there used to be row after row of permanent vendors selling overpriced beer and pretzels and the usual stadium fare. Decades of dust and grime coated the empty stalls and counters, giving it the feel of a ghost town. The action was now in the middle of the wide walkway, where the same kinds of food and souvenirs were sold relatively cheaply at kiosks and rickety tables.

"Step right up, get your all-beef frank, Chicago-style," called a balding guy dressed in retro bebop. As we walked past, he stepped in front of Mike and practically shoved a hot dog in his face. "Hey, Kung Fu, you hungry?"

"Don't eat meat, fool," Mike said. He lifted his arm in a defensive martial arts move and the dog went flying out of the bun. Luckily, it landed back in the vendor's portable stand. Not so luckily, it splashed his 1950s guitar shirt with greasy water.

"Hey! Easy, man, I'm just trying to make a living."

"Sorry," I mouthed to him from behind Mike's back. "Let's keep going."

We wandered past a clown who sold glow-in-the-dark bracelets, an earth mother in tie-dye selling baseball caps and a macrobiotic vendor who sold brown rice shaped like wieners and hamburgers.

The array was endless. I wasn't sure what I was looking for. Jon told Hank the secret passageway was here, but he didn't exactly give me an address and key. I suppose he trusted I'd figure it out.

From the corner of my eye I noticed a magician in dark sunglasses. He wore a classic silk cape and top hat. He had a big black box, about the size of an upright coffin, apparently used for disappearing acts. He also had a pretty assistant in a tight, sequined outfit. I nudged Mike out of the flow of foot traffic and tugged him toward the magician, who worked under a banner that read Cosmo's Magic Emporium. "We gotta check this out."

When I got a closer look at the operation, I realized why business was slow. A sign written in bright red print announced that Cosmo the Magnificent charged a hundred dollars to make people disappear. Small print further explained it would take another grand to reappear. So a ten-minute magic trick would cost eleven hundred smackers, unless you were a masochist who enjoyed being trapped inside the false back of the rigged box. Used to grifters as I was, I had to admire the guy for his chutzpah.

"I want to do it," I whispered to Mike. "I want to see how he makes me disappear."

He frowned at me. "You nuts? We keep looking for secret door."

"I always begged Lola to take me to a magic act, but she never would. She thought magicians were beneath her."

Just then I got lucky. A family of four, munching caramel corn, strolled up to Cosmo's Magic Emporium. The father looked like a corporate executive. He had gray hair at his temples, tasseled loafers, a crisp sport coat and a striped open-necked shirt and polished fingernails. And this was obviously his slacker wear. He forked over his cash chip to Cosmo's assistant and his two giggling daughters went into the box.

"I'm scared, Daddy," one of the girls giggled.

"It's okay, honey. You'll be fine."

I was as fascinated by the impeccably dressed guy and his perfectly coiffed wife as I was by the magic act. These people obviously came from the suburbs. This was probably their night out to mingle with the common folk.

"You are about to witness, ladies and gentleman, an act so amazing that you will remember it for the rest of your life!" Cosmo began with a patter that he'd obviously given a thousand times before.

As he promised miracles and amazement, his assistant went around to the back of the box, proving my theory that she would help the girls step into a back exit space in time to amaze their parents. It was all a hoax.

"Come, Baker," Mike whispered. "We must find the entrance. Forget stupid magic trick."

"Shh-hh. Just a minute." I smiled as the girls tried to hold back their laughter. Cosmo pulled off the act quickly and flawlessly. When he opened the box to reveal its emptiness, the parents pretended to be surprised and worried about their missing children.

Cosmo reversed the routine before the children became impatient and—*voilà!*—there they were again. The girls rushed out of the tight box, hugged their parents and off they went, excitedly describing their adventure.

"How about you, madam?" Cosmo said, eyeing me almost seductively. "Would you like to know the secrets of the unknown?"

"Not really," I replied. "The less I know, the better. But I would like to see you make me disappear."

"Baker!" Mike said.

"Ah, but you don't seem like a woman who shies away from the truth," Cosmo murmured, turning so I couldn't see Mike's disapproving frown. "A whole world exists inside this box. A world that not many get to see." He lowered his sunglasses over his nose, as Jon had yesterday, and pierced me with hugely dilated eyes. "A world not many *want* to see."

At last I understood why a penny-ante street magician would set his prices so high almost no one would ask to see his trick. He was Emerald City's northside gatekeeper. I turned and gave Mike the thumbs-up sign. "Okay, Cosmo the Magnificent, how do we do this?"

He pushed his glasses up his nose and broke into a broad grin. "One at a time." When I pulled out my wallet, he waved his white-gloved hands. "No need, madam. I only charge idiots who insist on a real magic trick. My other services are gratis. I've been waiting for you."

He helped me into the tall rectangle and leaned against the doorway with his arms crossed, talking fast like an airplane flight attendant. "Hold on to the handrails on either side. When the door slides out from under you, don't panic. Look down and get a glimpse of the ladder. Move down slow until you get your footing, then go fast. The trick floor stays open only fifteen seconds. Be ready or you'll fall on your derriere. But it's only an eight-foot drop, so either way you'll survive. Any questions? No? Good."

He dusted his hands as if he'd just completed a difficult task.

"See you in a few. I hope." I gave Mike a little wave and grabbed the side handles as instructed.

Everything went as Cosmo had said it would. The door slid slowly open, I lowered myself until my foot caught on the top rung of the ladder leading down into the underground, and I quickly climbed down the ladder until I found myself standing upright in an oval tunnel that was surprisingly well lit.

What didn't go as planned was the arrival party. Just as the trick door closed overhead, I felt a shadow crawl over my shoulder and turned to find one very tall and mean-looking sonofabitch looming over me. His skin was pale but covered in ash. He had long black hair held tight to his skull in a black nylon do-rag and muscles that wouldn't quit. One huge fist curled around a nasty-looking steel pipe with dried blood on the tip.

"Uh, hi." I looked up with a weak grin. "Let me guess. You're a Shadowman."

He grunted and nodded slowly. Quite the conversationalist.

"Well, my name is—" Before I could even finish the sentence he cut me off.

"I know who you are. You're Dead Meat."

Chapter 15

The Cyclops

In a blaze of adrenaline, I twisted sideways and rammed my heel in his groin. When he doubled over, I uppercut my fist into his nose. The impact sent a jolt of pain through my shoulder. When he reeled back, I brought him down with a leaping roundhouse kick to the head.

Mike dropped down from the hatch above and immediately jumped into a dragon pose, ready to strike if the crumpled heap rose once more. "Who is it?"

"A Shadowman," I replied, panting. I wiped the blood from his nose off my knuckles. "I struck before he could. These guys are like animals. They kill for fun. And they don't usually travel alone." I looked in either direction. "We better get moving. But which way?"

I wished I had the crystal ball. I had no clue. No hunches. Not even a gut instinct. *Use your skills,* Marco had said. But how? I was like a natural golfer who takes her first lesson and suddenly becomes self-conscious and forgets how to swing. So, I resorted to my failsafe: eenie, meanie, minie, moe.

Pointing right, I said, "This way."

"No," the dirty brute said as he struggled to recover his breath. He put his forearms on the ground to try to push himself up.

I drew back my foot to wallop him in the gut, but Mike held me back. "Hold off. Listen to him."

"Don't go that way," the guy said as he pressed a fist to his bleeding nose. He looked at us with urgency. "The Shadowmen have a substation south of here. Go north two hundred yards and duck through to the right."

I knelt down beside him and looked into intelligent eyes. "Who are you?"

"Officer Erik Roper," he said hoarsely. "Chicago P.D."

My mouth dropped open. "Some disguise. I thought you were threatening me."

"No," he said on a moan, "I was warning you that you'd be dead if you didn't get out of here fast. The Shadows aren't far behind me."

"What are you doing here?"

"Undercover ops. I was assigned to follow your tracker."

"How? My tracker isn't live."

"Detective Marco said you wouldn't bother to engage, so he gave you a Lazarus Model EL. It never dies."

So Marco had tried to outsmart me. And *this* poor schmuck. "I broke your nose."

"It's happened before," he said, now breathing normally. "I was in the Universal Wrestling Federation before I turned to law."

The UWF. That would explain his uncanny resemblance to a Shadowman. "Any other police down here I should know about?"

"I'm it as far as the Shadowmen go. Now get moving. They'll be here soon. Get your quarry and get the hell out. I'll keep the Shadows away from this launch pad until you can make your exit."

"Thanks." I wanted to say I was sorry, but it would sound so lame I didn't even bother. I'd let him explain to the other Shadowmen how a tough guy like him got a broken nose. I was sure he wouldn't mention it had happened at the hands of a petite blond chick and a Buddhist monk.

Voices echoed thinly from the south, then grew more distinct. I heard a steady pounding and realized it was the thud of synchronized jackboots hitting the tunnel's concrete floor. Jon told us the Shadowmen ran in tandem, sometimes ten deep. They ran everywhere with the endurance of marathoners. If you got in their way, they mowed you down and trampled you, unless they wanted to filch your jewelry. Then you got a simple whack on the head with a steel pipe and were left for dead. God help you if you were considered an enemy. Then

they dragged you to their station where the L platform had been wired with pirated juice. They
stretched you out on the third rail for a fry job and
watched you twitch like bacon on a skillet.

"Go!" Roper urged us.

He didn't have to say it twice. Mike and I both
turned and ran at the same time. I pulled a flashlight
out of my Velcro leg organizer and led the way.
We were running on hard-packed dirt, and I realized
this narrow tunnel was not part of the Chicago
Transit Authority's twenty-first century public transportation system. I guess a century is long enough
to build a whole new underground passageway if
you have the knowledge and determination. I'd read
that over the years a few ministers, ultraliberal types
and loners, had voluntarily moved to the Emerald
City complex. I suppose some of them might have
been architects or engineers.

We veered right as the undercover operations officer had instructed. Quickly, we found ourselves
reaching a hive of activity. There were voices, laughter, but before we could get close enough to check
it out, two young men stepped out of the shadows
with automatic weapons.

Mike and I froze, but when the young sentries
called us by name, we relaxed. They motioned us
into the large underground station. We stepped out
of darkness into a yellow haze created by gas jets
blazing against the tile wall near the now-defunct
train ticket booth.

"Hello," a man greeted us with a warm smile. He
wore a serviceable brown omni suit that zipped up

the front. He looked like Jon, but with graying hair. "My son said you were coming. Welcome. I hope the Shadowmen didn't give you any trouble."

Mike and I exchanged a droll look. "No," I said, finally breathing easy. "No trouble at all."

It turned out that Jon's father was one of the elders who determined policy for five families that lived in and near the Addison station. He was self-educated and had spent his whole life in Emerald City. Cal Moore was the grandson of Jack Wendell Moore, one of the founding fathers of the underground society. He helped organize the homeless who took over when the CTA abandoned the underground lines in 2020 for the aboveground superconductor lines.

Moore had been a very successful engineer who worked at the Stone Container Building on Wacker Drive. He lost his job when American corporations sent white-collar jobs to join the blue-collar positions already overseas.

Overnight Moore lost his Winnetka mansion, his Mercedes, his wife and his faith in the system. But he believed strongly in the American Dream and set out to create a better form of democracy beneath the streets of Chicago. He never achieved his dream but died trying.

Cal proudly displayed a photograph of his grandfather on the wall of his family's large living quarters in the southeast corner of the station. We sat around a table lit by a candle, sipping water, and studied a map of the underground system.

"I don't know who down here would want your mother," Cal said after hearing our story.

He stroked his attractive, clean-shaven face. Like the others, he was pale and his wide, unprotected eyes seemed omniscient. "Most of our folks are good people. Of course, the Shadowmen are savages. Bred in mayhem, they're raised without consciences, but they do have a strong tribal sense, so they're organized. Still, I can't imagine them kidnapping your mother."

"I believe she was taken by the R.M.O.," I said. "But then how would she end up down here?"

"Tell me again what clues brought you here?"

"A vision," Mike said.

I nodded. "I saw Lola someplace very dark, devoid of light. And I heard creaking chains. I saw this…this enormous eyeball. Very creepy."

I shook off the memory and turned my attention back to Cal. His wide eyes glimmered with something that looked a whole lot like dread.

"What is it?" I leaned forward. "Cal, did I say something wrong?"

He swallowed thickly and pursed his lips. "No. Not really. It's just…it's just that what you described can point only to one man."

That was good, I thought. No running in circles. We could grab Lola and get the hell out. "Who is it?"

"Cy."

"Cy who?"

"Just Cy. It's short for Cyclops."

When we reached Cy's prison forty-five minutes later, I mentally thanked Cal for great directions.

The path had been incredibly convoluted. We would never have found it without his help. His runners led the way until we almost reached our destination, but they turned back, clearly nervous about wandering so far from home base in the darkened tunnels.

I could well understand why. According to Cal, the so-called Cyclops was a deranged young man who had been badly burned in the gas explosion Hank had talked about. While others in his clan had either died or reluctantly accepted their fate as scarred survivors, this guy had lashed out at the world. He'd built a stone prison, somehow managing to install mechanical wrought-iron gates that he operated on a pulley system.

Cal said sometimes Cy sent his hired Shadowmen in search of someone randomly to imprison. Then he'd rant at his terrified and innocent prisoner, quote Shakespeare and rail against the world that had disfigured him so badly. Usually, however, Cy's prisoners were people he'd been paid to keep for others. Cy would hold prisoners for a fee, and it was widely known in Emerald City, if not above, that the R.M.O. employed him regularly. There was some speculation that a skeleton in the first cell to the right was all that remained of Chicago's last powerful Italian don. He'd gone missing two years ago and the moles down here said he would have been better off sleeping with the fishes than spending an eternity listening to Cy's melodramatic rendition of Shakespeare's plays.

I didn't care whose bones I'd find as long as they

weren't Lola's. At least I didn't care until we unex-
pectedly found the prison after turning a sharp
corner.

"This is it," I whispered.

Mike had already come to a stop beside me. We
faced a short hall carved in stone that opened to a
big stone support beam. Through the side bars of the
first iron prison to our right, I could see an open area
beyond that was domed and bore a sign that read:
The Globe. I guess that's why Cy named it after
Shakespeare's round Elizabethan theater. A torch
blazed on the support beam, giving the whole area
a golden glow. Cal said that Cy had been unwilling
to tap into underground gas lines, for obvious reasons.

Mike looked to me for guidance. Should we go
forward? What would we face? I sensed no one was
here—no one who could harm us, anyway. I jerked
my head toward the dome prison, gave a silent
follow-me sign and led the way. After a few steps, I
could fully see the first cell.

Sure enough, it contained a skeleton propped
against the back stone wall, legs straight out, hands
on either side, head slumped forward. It was still
fully dressed in expensive, though tattered, clothes.
A mouse had made a nest in the dead prisoner's remaining gray hair. Another poked its head out of the
dead man's eye socket to see who had come to visit.

Cold prickled over me and suddenly I didn't want
to be here anymore. Mike stared in dismay at the
skeleton, as well. If this person had simply died in
that position waiting for another crust of bread and

had decomposed there, the stench must have been unimaginable. Much later Mike and I would debate whether this was a hoax designed to frighten away unwanted visitors or a sign of Cy's dereliction of duty as a prison warden. Right now all we wanted to do was get Lola and get the hell out.

"It's now or never," I whispered. "Let's go in."

We were drawn by the soft crackle of a torch adorned with the wrought-iron head of a dragon. The flames licked out of its mouth.

As we drew closer, we could make out more cells—six in all. All were empty save for one that contained a prone figure on the floor, dead to the world. My heart started to race and my throat tightened. No, she couldn't be dead. She was simply sleeping. While Mike kept watch at the entrance, I walked soundlessly toward the prisoner until I saw a glimpse of brassy red hair and heard soft snoring. Hugely relieved, I rushed the distance.

"Lola," I called sotto voce. "Wake up!"

I grabbed the black bars that separated us and confirmed in my mind that this crumpled heap in the corner could be no one but my crazy mother. Her hair—chaotic in the best of circumstances—was riotous and knotted. Her brown, flowing shift, gathered around her knees, exposed her wrinkled legs. The shadows deepened the wear and tear on her once beautiful face.

She looked so helpless. And old. She wouldn't live forever. My hands tightened around the bars and my legs felt weak. *Oh, Mom.*

"Baker," Mike whispered. "Hurry."

I nodded, clearing my throat. "Lola. You have to wake up."

Suddenly her head snapped up in surprise, instantly awake. She looked at me with a blank expression while she struggled to sit up. She made an effort to straighten her hair, which she would do even if the devil himself came to call. *Appearance is everything, Angel.* I'd heard her say that a million times, which she invariably followed up with a cheerful, *Fake it till you make it! Fake it even if you don't make it.*

Lola sat up and her confusion vanished. She squinted at us against the yellow and black dance of light. Then recognition transformed her face—briefly into the woman I had known and loved when I was about five years old.

"Angel!" she cried.

With tears brimming in my eyes, I reached my hand through the bars. "How can I get you out of here?"

She crawled toward me, then grabbed my hand and pulled herself up. She flung herself to the bars and squeezed one plump arm through to hug me. I wrapped my arm around her. "Oh, honey, I knew you'd come. My baby, my baby, I knew I could count on you."

Tears burned my eyes. "Lola, we have to go," I whispered, pulling out of her powerful hold. "How do I operate this thing?"

"Over there." She pointed against the wall. "Pull the fourth lever from the left and then…then crank that handle."

I rushed over to the primitive control panel that linked to the chains that raised and lowered iron grates like you see in pictures of castles. I cranked hard and the front of Lola's cell started to open. At the same time I heard a guttural shout and the slap of fists on skin and the thwomp of feet meeting flesh and bone.

I glanced over my shoulder and saw Mike fighting a leather- and muscle-clad Shadowman who was a foot taller than him. My first impulse was to run to his side, but the pointy teeth of the iron grate began to lower just as Lola was halfway through on her hands and knees. I grabbed the crank before the leaden arrows impaled her and continued cranking until she scrabbled out. I helped her up and we ran toward the entrance.

"Go, Lola, run!" I pushed her to the right and came around to help Mike.

"No," Mike shouted. "You go with Lola. I'll fight."

"Together or nothing, Mike," I said as a second brute came loping toward the sounds of the fight.

I shoved Lola toward the corner. "Wait outside," I whispered, not waiting to see if she'd obey. No time. The second Shadowman bypassed Mike and his foe, coming directly for me, raising a nasty wooden cudgel. I slammed the toe of my boot against his kneecap, eliciting a grunt of pain. His leg buckled, but it wasn't enough to stop the downward arc of his powerful swing.

The club grazed my shoulder, scraping a bloody path down my arm. Better that than a broken clavicle. I moved in and landed a solid punch to his solar plexus, putting the full force of my body into it, driving deep enough to double him over this time. As he started to crumple, I raised both fists locked above my head and crashed them down on the back of his neck. He was out cold. I turned in time to see Mike's opponent hit the stone floor.

Two more thugs lumbered down the corridor, brandishing knives and clubs. Whatever possessed these guys to use primitive weapons instead of modern firepower? Hey, I wasn't complaining, just curious.

Mike and I stood back to back, each poised to take on a Shadowman as the pair split up, approaching from two sides. Mike seized his opponent's outstretched wrist just as the thug swung his club. Pivoting on his right foot, Mike used the forward momentum of his attacker to slide the thug's arm over his shoulder and catapult him into the iron bars of the cage six feet away.

I couldn't pay more attention to their contest because I was occupied dodging the flashing blade of my Shadowman's knife. He was big but surprisingly quick. I was little and quicker.

"Getting tired, Ace?" I sassed, spitting on the ground in front of him. He let out a guttural growl and tried again. "Don't any of you creeps know how to talk?"

All I got was a grunted "Huh?" I kept out of reach, waiting for my opening. He was breathing harder. Good. But then another Neanderthal engaged Mike just as he put the finishing touches to the one he'd been fighting. Damn. No help for me now.

I'd have to handle this one myself. He slashed just low enough so I could reach his knife arm from above. One of my hands was too small to reach around his wrist, but I knew the pressure point I needed to hit. It would take two hands to do it. Dangerous. Like I had a choice! I wrapped my hands around his wrist while his knife inched too close for comfort.

Fingers busy, I used every ounce of my strength to press on the inside of his wrist. He dropped the knife with a squeal of surprise, his good right hand numbed. But there was nothing wrong with his left. He tried to grab hold of my hair. There's a good reason I keep it short. His hand came away empty. Just as he made a fist and swung at me, I whirled away and sent my leg flying under the blow. My foot connected with his groin and he folded like a circus tent on traveling day.

Then the sound of a theatrical voice echoed around the macabre vault of horrors. "A horse. My kingdom for a horse!"

Seeing Cyclops up close and personal hadn't been on the agenda, but here the creep was, lurching toward us. Since Cyclops had been your average mole until he'd been horribly burned in an underground fire, I guess it was only natural that he would identify with the king Shakespeare had portrayed as deformed. How inventive of Cyclops. It was a little grandiose, but admirably literate of him.

Cyclops moved in the odd way someone who had

suffered crippling burns would, shambling to favor ru-
ined muscles and skin twisted into knotted scars.
Briefly, I felt sorry for him. In the torchlight I could
see that searching, hideous eye—the one I had seen
in my mother's crystal ball. And it was fixed directly
on me.

"Okay, so maybe telepathy really exists," I muttered to myself.

He charged toward us, flanked by two more of his
minions. Mike quickly tossed the first of them like
a ragdoll, stacked on top of his pals in the corner. He
engaged the second and they commenced to spar
while the deranged Richard III paused and studied
me with that ghastly, single bloodshot eye.

"You," he rasped from beneath his black, hooded
cape. "I know you…glorious sun of York," he
rasped.

His voice was hoarse from smoke and fire damage but his body was squat and powerful in spite of
his scars. There was something eerily hypnotic
about him as he advanced on me with arms outstretched as if greeting a long-lost sister.

Ugh! What a thought. Lola might have been a little off-kilter but she hadn't given birth to any luna-
tics…that I knew of. I backed away, forgetting the
brute lying curled in a fetal position behind me until
I tripped over him and fell backward. My thespian
adversary followed me down, pinning me. I felt as
if I were living a nightmare and longed for insom-
nia.

Just as I started to twist my body so my knee could
do some serious damage to Cyclops's gonads, a high-

pitched screech filled the air. Lola, armed with what looked like a broomstick, was pummeling "the usurper." He turned to swat her away like a bothersome fly, but when he raised his head toward her, instead of backing away, she surprised me—and probably herself.

Lola jabbed the end of the stick into his good eye with a yowl of fierce pleasure that froze even Mike in his tracks. Luckily, he'd finished off the last of the Shadowmen. Cyclops emitted a horrible moan and grabbed at what had been his good eye, rolling away from me to writhe on the floor.

"In the kingdom of the blind, the one-eyed man ain't king anymore," Lola said with gusto, tossing her wild red hair back with a triumphant twist of her head.

"You all right, my brave baby?" she asked me as her face transformed from Boadicea to Earth Mother.

I simply stared at her in amazement.

"Quickly," Mike said, motioning frantically. "We must go before others come."

I jumped to my feet. I could hear what sounded like a legion of Shadowmen rumbling down the stone corridors. "Let's move," I said, grabbing my mother, the unlikely lioness, by one withered arm while Mike took hold of the other.

As we raced away from the hellish version of a Medieval Times performance with Cyclops's knights in hot pursuit, I wondered if I'd ever get the vision of that hypnotic single eye out of my mind again.

Chapter 16

Hot and Bothered

When we finally climbed out of the hellhole—
scraped, bruised and shaken—we found Marco and
Detective Hoskins standing by with a retinue of police officers and emergency technicians. While I
wanted the cops to go after Cyclops, I knew they
wouldn't. The moles had negotiated treaties with
the City of Chicago, giving them limited sovereignty
over their territory. A few undercover officers, like
the one we met, kept surveillance but couldn't
legally interfere with what went on below.

In a parking lot on the north side of the crumbling
stadium, we were debriefed while the police pep-
pered us with questions, filled out reports, fed Lola
burgers and told us we were lucky to be alive.

Lola cried when she heard about her cleaning lady's murder. When Hoskins advised her to stay away from her apartment, she showed surprising good judgment by promptly agreeing. So did I, though I dreaded the fact that this would mean Lola had to move in with me for a while.

After extensive questioning, it became clear that one of the scenarios Henry and I had batted around was right on. Lola said she was kidnapped by R.M.O. thugs shortly after she did a reading with Vladimir Gorky. She said she'd been advising him for years. During their last reading, Lola mentioned a lost fortune. When she made a reference to an eagle, the symbol of Russia, Gorky had turned white and pressed her for more details. It seemed Lola had hit on an unresolved mystery.

Gorky had been searching the past ten years for a fortune that someone in his organization had stolen and hidden. Thinking that Lola actually knew the location, he became angry when she wouldn't provide more details. He was convinced she was holding out on him and imprisoned her for future questioning. I broke out in a cold sweat when I realized how easily Lola could have become a forgotten skeleton in Cyclops's prison. What if I hadn't come through for her?

Even though Hoskins questioned Lola, it was clear that Marco had been the driving force in the search for her. He walked us out to the squad car that was going to take us home. Mike stayed behind to tell them about our encounter with Officer Roper. Like the gentleman he was, Marco opened the back door for Lola and helped her in. He then came around to my side and leaned against the door before I could open it.

"You look like hell," he said, crossing his arms and eyeing me closely.

I laughed and ran a hand through my hair. "Thanks. Bad hair day. Remind me to curl it next time I go underground."

"I hope there won't be a next time."

"But you never know."

"Nope. Not with a stubborn broad like you."

"I'll take that as a compliment whether it was meant as one or not."

He smiled openly. God, what a spectacular smile he had—white teeth, bright eyes framed by ruggedly handsome crow's-feet marking healthy, tanned skin. He was all man. Confident. Stubborn, too. I smiled back.

"I like you, Baker. I really do. Too bad things can't be different."

"Yeah, well, you can't have everything." I added in a tight voice, "I suppose you want me to say thank-you."

"What for?"

I put my hands on my hips and eyed him with exasperation. "As if you don't know. For one, risking your reputation for helping a CRS in a covert rescue mission that wasn't authorized by police assigned to the case. For another, planting that tracker on me. I'm not sure we would have made it without Officer Roper's help. I thought he was a Shadowman. Poor guy, I think I broke his nose."

"It's happened before."

"That's what he said. Talk about tough."

"Yeah, you are," he said, willfully misinterpreting my comment, and I thought I heard a note of admiration in the wry statement.

"Flattery will get you nowhere, Detective."

He pulled a grimace. "Damn. It's always worked before."

"I have no doubt. But don't forget that while you were busy saving my ass, you also lied to me. You told me that tracker would be dead until I activated it."

"Lucky for you I lied. And to think you accused me of being a Boy Scout." I really hated the ambiguous lines between truth and lies, right and wrong, love and hate. As Hank had said, those lines grew blurrier by the day. It made self-righteousness damned near impossible. At this rate I was going to have to adopt an entirely new modus operandi.

"I'm going home now, Detective, and I'm going to sleep for a very, very long time. But tomorrow night I'm going to celebrate our success with a little soiree. I think Lola deserves a party. You should have seen how brave she was. Want to come?"

"Sure. What time?"

"I'll call you. Don't keep Mike too long."

"I'll drop him off myself in ten minutes. See you tomorrow."

He shut the door and waved at the officer behind the wheel. As the car pulled out of the lot, Lola's curiosity blasted me from the other side of the seat like a wood-burning oven. I turned to her and instantly recognized her meddling smirk for what it was.

"Forget it, Lola. I can't believe you'd even think about something like this after you barely escaped with your life."

"O-oh, but honey, he's handsome."

"That's the problem. I don't trust handsome men."

"Who's talking about trust? Just one night with a man like that—"

I stopped her with a vicious glare. "Do you want to stay at my place or not?"

She went pale. "Yeah, honey, I got nowhere else to go."

"Then don't ever talk to me about Detective Marco again. He's not my type. Got it?" I said it harsher than I'd intended, but there was never going to be anything between me and Marco. Period.

She nodded obediently. "Yeah, honey. Yeah, I got it. Not your type. Yeah, that makes sense." Then she muttered to herself, "O-oh, but is he ever a hunk."

When we got home I cooked an omelette, which Mike and I inhaled. Lola had already stuffed herself with the burgers and fries she'd gobbled down in the back of a squad car. The three of us rehashed the night's surreal events over cups of oolong tea, still buzzing will adrenaline, until exhaustion finally set in. We congratulated ourselves once more, said good-night, showered and prepared for bed.

I set Lola up in the studio downstairs. That way she could sleep until noon if she wanted without being disturbed. I made sure the futon in the corner had sheets, and when she climbed under the covers,

she looked like the subject of a modern art paint-
ing—a Raggedy Ann doll, with a head of tousled red
yarn and doleful dark eyes, tossed on a white bed in
a black room. Before I went upstairs, I sat on the
edge of the futon and smoothed away a lock of hair
from her forehead. "We've been through a lot today,
Lola."

Her eyes puddled and she squeezed my hand. "I
couldn't have done it without you, honey. You saved
my life. I knew you would."

"Sure, Ma. We're family. That's what family
does."

Lola's face lit with joy, then she sat up and
yanked me into a bear hug. Her strength surprised
me. It always had. I let her hug me as long as I
could, then pulled gently away. It would be a long
time, if ever, before I overcame my natural instinct
to keep her at arm's length.

She sank back onto her pillow and gazed at me
with blatant admiration. "How did you do it, Angel?
How on earth did you find me?"

I swallowed hard. "Uh, well, it's like this. I—I
had a vision." I stopped and listened to the pounding of my heart, but knew I couldn't stop there. "It
seems I have a special ability to…to see things.
I'm…you know…psychic. I guess."

I gave her a quick look. She wasn't gloating, as
I'd half expected. Incredibly, her eyes were soft with
compassion.

"I'm so sorry, baby."

I tilted my head. "Why?"

"I know how you hate that psychic crap."

I bit my lower lip and took her right hand in both of mine. Age spots speckled her pale skin. "But it's not crap, is it, Lola?"

She shook her head. "No."

I covered my face with my hands. "Oh, God, I was so unfair to you."

"No, baby, you weren't."

"Yes, I was! All these years I thought you were a fake. I never imagined it could possibly be real. I don't know how you can ever forgive me."

"Forgive *you*?" She laughed. "Oh, sweetie, there's nothing to forgive. You were just a kid, and I was a lousy mother. You had to hate me for something. Being a psychic was just as good as anything. I'm just sorry you have to have the gift, too."

I shrugged. "I simply have to use it for a good purpose and everything will be okay."

She huffed doubtfully. "It ain't always that easy, kiddo."

I studied the layers of dark circles under her eyes. "What do you mean?"

"It's not like turning on a faucet. That's why Vlad was so mad at me. He thought I knew where to find his lost fortune, but I didn't. I just couldn't come up with enough information."

"Don't worry about it, Lola."

"I got to, honey. As soon as Vlad is done dealing with those Chinese girls, he'll start worrying about his fortune again and he'll come looking for me."

"I'll ask Detective Marco to make sure the police keep an eye on this place," I said. Then I realized what she'd just said. "Wait a minute. Did you say Chinese girls?"

"Yup."

"So Vladimir Gorky has something to do with those missing girls I've been reading about in the newspaper?"

She sighed and nodded. "Yeah, I felt sorry for them. But there was nothing I could do to help."

"You mean you *saw* them?" I practically shouted.

"They were at the Gorky mansion on the north side. Vlad's thugs took me there for one last reading before they handed me over to that one-eyed lunatic in Emerald City." She shivered at the memory. "Can we talk about this tomorrow, honey? I need a good night's sleep."

"Sure." I nodded, my mind reeling. We knew where the girls were. They would have to be rescued.

The police would never interfere without proof positive that Gorky had them, and they certainly wouldn't take Lola's word for it. Somebody had to help those girls. They needed a real home before they were scarred for life. I knew that better than anyone.

But I was too tired to solve all the world's problems…tonight.

I slept until noon, then made arrangements for the small party.

By nine o'clock the next evening everyone had arrived and mingled in the garden. Soft jazz music floated through the hibiscus-scented air, mingling with the animated conversations and heightened laughter. I wasn't typically big on social events, but after a close brush with death, we all felt immortal and needed to celebrate our victory.

I'd ordered from a Chinese restaurant that delivered, and there were plenty of dishes for vegetarians and carnivores alike. The small gathering split nearly down the middle on that score.

My foster brother, Lola and Marco were unabashed meat eaters. Hank's girlfriend Soji and Mike were vegans, which is what I call vegetarians with an attitude. They don't even eat eggs and cheese because they come from animals. I split somewhere down the middle. I preferred lighter vegetable dishes, but I wasn't above using my incisors on occasion.

After we ate and I brought the dishes back up to the kitchen, Soji cornered me at the bottom of the stairs on my return.

"Hey there, hero," she said.

I laughed and gave her a one-armed hug. "I'm just glad Lola made it out alive."

I motioned to two Adirondack chairs positioned in front of a semicircle of flowers and foot-high Chinese lanterns. She'd brought me a glass of white wine, and we sat side by side. I could finally relax.

Soji was a cool woman. Hank had been dating her for a year and I really liked her. I didn't want to jinx anything by telling him I hoped they'd get married, but I think he had that in mind, as well. She would be a hard one to lasso, though.

Soji, which was short for Sojourner, was a gorgeous television reporter who hailed from Mozambique. With an exotic accent, a luscious caramel complexion, a svelte supermodel figure and cheekbones to die for, she was destined for network stardom. Right now she was one of the Chicago market's hot commodities. I'd given Hank a hard time, asking him how a guy with freckles and baby fat could snag a woman like Soji Wilson. He'd taken the ribbing in good humor, flushing with pride over his apparent victory. I suspected Soji was attracted to Hank's intelligence and his great news instincts, not to mention his journalism pedigree. And while he wasn't particularly tall or dashing, Hank was like a young Spencer Tracy—rock-solid and dependable.

"So may I have the first interview?" Soji asked me with a conspiratorial smile.

"Oh, no," I said, waving her off with a weary laugh. "No interviews."

"Come on, Angel. Mike won't talk and you're a hero, too." She uncrossed her long, trim legs and leaned forward. "Think about it. Defying the constraints of the criminal justice system, a retributionist risks her life and confronts the terrifying underworld to save her own long-lost mother. What a story!"

"The last thing I need right now is publicity."

"Maybe you don't, but your profession does."

I gave her a weary look. "You mean, because of the Gibson Warrants?"

"Yes. Those warrants are just the ammunition the establishment has been looking for to knock your profession out of the box."

I gazed at Marco, who stood at the other end of the garden. Lola had cornered him. He nodded politely, even charmingly, while she regaled him with her nonsense. A man who took the time to charm an old woman couldn't be all that bad.

"Maybe it *is* time the police took back the streets," I said.

"But they can't," Soji said. "Things are too far gone. Until Congress can get organized crime out of the criminal justice system, it's every man, or woman, for himself. The common people have to have recourse. CRSs came out of a genuine need in the community. That need will be there for a long time to come."

I looked at her askance. "Boy, you're sounding bleak tonight."

She sipped her wine and smiled wistfully. "I just see what's going on out there. And I'm not sure your mother would have come out of this alive if not for you. Well, I won't pester you. If you decide to talk to the media, you know where to find me."

Hank came up behind her and leaned down to kiss her cheek. "We call her Killer," he said to me. "She'll hound you until you surrender. She's relentless in her pursuit of a story and skeptical once she hears it. When she was little and her mother would say 'I love you,' Soji would always verify it with at least two sources."

"Stop!" Soji said, playfully slapping his hand, which rested on her shoulder.

I smiled, recognizing the signs of true love. Funny how easily I could see it in others, but could not even imagine it for myself. I made an excuse about wanting more wine and left the lovebirds so they could tease each other in privacy. I headed toward Marco and my mother.

After our heart-to-heart last night I felt closer to Lola than I had in years, and I had new respect for her. But she still had a knack for getting on my nerves, and I was afraid if I didn't rescue Marco she'd soon be dropping hints about me to him and planning our wedding.

"I'm sorry to interrupt," I said, "but you have to come with me, Detective. We need to talk."

I slipped my arm in his and pulled him away as he still listened politely over his shoulder to Lola, who hadn't even paused to take a breath. She continued a long-winded story about how perfect I was as a child, adding that there was, nevertheless, no accounting for how kids turn out and she had done her best. She grew louder as we receded. She was like a press agent who didn't know she was supposed to downplay her client's faults.

"I'm sorry," I muttered as we broke from Lola's gravitational pull. "You're a very patient man."

"Don't worry about it," Marco said. "She's charming."

"In the last few days I've grown to appreciate my mother, but she's still easier to take in small doses."

"She's one of a kind."

"Thank God." I looked back just as she followed Mike into his coach house. "This will be interesting. I give Mike five minutes before he touches her third eye and puts her into a trance."

"Now, that's a good skill to have. I heard you did that to one of the officers outside of Lola's apartment. He thought it was some kind of voodoo."

"Nah, just old-fashioned concentration." I tried to pull my hand away from his arm, but he squeezed it against his ribs and wouldn't let go. I looked up, brows furrowed.

"I want to talk to you, Baker."

"May I go first?"

He smiled. "Sure."

"I need you to help me find those Chinese girls who were kidnapped from the Mongolian Mob. I know where they are."

"Okay," he said.

I raised a brow. "Okay? That means yes?"

"Last time I looked it up in the dictionary it did."

I crossed my arms and squinted doubtfully. "Why are you being so easy?"

"I'll agree to anything as long as we don't have to talk about it tonight. This is a party, remember? You do know how to have a good time, don't you?"

I exhaled. "Oh, yeah. I'm supposed to relax."

"Enjoy yesterday's victory before you set out tomorrow to save the world. Besides, you and I agreed we can't work together, remember?"

I rolled my eyes. "Oh, yes. I forgot about that. So what did you want to talk about? It had better not be business."

His eyes turned sultry. "My conversation requires privacy."

"Okay, come on up to the deck."

He took my hand in his and tugged me up the

stairs. When we stood in the privacy afforded by the surrounding tree branches, his presence engulfed me. We were still holding hands, but I couldn't quite look him in the eye and acknowledge the intimacy. Together we gazed down on the beautifully lit garden.

"For two people who can't work together," I said, "we seem to be getting along rather well."

"But this isn't work." He pulled my hand, forcing me to turn and face him. "At least not for me."

He reached out and very carefully stroked my cheek with the tips of his fingers, like an alien wondering at the miracle of human skin. Then his hand moved in and cupped the back of my neck. A shiver coursed through me from head to foot as I shut my eyes.

"You'd better go, Marco, before we get into trouble," I forced myself to say.

"I've never been able to resist trouble."

I opened my eyes, knowing we stood at a cliff and wanting to measure just how many inches remained until we plunged over the edge. He pulled me into his arms, bending just enough to make the fit perfect. A flash fire spread over me. I gripped his strong shoulders, and instead of pushing him away, I tugged him closer.

"Angel Baker," he whispered in a husky voice, "I want you in a way I've never wanted anyone before."

His mouth was a magnet, pulling me in. I somehow managed to put the breaks on two inches from his mouth. His breath was warm and sweet.

My hands clawed down to the small of his back

and settled on the taut, narrow muscles thinly covered by his damp dress shirt. My mind was racing, screaming to push away. Our mouths moved closer while every other muscle in my body strained in a last attempt to keep some distance. With our noses almost touching, we breathed in sync, ragged and hot.

"Marco, kiss me," I murmured, shocked by the words coming from my mouth. *Kiss me like it's the last time.*

His lips brushed mine with a hello caress. His day-old whiskers brushed my chin. The friction pricked a sudden urge to screw him until he begged for mercy. Hungry, I parted his mouth with my own and delved inside. Then all bets were off as our mouths fused.

With a fierce groan he lunged, briefly bending me back, then pulled me upright. Our bodies pressed to get closer. It was impossible. But we tried, melding lips, chests, hips and legs into one.

When the phone rang, I didn't hear it at first, even though it was pinned to my blouse, perhaps because it was. The sound couldn't escape. But my brain, which was floating in the stardust clouds of planet Venus, finally registered the Morse code-style ring I'd programmed for urgent calls from Mel Goldman. It took a moment for my head to clear enough to remember my P.I. was still staked out at Lancaster's Shelter. I'd told him to use the urgent-only number if Tommy Drummond showed up.

I pushed Marco away. "Shit!"

"What is it?" he asked.

I popped the ear button off the receiver and planted it in my right ear. "Baker here. Make it fast."

"Angel," a frantic voice replied. "It's Mel. He's here!"

"Drummond?"

"Yeah, the big ape is on a rampage. He busted into the shelter."

"Call the police."

"I did. But I don't think they're gonnà get here before he blows away his wife and kid. He already gunned down the guard Myrtle had on duty."

"I'm coming," I said tersely, then hung up.

Three strikes and you're dead was Judge Gibson's now-infamous warning to restraining order violators. But in Drummond's case, I was afraid it was his wife and kid who were about to die.

Chapter 17

Life Interruptus

Unfortunately, Marco had driven to my house in his hydro SUV and not in one of the Chicago P.D. aero cruisers. I wanted to fly over the broken pavement quaintly referred to as roads that lay between Wrigleyville and the northwest side. Instead, Marco's land vehicle negotiated every pothole along the way with teeth-clattering determination.

I briefly considered going alone but couldn't take the time to use public transportation. Besides, Marco would have followed me. Hank and Sojourner jumped into the television station's solar Humvee they'd driven from work and followed at a breakneck pace. I hoped they were coming as friends, not journalists. Either way, I had a bad feeling we'd need witnesses to whatever we'd find at Lancaster's Shelter and was glad they were coming.

I asked Mike to stay and watch over Lola, just in case Vladimir Gorky decided to pay a visit. Besides, I didn't want her to burn the house down smoking contraband. And I certainly didn't want Mike to chance taking a bullet from Drummond after he'd already risked his life for me in the tunnels.

With Marco yanking the steering wheel left and right every two hundred yards to maneuver around vehicles that crawled at a turtle's pace, I briefed him on the Drummond case.

"Whatever does or does not happen tonight," I said in conclusion, "will be on my conscience forever. It was my job to intimidate him."

"You were doing this pro bono, Baker, get over it." He risked taking his eyes off the road long enough to skewer me with a razzing frown. "Why do you think everything that goes wrong is your fault? You did your best. What you *should* feel bad as hell about is trying to handle Drummond without going to the police."

"I didn't think they'd help," I said softly as I watched the brick bungalows whiz by. I didn't want to tell him the rest of the story: that I'd forged a Gibson Warrant and used it to threaten Drummond, a threat that apparently failed.

We arrived an amazing fifteen minutes later and parked on the opposite side of the street. Two police cruisers hugged the other curb, red strobe lights flashing.

"Stay here," Marco said.

"Hell no!" I shot back.

"That's an order," he growled through clenched teeth. "I don't want this getting messy. I'm not going to jinx my career at the starting gate because a CRS was stupid enough to think she could handle a creep like Drummond instead of letting the authorities handle it."

I punched him hard in the arm, then grabbed his shirtsleeve and said with feral intensity, "Fuck you, Marco. This is my case, dammit. *Mine*." My case. My fault. No one else's.

Adrenaline ricocheted through my body and my muscles flexed and pumped, ready for a fight. I threw open the door and bolted around the front of the SUV, but stopped when I saw how eerily quiet it was. The drone of an obscenely loud police radio grated the silence. Two officers filling out forms on electronic clipboards stood behind yellow laser beams blocking off the crime scene.

Crime scene. I was too late. I broke out in a cold sweat. What had happened? Just then Mel Goldman came hobbling over, rubbing his shiny bald crown in the manic way he reserved for tragedies.

"Angel, oh, thank God. Angel, it happened so fast."

Numb, I turned and tried to focus on what he was saying. Most of it was a blur drumming in my ears. With beady eyes full of woe, Mel recounted the events like a machine gun, his stained teeth shooting out words like bullets.

"Nothin' happened for days," he said, wringing his hands. "Like you told me to, I notified the cops

I was here and what the situation was. I had a special number to call and everything in case Drummond showed up. I didn't say nothin' about the fake warrant, but told them Drummond could be lethal. I had my partner here when I was sleeping, so we never missed a beat."

"Yeah, yeah, get to the point, Mel."

"But suddenly Drummond shows up an hour ago, I'd say. He sprays the storefront with bullets then walks right through the door where the glass was a second before. I called the cops, then you, and officers were here not two minutes later, but by then he was back out here. Suddenly a vehicle zooms by spitting out bullets a mile a minute, splattering his brains on the sidewalk. He—"

"Shut up, Mel, I don't want to hear any more."

I turned to the crime scene. Marco had crossed the street and was talking to the two officers. Sojourner and Hank had parked and came jogging my way. Impatiently, I held up a hand.

"Don't bother me now. Talk to Mel."

They stopped abruptly, nodded in understanding, then went to grill the P.I. I had a funny feeling Soji had placed a call into the newsroom, but I hoped not. The last thing we needed was a media circus.

Marco must have resigned himself to my presence at the crime scene. When I crossed the street, one of the officers briefly disengaged the yellow laser so I could join them in the containment zone. Marco was deep in conversation with the lead officer.

I took a moment to look closely at what had been

hidden by the police cruisers—a dead body laying in a pool of shiny, candy-apple-red blood. Pink brain matter littered the sidewalk. I recognized the lily-white beer gut hanging out from the bottom of his shirt and the beefy hands. Definitely Tommy Drummond.

Dear God, I prayed, let this be the only casualty tonight. Please let his wife and child be safe.

"I'm going inside," I said to Marco.

He frowned at me, then nodded his permission to the junior officer, who radioed my clearance to the investigators inside.

I made my way through the front office until I found the hall that led to the large communal family room. My feet were leaden, unwilling to go farther. I saw two uniformed officers, but otherwise the room was empty. I pushed onward and saw as I drew closer that the door on the far wall was open and people mingled outside in the playground area. Probably shelter residents. I prayed they had suffered no more than a terrible fright. Where were Janet and Lin? I couldn't see them.

When I stepped inside the room, my gaze found blood spots on the carpet, a spray pattern that grew denser as I followed it to the left, near a corner. There in an awkward pose lay Janet Drummond, dead. Her blood-drenched body seemed frozen in time. Life interruptus. With her head tilted back, her pale blue eyes seemed to beseech a heaven that had not heard her final pleas.

I took two running steps forward, as if I might be able to do something to help her. *She's dead. Dead.*

Not even "I'm sorry" would help her now. And I was. So very sorry.

I stopped abruptly, then reeled back a step when guilt hammered me. Pain seared my forehead, then flowed through my body like hot, sick lava. I covered my face with trembling hands.

"Don't blame yourself," came a familiar voice. Myrtle. She cupped my upper arm with a warm hand. "He would have done this to her eventually. It was just a matter of time. You gave her hope, Angel. In the end, Janet was really hopeful she could make a new life for herself."

Was it better to die with hope unfulfilled or embracing despair? I didn't know.

"Angel, you did the best you could."

I lied, Myrtle, I wanted to say. *I lied to him about the warrant because I didn't have the guts to shoot the creep. And he deserved to die. I lied because I thought I was clever enough to bluff him into leaving Janet alone, and cleverness is never enough when you face pure evil. I misjudged everything. I'm a disgrace to my profession. Worse, a fool.*

I lowered my hands and took in a shallow breath. "Is Lin…?"

"She's alive. She's upstairs."

"How is she taking it?"

"Well." Myrtle's eyes moistened. "Too well. I don't understand that child. She doesn't seem to feel anything at all."

"She won't until she's safe." I turned away from the body and Myrtle turned to face me.

"Are you going to be all right, dear?"

"I always am, Myrtle, it's my curse. But what about Lin? What will happen to her?"

"She'll have to go into temporary foster care until a long-term foster arrangement can be made. When the social workers sort out her legal status, I imagine she'll be adopted."

Foster care. If she landed in the wrong place, she'd never be safe enough to feel like a normal child should.

"Let me take her." The statement shocked me as much as Myrtle. It was a huge commitment.

"Angel, are you sure?"

"Yes," I said with more confidence. "I went through the foster parent training program a few years ago, even though I never actually took anyone in. I'm still registered. My house would be perfect. Mike speaks Chinese. And I...I know what it's like for a child. I'll be kind to her, I promise."

"Of course you will," Myrtle said as she stroked her chin. "Well, it would only be for a week or two at the most. And she really does need someone who can speak her language. I'm sure she feels very isolated. I'll make the recommendation tomorrow. Meanwhile, you go home and get some rest. *And don't blame yourself.*"

"I won't."

We shared a rueful smile, both knowing I would.

But guilt and other indulgences would have to wait. First I had to deal with the media circus that was forming under the big top outside.

Chapter 18

A Hill of Beans

By the time I stepped·outside, a WFYY satellite cruiser was camped across from the shelter. Soji had already cornered Marco. The handheld digicam her photographer aimed at Marco's face put out a blinding light. Marco strained not to blink as he smoothly answered her questions about the murders. Cruisers from two more television stations pulled up and reporters jumped out with e-pads, clearly frustrated to see Soji scooping them on the first interview.

"Damn it," I muttered as the zoo got bigger. I spotted Hank, acting as field producer, standing behind Soji's photog, and headed his way with steam coming out of my ears. I pulled him aside. "Hank, how could you do this?" I hissed.

"Soji—"

"I don't care what kind of a shark reporter she is. Does she chew everybody up and spit them out? Even your family?"

"Calm down," he said, grabbing my shoulders and roughly spinning me around. "Get back in Marco's vehicle."

The reporters ran past me. "Hold it," Hank said, stepping in their paths. "Soji has an exclusive with Detective Marco. You'll have to call down to HQ to get somebody else to talk to you on camera."

The reporters and their cameramen grumbled, but there was no serious mutiny. Nobody wanted to mess with Sojourner Wilson. She was known for her uncanny ability to get payback against competitors who tried to steal an exclusive from her. Hank deftly moved me out of their line of sight and took me across the street, bringing me around to the relative privacy of the far side of Marco's SUV. I crossed my arms, leaned against the vehicle and waited with a truculent frown.

"Soji and I talked about this with Detective Marco while you were inside. On our way over here, our assignment editor called us in the Humvee after hearing about Drummond on the police scanners. The station would have sent a reporter out here anyway. Soji offered to cover the story so she could put her own spin on it."

"I thought reporters were supposed to be unbiased," I fumed.

"Come on, sis," he said. "Lucky for you that's not always the case. Soji's going to keep your name out of the story, and she can justify her decision by following the basic guidelines of what constitutes news. You have a signed contract with the shelter, not the victim, so there's no need to even bring in the fact that a CRS was involved. You weren't here when it happened. You didn't have a Gibson Warrant."

I winced.

"What is it?" He frowned. "Did you have a Gibson Warrant on this guy?"

I shook my head and swallowed hard, saying weakly, "No. No, I didn't. She couldn't afford to take it back to court."

"Okay, then. No Gibson Warrant, no news. Basically, you're not newsworthy."

"Gee, thanks, my self-esteem rises by the minute."

"There was a P.I.," he continued, ignoring my barb, "and he was keeping an eye out for Drummond. He called the police as soon as the shit hit the fan. The cops responded promptly, but not soon enough. It was an unavoidable tragedy."

Was it? I was drowning in a black sea of doubt.

"End of story," Hank said with finality. "Marco agrees it's best to keep you out of this."

"Only because he's ashamed to be seen with a lowlife retribution specialist."

Hank's eyes narrowed knowingly. "Ah, so that's what this is all about. I wondered what happened between you and Marco at the party."

"Look, little brother, the man is a fascist. He thinks he's the incarnation of Elliot Ness and he's going to clean up not only all the criminals in this town, but the renegade vigilantes, as well. That's what he thinks I am."

Hank crossed his arms, not immediately protesting the characterization.

"But regardless of what I think of Marco, you put him in a terrible position. He only came here to help me. This isn't even his case."

Hank looked over at Marco and Soji. "It is now. But don't feel sorry for the guy. He was in psy-ops, for God's sake. Look at him. He has a body like a movie star—he's smart, a smooth talker. He knows how to handle the media."

I wondered if there was anything or anyone Marco didn't know how to handle.

"Marco agreed to give WFYY an exclusive on the story," Hank added. "That means the other stations will only be able to rehash and confirm whatever information Soji gets. It was the best we could do for you under the circumstances."

I unfurled my arms and looped them around his torso, then kissed his cheek. "I know I don't act like it, Hank, but I'm grateful for your support."

He gave me a bear hug. "Hang in there, kiddo. This is all smoke and mirrors. It will evaporate by morning."

He hurried back across the street to make sure none of the other reporters snagged Marco when Soji's interview was over.

I saw Mel standing by a tree, talking to a man

who looked just like him. They were both in their fifties, both short and stocky, both wore argyle socks that didn't quite reach the hem of their flood pants, and both had a permanent and charmingly surly curl on the left side of the mouth. They had to be brothers. Maybe twins. Now that was a scary thought.

I headed their way. Mel was recapping the night's horrors to his look-alike. The reporters hadn't discovered them yet, but it wouldn't be long.

"Hi, Mel," I said.

"There she is now! Hey, Angel, meet my partner. He's my brother, too. Marvin Goldman. He was the one who was watching this place when I slept. I've told him all about you."

"Hello, Marvin." I shook hands with the man who was obviously Mel's identical twin. I was surprised. Mel had never mentioned that. The only thing that set them apart was hair. Mel had virtually none and Marvin had a full gray mane. Correction upon closer inspection: Marvin had a halfway decent rug. "You fellas may want to make yourselves scarce. Those reporters are going to be combing the neighborhood soon, looking for somebody to go on camera."

"I been on TV before. I can handle it." his voice even sounded like Mel's, except he was clearly the more confident of the two. Must be the rug.

"No," Mel said, clearly the smarter of the pair. "No interviews. We're going now, Angel, but I wanted to have a word with you."

"Me, too, Mel." When he pulled me aside, I said, "I'm sorry about this. I don't want you to think any of it was your fault."

"It's not your fault," he said at the same time. We stopped and smiled at each other. "We've been workin' together, Angel, what now...three years?"

I nodded. "Yeah."

"Nothin' like this ever happened before and never will again."

"I was wrong, Mel. So wrong."

"Nah."

"I made a terrible error of judgment and I'm sorry I made you witness this."

"Nah, Angel, you did nothin' of the sort. That pig Drummond did it all, the crazy, greedy bastard."

I nodded, tears burning the backs of my eyes. Why was it that older people were always so much quicker to forgive than the young?

"Look, hon," he said, taking my hands in his. "Uncle Mel's gonna tell you somethin' you don't never wanna forget."

I raised my eyebrows in feigned anticipation.

"Nothin' you do," he said slowly and tapped my breastbone, "that comes from the heart is wrong. *Nothin'*. Things may not always turn out right, but that's not the same thing as being wrong. And don't you never let nobody tell you different." He emphasized his point by winking.

I could have broken down and cried right then and there, but there was no time. The pack of reporters had spotted us and were heading our way.

"Thanks, Mel. I'll call you tomorrow." While he and Marvin hurried to their car, I jumped into Marco's SUV. His interview had ended and he headed my way, climbing into the passenger's seat.

He placed his palm on the start pad, which read his fingerprints, and the engine roared to life. I threw the vehicle into Drive and floored it. The force of acceleration slammed him against the seat.

"Whoa!" he said as we careered around the corner without slowing. "You do have insurance, don't you?"

"No," I said with dark glee. "I don't even have a driver's license."

He didn't say another word for the rest of the white-knuckled trip. I'd finally found a way to get in the last word with Detective Riccuccio Marco.

I brought the car to a screeching stop in front of my two-flat. When we stopped rocking back and forth, Marco let out a breath I think he'd been holding since we'd left the shelter.

I looked at him in the shadows of the early morning darkness and said, "I let my license expire because public transportation is more convenient in the city. But when I was in college I placed third in the National Championship Road Race competition. Land vehicle class."

He whistled low. "What else haven't you told me about yourself, Baker?"

"Everything," I said, going monotone. "You don't know anything about me."

"I know you're feeling guilty about Janet Drummond's murder."

"Don't psychoanalyze me, Marco." In a whisper, I added, "Please."

He smiled sadly and reached across the seat to

clasp my hand. I let him, then said impulsively, "Marco, you and I were not meant to be…involved. But thanks for the…for the possibility. It was fun."

He frowned. "You sound like you're going away."

I am, I almost answered. *I'm going to that deep, dark place where Lin Drummond lives. That sterile, safe place where no one else can visit.*

Instead of pulling himself up with wounded pride, he leaned forward and pressed my hand harder. The damn fool wasn't going to give up.

"Baker, don't make any rash decisions. You've been through a lot tonight. Get some sleep and we'll talk in the morning."

I saw a flash of light in the shadows a few feet away. A blue and yellow match flame revealed a craggy, noble face shadowed by a slick fedora. I'll be damned. My deus x machina had arrived. Humphrey Bogart, aka Rick Blaine, sauntered into the yellow pool of the streetlight. He dragged hard on his cigarette and blew out the match with a smoky breath.

"My date is here," I said.

Marco looked out the windshield, then leaned back. "Don't do this, Baker," he said in a tight voice.

"You're going to have to go. Just remember this moment so you never think about touching me again."

I climbed out of the car. I was so tired I felt like a zombie but forced myself to step lively. He had to think I couldn't wait to climb into bed with Bogie. I knew how much that would appall a straightlaced guy like Marco. I had to convince him that my judgment was as terrible in my personal life as it had been recently on the job.

"Hello, Angel," Bogie said. His voice was a balm to my ears. He was safe and predictable.

"Hello, Rick." I took his hand and led him to my door, watching Marco's reaction from the corner of my eye. He moved to the driver's seat and watched us until I opened the door. Then he drove off, leaving a peal of rubber on the pavement as a memento.

Finally the curtain had fallen, signaling the end of the show. I slumped in the foyer, then sat on the bottom step, dropping my head in my hands.

"What is it, Angel?" Bogie asked, clearly befuddled. We had our routine and this wasn't part of it.

I couldn't answer. Overwhelmed, I burst into tears, something I hadn't done in a long, long time. After a while, I wiped my eyes and found Bogie still staring at me. I almost felt sorry for him. He didn't have much of a repertoire in terms of reactions. He was waiting for some cue that seemed familiar.

"I'm sorry, Rick," I said and stood. I unfastened his trench coat and slipped my hands up under his suit coat, caressing his back.

"Now that's more like it," he said with a relieved chuckle. Too late, he realized what I was doing.

I grabbed his dress shirt and pulled it up so I could touch the small of his back. I felt for his program chip and pulled it out. He was just about to say "No!" when his system shut down. He went into synthesleep mode—arms down at his sides, posture erect, eyes closed.

"I'm sorry, Rick," I whispered in his ear, just in

case the synapses in his digital brain were still clicking from that final surge of shutdown power. "But the world doesn't care a hill of beans about the problems of two little people like you and me."

He hummed momentarily to life. His eyes flashed open and focused on me with fond recognition and, I thought, perhaps even sadness, then they closed again. He was, for all intents and purposes, dead to me.

I flipped on the foyer light and punched up the program in his portable chip. I tapped new coordinates into the palm-size disk and permanently reprogrammed our relationship. I'd only done this once before, the first time AutoMates, Inc. sent Bogie over so I could activate our relationship program, so I hoped I was doing it right. I returned the chip to the small of his back and stepped away.

His eyes opened and he gazed at me wistfully. "Goodbye, Angel. Remember—we'll always have Paris."

I felt a surge of affection that wasn't quite love but was frighteningly close. Then I kissed him on the mouth one last time. "Yes, Rick, we'll always have Paris."

He turned and opened the door, looking back at me just once from beneath his suave fedora. "Here's looking at you, kid."

Then he walked out of my life for good.

Chapter 19

Stop the Mandala, I Want to Get Off

I woke to the scents and sounds of my early childhood: sizzling bacon, frying eggs and burnt toast. Lola sang as she cooked in the kitchen. I hadn't had bacon and eggs in years, so I assumed she'd bought them at the corner store.

"Angel," she said in the doorway. "Wake up, honey. It's ten o'clock. Time to eat."

Actually, I usually ate at seven after an hour-long workout with Mike, but I didn't want to say that or Lola would consider it an invitation to conversation. I didn't want to talk about what happened last night, so I tried to go back to sleep. About a half hour later, I heard Mike's precise footsteps in the doorway and inhaled the scent of coffee. Now here was temptation.

I peeked out from under the covers and found him standing by my bed with a steaming mug in hand. Wow. He really had to be worried about me to willingly offer me coffee.

I grudgingly sat up and leaned against the headboard, taking the mug without looking him in the eye.

"Hank called this morning," Mike said, sitting on the edge of the bed. "He tells me what happened with Drummond and wonders if you are okay. I say yes, but now I wonder."

I took a sip from the mug, then rested it on the flat plane of my abdomen. "I can't do this anymore, Mike."

"Do what?"

"Try to bring justice to the victims of the world. There are too many of them. And I'm not very good at it."

"Why not?"

"I'm not God." I gave him a pained look. "I can think I know what's right, but I can also be wrong. And when I am wrong, the consequences are unbearable. I'd be better off doing nothing at all."

"Do not be so full of yourself that you think you cause what happens last night."

I took another sip and looked into his eyes.

"Janet Drummond dies not because of what you do, but because of what she does. Maybe not in this life, but in past life."

"Karma," I whispered.

"Yes. Only a buddha—one who achieves enlightenment—can see the big circle of one's life, can know how many reincarnations a person must endure before his karma is cleared. Not you, Baker. You are a smart girl, but not enlightened. Not yet."

I cradled the warm mug in my palms. "I cannot believe Janet did anything in this life or any other to earn a death like that."

"It is not for you to say or know how or when someone dies. You only can know about your own karma. When you lie about the Gibson Warrant, Baker, you start a cycle of bad karma. But that karma comes back to you, not Janet Drummond."

"I thought I had chosen the lesser of two evils. I didn't want to kill Drummond, even if I could have gotten a real Gibson Warrant. But I needed more leverage than I had without one. That's why I lied."

"A lie to Drummond is better than to murder him. Still, everything has cause and effect. But you and I know that." He smiled deeply. "I was a terrible monk. That is why I quit. You are a terrible angel."

I smiled. "That name is on my birth certificate. It has no symbolic or hidden meaning."

Mike looked off in the distance. "We both know we must try to make a better world. We have special talents." He turned his remarkable focus to me. I unconsciously straightened. "You see with the inner eye. And I know the way of Shaolin. Okay, the Buddha says we should live in a cave and ignore the world. But we can't—you and I. So we do our best and pay for our mistakes in this or the next life. Small price if we make this world a little bet-

ter for others. Even if we make it better for just one
person."

I nodded. Hopefully, I was about to do that for
Lin. But could I have done more for Janet? "If I'm
such a talented psychic, why didn't I see Janet's
murder coming?"

"You have been a sleeping dragon, Angel. But
now you wake. Like a dragon, you will ride the wind
to your destiny. Use what is around you to borrow
the strength you need. Become the dragon before the
eagle comes to claim you."

For the second time Mike had made an ominous
reference to the eagle. That had to be Vladimir
Gorky. If the Russian eagle was coming for Lola and
me, that meant Gorky was no longer distracted by
the kidnapped girls.

"Oh…my…God." I looked at Mike slowly. "Now
is the perfect time to rescue those girls."

"What?" he pressed.

"If Gorky is coming after me, then all I have to
do is an end run around him to snatch the kids out
of his own nest when his guard is down."

"What girls?"

"The pure-blooded Chinese girls that Gorky stole
from Corleone Capone, head of the Mongolian Mob.
The same girls that Lola saw at Gorky's mansion!"

Mike waited expectantly for the other shoe to
drop. "What does this mean, Baker? What do we
have to do?"

"It means," I said, standing up abruptly, "that it's
not enough to save just one orphaned girl. No, Mike,

not when you have skills like we do. We have to save all of them."

"Save who?"

"The Chinese orphans. We have to find them now!"

I put in a few calls to Hank, Mel and others who might help me in my rescue attempt. I struck out with almost every call and had to leave messages. I ate a quick bite and was surprised when the doorbell rang moments later. I wasn't expecting anyone and had no appointments.

When I opened the door, I was stunned to see Lin Drummond in four feet of thin grace and long black hair, clinging to a pathetically small bag of clothes and toys.

"Oh!" I pressed a hand to my chest. "Lin. I wasn't expecting you. But...but that's okay, that's... great!"

She didn't look me in the eye, but stared somewhere just above my right shoulder; her feelings of disdain for me couldn't have been clearer.

I finally noticed a pretty, middle-aged black woman standing behind Lin. "You must be the social worker," I said and invited her in for tea.

She introduced herself as Harriet Gross and accepted my offer, adding, "But I can't stay long. I'll have to leave you two alone sooner than I'd like, but I'm sure you'll be just fine."

God, was she really going to entrust this sullen, hurting child to my care? Had I really offered to take on this responsibility? Was I *nuts?* I didn't know how to be a mother, and I certainly didn't want to make the same mistakes Lola had. I didn't even know how to be a daughter, for God's sake.

"Can't stay long?" I said like a doll who has just had her string pulled. "No problem! Come in. Come in."

Ten minutes later we were sipping iced tea on the patio under the porch. Harriet offered a dozen papers for me to sign as a temporary foster parent. The pulse in my temple throbbed more loudly with each signature. I hadn't been this nervous since I'd closed on the mortgage for my house. Commitment always affected me that way. If I ever walked down the aisle, I'd probably keel over from an embolism before I made it to the altar. Damned good deterrent.

"Myrtle said you would be the best possible place to put Lin, and I agree," Harriet said. "This will only be for a week or two, until we sort out her case and find a long-term foster family for her."

I nodded. Unfortunately, Lin and I would just have broken the ice about the time she would have to leave and start all over with someone new. "I understand. I was a foster child myself, Mrs. Gross."

She nodded sympathetically, then looked at Lin. "She shouldn't be too much trouble. Myrtle says Lin keeps to herself."

We chatted awhile about the mundane but important details of temporary parenthood, like emergency contact numbers and follow-up visits from the Department of Children and Family Services. Then, all too soon, Harriet Gross stood to leave.

I looked at Lin, who still gazed out at nothing in

particular, and felt a moment of genuine panic for the first time in years. Volunteering to be a foster mother had been a bad idea, a cosmically bad idea. But I had to remember the big picture here. I could keep Lin safe and she might even be able to help me find the other girls.

I assured Harriet Gross that everything would be fine, escorted her to the front door, then returned to the garden. I paused before stepping out onto the patio. Lin still sat at the edge of the garden chair, the little duffel bag on her lap. Her spindly little legs extended below the seat like matchsticks. She still held her shoulders back with determined dignity, but now her head tilted forward and her eyes blinked sorrowfully beneath her straight onyx bangs.

When I cleared my throat to announce my return, her head snapped up and she stiffened. God only knew what she'd experienced in the Drummond household to warrant such wariness. I could hardly blame her for being on her guard around adults who pretended to care but could give no meaningful comfort. I understood. I'd been there myself. It seemed like just yesterday.

And that had prepared me better than most for foster motherhood. Enough of this hanging back and letting a pouting child intimidate me. I could do this. And I knew from experience that being direct was the best approach.

I walked forward with a brave smile and sat in the plastic lawn chair next to hers. "So, Lin," I said, even though she couldn't speak English, "what do you think of your new surroundings?"

Her head turned my way with astonishing precision. "I *hate* it. I hate *you*." Then she slowly, almost regally returned her head to its stiff, forward position.

I leaned back from the blow. Round One went to Lin the Invincible. I guess I was wrong about taking the direct approach. Then it hit me. "Wait a minute, you spoke English."

Just then Mike came out of his coach house and joined us.

"Boy, am I glad to see you," I said. He kept a respectful eight feet or so of distance from Lin. She eyed him warily. He studied her quietly as I went to his side. "This is the girl I told you about. Her name is Lin. She's going to be staying with us for a couple of weeks."

"*Ni hao,*" he said, which was hello in Cantonese.

"*Ni hao,*" she whispered, looking away from him.

"Ask her how she's doing," I whispered to him. "I think she speaks English but she won't talk to me."

He spoke rapidly in Chinese, which to me was always a mystical and incomprehensible language of strange sounds and staccato delivery. As soon as he was done speaking, she turned to face him fully and spat back her response in an impassioned diatribe of indignation that had her pounding the cushion and left tears brimming in her eyes. If I had to guess, I'd say she'd just cursed his ancestors from now until kingdom come.

Just as quickly as she had launched into her attack, she fell silent. She wiped at a tear that had spilled down one perfect, porcelain cheek and went back to her Sphinx pose.

I pulled Mike aside. "What did she say?"

He gave me a pat smile. "She says she is very grateful for your hospitality and she is sure she will be very happy here."

My lips thinned with cynicism. "Nice try, Mike. What did she really say?"

"She say she hopes you bring shame to your family and that you come back in next life as an ant."

I nodded approvingly. "That's a good start. What else did she say? She shouted at you for a full two minutes. There had to be more than that."

"She say more than that, but it all comes out to same thing. She does not want to be here."

"Tell her she has no choice."

"She knows that," Mike said.

"She spoke English a moment ago. See if you can determine how much she knows and where she came from. I want to find out exactly how she got to the Drummonds' before D.C.F.S. does. I have a feeling this is no ordinary adoption gone wrong. We need to find if at any point she was with that group of kidnapped orphans."

"Yes, Empress Cixi." He always called me that when I got bossy. Empress Cixi was the last dowager empress in the court of the last emperor of China. She was nicknamed the Dragon Lady and was so vindictive she once was said to have dismembered a concubine who angered her, then kept the girl alive in a big vase with only her head sticking out of the top.

"Hey, whatever it takes to find those girls." And maybe make something good out of the Drummond nightmare. Even if this time I paid the ultimate price to finally find some peace of mind.

Chapter 20

Chinese Puzzle

I left Mike and Lin in the garden and went back inside to make some more calls. I had to turn down a retribution gig for later in the week. I didn't want to commit to anything until Lin was settled. Then I put a call into Mel but he wasn't home. Marvin answered the phone, and for a minute I mistook him for his brother. I wondered how often that had happened without my knowledge over the past three years. They were, after all, descendants of actors. That would definitely be a new take on job sharing.

I decided to give Lin the guest room and asked Lola if it was okay if she stayed down in the studio. Lola seemed delighted with the setup, I think because I was moving her somewhere other than out on the street.

And in a strange way, she and Lin had a lot in common. They longed for loved ones but deep down they didn't believe that family would be there for them any more than a stranger would be. Even though I'd just proven to Lola I would go to the ends of the earth for her, I knew she couldn't fully depend on me any more than I guess I could on her. So I'd just settle for coping with them. Love was still way too ambitious for me.

When Lola joined the others in the garden, I went back upstairs and punched up Mel's mobile number on the omniphone. He answered and his voice projected over the in-house speaker system.

"Angel, Marvin said that you called. How ya doing?"

"Fine." I plunked down on the couch and propped my legs up on the coffee table. "Mel, this morning I was thinking about something you said in passing last night. Everything was so crazy I didn't have time to ask you about it."

"What is it, doll?"

"You said that Drummond was a greedy bastard. What did you mean by that?"

"Oh, that. I meant he was a pig to think he could take a girl who would sell for ten million dollars on the black market and keep her for himself, raise her and then broker her into some kind of arranged marriage for twice that amount. It ain't gonna happen."

"So you don't think the Drummonds paid for an

adoption so they could raise Lin as their own daughter."

"Are you smokin' the funny stuff? Where would a putz like him get that kind of money?"

"Well, then, where could he get the money to buy her on the black market? That costs more than a legitimate adoption."

"I dunno," Mel said. "Maybe the lame nut got a freebie. Look, doll, I gotta go. Was there anything else? I'll call you when I get back to the apartment."

"No, that's okay. Thanks, Mel. I just…I just wonder how Drummond could land such a prized commodity on a carpenter's salary."

"I'll try to do some snooping around Little Beijing. Corleone Capone's the one who has the slave trade on kids from China locked down tight."

"I'm thinking that Tommy Drummond somehow got in good with Capone when he did some rehab work for the mobster."

"Well, that's gotta be the connection. But that's some compensation for rehabbing Capone's bathroom. Maybe he stole her right out from under Capone's nose. And maybe that's why he was gunned down outside the shelter."

"That makes sense."

"Don't forget that five years ago Capone spent six months in the slammer for slave trading a dozen girls he purloined from mainland China. Looks like he's up to his old tricks."

I sighed heavily. "Lots to think about. Thanks, Mel. I'll talk to you later."

I made a few more calls, then went out on the

back porch to gaze down on Lin's progress in the garden. What I saw had me gaping in disbelief.

Mike knelt in the grass, plucking weeds out of a bed of zinnias. Lin and Lola sat facing each other cross-legged on the ground nearby. Lin looked downright American in her pink Barbie shirt and shorts. Lola, as usual, looked like a circus clown in a muumuu so colorful I feared it would induce epileptic seizures.

But that wasn't what amazed me. Lola and Lin slapped hands in a game of patty-cake. Every time Lola got confused and missed, Lin broke out in a peal of elated laughter that she tried to stifle behind cupped hands. Then Lola would let loose with her guttural smoker's laugh. High and low, the sounds were the sweetest I'd heard in a long time.

Then it hit me. This was what irritated me about Lola. When she put her mind to it, she could charm the stripes off of a tiger. Why did Lin warm up to her and not me? I was the one who saved Lin. I was the one who would pay for her meals and make sure she found a good long-term foster home. Why didn't Lin tell Lola she hated her?

More important, why hadn't Lola cared enough about me to keep herself out of jail when I was young so I could have laughed and played with her?

I called over the balcony and asked her to help me prepare some lemonade. She was breathing hard by the time she climbed the stairs and entered the kitchen.

She looked at me in confusion. "Where's the lemonade?"

"We'll get to that in a minute. I need to talk to you."

"Oh, Angel, that kid is terrific." She sank into a chair at the kitchen table, looking flushed and happy. "I love her like she's my own, honest to God."

"But she's not your own!" I nearly shouted and was satisfied to see Lola's jaw drop. I'd hit a nerve and was perversely glad. "She's my foster child, not yours. I pray to God I can do a helluva lot better as a mother than you did with me."

"Yeah," Lola said breathily, taken aback. "Yeah, me, too."

"I don't even think you know what I'm talking about."

"I do, honey, I do."

"No, you don't. You don't know what it was like when I went to live with Jack in Schaumburg. Did I ever show you the cigarette burns on my back?"

Lola shrank back in her chair. "No."

"They're real pretty, Mom. I'll show you next time we go swimming in Lake Michigan. We haven't done that since I was seven, when they hauled you off to prison."

"You turned out okay," she said.

I punched the refrigerator, leaving a dent, then rubbed my sore knuckles. Calmly I said, "Do you know that I still question what I'm worth? That happens when your foster father sells you like cattle."

"What do you mean?"

"Jack made Henry Bassett pay him five thousand bucks to get out of my life. And Henry, God love him, paid it. I'm not sure you would have cared enough to do the same even if you had had the money."

"How could I? I was in prison!"

"My point exactly!"

"I wanted to be a good mother to you, honey. I was left alone to raise you. It wasn't easy. But you can do better."

"Can I?" I looked at her bitterly.

"Here's how you do it, honey." She scooted forward and leaned her weight on the table as if she were about to deal a hand of cards. "Here's how you deal with Lin."

I rubbed the back of my neck, praying for patience.

"You don't mention a thing about China to that girl. You know yourself how painful the past can be."

"What?" I scowled at her. "What are you talking about?"

"I'm talking about her emotional well-being," Lola shot back emphatically. Many years of self-inflicted melodrama had rendered my mother's face so expressive she often reminded me of a silent-film star. Unfortunately her exaggerated expressions came with a sound track.

"Lola, what does this have to do with Lin's well-being?"

"She's obviously been traumatized by something that happened in China. You shouldn't talk about it or you'll upset her."

"Oh, boy, here we go." I rubbed my eyes as I silently counted to ten. When I was done, I was still pissed. "That's your answer to everything, isn't it?

Let's just don't talk about it. If you pretend a problem doesn't exist, it will go away."

"Sometimes that's exactly what you have to do."

"Lola, do you know what that poor child has been through?" I railed at her. "She was kidnapped and sold! Her friends are imprisoned with Gorky. And you want her to just forget about it and act as if nothing ever happened?"

"Honey, she has to move on. You can't dwell on your problems."

"Oh, Jesus," I hissed, covering my face with both hands. I wanted to smack her. Instead, I tried one more time for reason, like a kid who wastes her last token on a carnival game she knows is rigged against her. I sat and said as calmly as I could, "If I don't find Lin's friends and prove that she's been the victim of a serious syndicate crime, she's going to end up in the foster care system, just another faceless number to get lost in the shuffle."

"So?"

"Did you hear what I said?" I nearly shouted. "Foster care!"

"What's so bad about that? You were in foster care and you turned out great."

I dropped my head, so frustrated I wanted to either drool or cry. That was so like my mother. She was too dense to know how much her actions had hurt me, but still smart enough to know a kid needed praise. Even an old kid like me.

"Okay, Lola, I guess that's enough talking."

"That's right, honey." She patted my arm. "Talking won't do you any good."

"Let's get some lemonade down to the garden," I said. "We've got work to do."

In silence we made frozen lemonade and collected a tray of glasses. Before we carried them down the porch stairs, I turned to my mother.

"Lola, why didn't you ever let the Bassetts adopt me?"

She was quiet for so long I thought maybe she'd fallen asleep standing up. I couldn't see her eyes in the glare of sunshine through the window.

"They really wanted me in their family. They loved me. I could have had a real family. I came so close to fitting in. Why wouldn't you let me go?"

"Because you were the best thing I ever had, honey," she said in a shaky voice. "I knew I didn't deserve you, Angel, but I couldn't let you go. I'm sorry. And I'm sorry I wasn't a better mother. But I know, honey, I just know you will be a great mom."

I played awhile with Lin in the yard, showing her some of my martial arts moves, and was surprised at how easily she opened up once I decided to open up myself. She still wasn't talking to anyone in English, but it was clear she understood everything we said and even laughed at my jokes.

I quickly realized that loving a child is an action more than a feeling. The feelings come later as the reward. First you have to show the kid love means being there. Always. No questions asked.

Later in the afternoon I went downtown to get some more information on the Mongolian Mob and the R.M.O. from Hank's news database. I wanted to have all my ducks in a row before I presented my case to the police. While I knew Marco would help me rescue the girls, stubborn pride kept me from calling him. I couldn't turn him away and then come crying for help every time I was in trouble. That wouldn't be fair to him. I had to do this myself. And I was afraid if I turned the case over to a detective I didn't know, the police might take Lin into custody for "safekeeping." I wasn't about to let her get lost in the system. Any system. I'd save the girls first and present an airtight case for prosecution after the fact.

By the time I returned home from my trip downtown, Mike had fixed a healthy and tasty vegetarian meal that even Lola claimed to have enjoyed. Lola had found some of my old pajamas and pointed Lin in the direction of the bathtub. I was impressed. As I recalled, when I was little, Lola would sometimes have me wear the same outfit for a week—in and out of bed. When I moved in with the Bassetts, I didn't quite believe Sydney when she told me you're supposed to change clothes every day.

By the time I found them, Lola was taking a nap in her makeshift apartment downstairs, Lin was in her guest room, door shut, and Mike had just finished cleaning up the kitchen.

I was glad to see him, and not just because I needed a translator. Whenever I walked a tightrope without a net, I liked to have Mike there to catch me if I fell. Together we went to Lin's room, knocked, then entered.

Lin sat on the bed in a pool of amber-tinted light from the bedside lamp. She'd locked her arms around her drawn-up knees, looking like a strong little scarecrow in the oversize long-sleeved and -legged cotton pajamas. With her black hair falling in jags around her bony shoulders and dashes of pink on her cheeks, a sliver of a mouth beneath solemn, almond-shaped eyes, she seemed like a young heroine in an anime cartoon, capable beyond her years, yet bighearted and innocent.

But I knew all too well that she was really a wounded little waif who had only a few years to decide once and for all whether the world was a good or bad place and whether that heart of hers would ever again be safe.

"*Ni hao*, Lin," I said, standing in the doorway.

She looked up warily at me, as if she knew we were going to have a difficult conversation. Yet she seemed more at ease than I'd ever seen her. It didn't hurt that Mike had probably fed her the best meal she'd had since leaving China. Green soy beans stir-fried with mong beans, tofu, yu-choy and black bean garlic sauce can be persuasive to a stomach that has probably been surviving on the Drummonds' likely fare of starchy pirogi, mutilated broccoli and white bread.

"We want to talk to you, Lin," I said, stepping inside and settling at the end of her bed. Mike sat on a chair against the wall, about two feet away. "Are you doing okay?"

She nodded.

"Lin, I think you understand English, but what I'm going to say is very important, so I've asked Mike to translate into your native language." I paused, allowing Mike to translate after every sentence. "I know you've been through some difficult times, but the bad times won't be over until we find out what has happened to you and where you belong. Do you understand?"

She blinked and, after what seemed an eternity, she nodded.

I let out a pent-up sigh and shared a hopeful look with Mike. "Good." I went on to explain what we knew about the Drummonds, which was very little, and the plans for her temporary and long-term foster care. "Lin, we can send you home relatively quickly if you will tell us more about where you're from. I believe you were with a group of girls who were kidnapped by a man named Corleone Capone. Is that right?"

She nodded and tears filled her eyes.

"Where are you from? Where did you live before you were taken?"

Her little body went stiff and her eyes seemed distant. "Peking," she said through tight lips.

"Peking doesn't exist anymore," I said gently. "Do you mean Beijing?"

She shook her head. Mike and I shared another look. "Ask her to describe her home," I suggested.

Mike translated her reply, which described a vast palace, jade statues, gold-tiled ceilings and giant pillars.

"Wow," I said, "that's quite a place to grow up in. Her parents must be rich."

"No," Mike said, "they must be royal. She described the Gugong in Beijing."

"Translation, please."

"The Imperial Palace, where Chinese emperors live for five hundred years, starting in the Ming dynasty and ending with the last emperor, Puyi, who lived there until 1924."

"So how could Lin have been raised there? Isn't it now a tourist attraction?"

"Yes. Where once there live three thousand eunuchs and hundreds of concubines, there is now over eight thousand empty rooms for tourists to see. No, she is confused."

"Or she's trying to confuse us," I mused. She looked at me sharply and I remembered she could understand most of what we'd said.

He spoke quickly in Chinese and she responded in kind, then broke into tears. She tried so hard to hold the tears back that her sobs came out in spurts. I wanted to pull her into my arms and soothe her, but I didn't know how. I turned questioningly to Mike.

"She says she was stolen from her sister by very bad men who murdered her," he said.

"Oh, no. That's terrible. What of the other girls? What happened to their families?"

Mike pressed on with questions and she sputteringly told him there were eleven other girls who grew up with her in the palace. Lin began crying again and I went into the bathroom, retrieved a couple of tissues and handed them to her. As she dabbed her eyes, I lost all desire to question her further. I didn't want to cause her any more pain. But I also needed more information to give to the police. I couldn't very well tell them the girls had been stolen from a royal palace that hadn't been used in more than a century.

"There's only one way to find out what I need, Mike, without causing her more pain."

He looked at me questioningly.

"Let's go to your shed. I'll bring my crystal ball."

He gave me one of his rare smiles and his black eyes gleamed approvingly. "Now you are talking, Baker."

I smiled at him, then at Lin. "Come on, sweetheart. Let's see if we can't get you back to Kansas without a trip to Emerald City."

Chapter 21

No Place Like Home

Talk about performance anxiety. Here I was in Mike's portable meditation hall, with paper amulets pinned on planked wallboards to ward off evil spirits, a Chinese Book of Days open on his bamboo writing table, *I Ching* coins scattered on his futon and charts showing the twelve palaces of purple astrology, and *I* was supposed to be the one to have a vision?

Mike lit several candles and placed the ball and tripod stand in the middle of the floor on a one-foothigh mah-jongg gaming table. I sat on a meditation pillow on the grass mat in front of it and adjusted the position of the ball.

"Ask Lin to sit across from me."

Mike began to translate, but she stopped him, saying, "I speak English."

We gaped in silence. She continued with only the slightest accent. "My sister taught me. She said someday I would need it."

Mike and I looked at each other and stifled grins. "Well, then let's continue. In English," I add wryly.

I tried to remember what Dr. Hunter had done at IPAC. I needed to start using my psychic powers in a more proactive way. "Lin, I need you to concentrate on your own experiences. As painful as this may be, I want you to try to remember what's happened since you left China. You don't have to talk about the events, just think about them, okay?"

She nodded, but her smooth, flat features went still and assumed a faraway look that I recognized well. She'd tightened the spigot on the pipeline to her feelings. It was, understandably, a defense mechanism that children used when they were afraid of getting hurt again or reliving past pain. Sometimes it was just too painful to keep the pipeline open. Lin eyed me warily, perhaps as she contemplated giving one more adult a chance to disprove her theory that none of them could be trusted.

"Okay, sweetie," I said, smiling reassuringly, "now I want you to shut your eyes and picture where you were before you went to the Drummond's apartment. Who was there with you? What did you smell? What did you hear and see? Think about how things felt to touch. Understand?"

She pulled her hair back behind one ear, sniffled and nodded.

"Good. Mike, turn the lights off. I only want candlelight."

Mike did as I asked and settled like a shadow in the corner of the room. I put my hands on the ball. Images popped into my head, but they were familiar and ordinary scenes from my daily life. Even after only a few attempts at reading the crystal, I knew the difference between active imagination and a real vision. I simply had to wait.

It was like waiting for slumber. Your mind whirls, replaying events from the day, and it seems you'll never fall asleep. Then you realize the scenarios have become bizarre, even impossible, and you think, "I'm starting to dream. Awesome."

I focused on the reflected candlelight on the smooth orb under my hands. In my mind, I saw Janet Drummond frozen in her own blood, Mel and Marvin Goldman's argyle socks, Soji doing her live shot, Marco on the beach. Then I saw a Chinese girl, but it wasn't Lin. And it wasn't in my mind. Her image appeared in the glass. A vision. Awesome.

I moved my fingers aside so I wouldn't block the view, but kept my fingertips on the glass. The girl suddenly seemed so real I thought I could reach through the glass and pull her out. She had short, black hair and was smiling. She looked to be no more than four. I saw others playing, including Lin. So this was the past.

"I see Lin with other Asian girls. One has short black hair and...huge dimples."

"Pei," Lin said in a small voice.

I didn't look up, afraid to lose the vision. Where

was Pei? I tried to expand my focus, like a camera lens, and it worked. I saw a flash of color behind Pei. "She's in a big red room. So big I can't see the ceiling. She...you and the other girls are filing out into a garden. I see...rocks piled up to look like little mountains, and gnarled pines, a bronze incense burner...and a winding footpath with colored pebbles."

"The Imperial Garden," Lin said.

Innocent laughter filled the ancient courtyard and a distant gong reverberated. I was actually hearing things. The girls played and laughed while older girls dressed in colorful red-satin Chinese dresses watched.

Suddenly there was a scream. Several men ran into the garden and started herding the girls into another big room with high, painted ceilings and incredible jade murals. The girls began to cry. "Sister, where is Sister?" several of them whimpered.

Again, as in a dream, the scene changed abruptly. I felt queasy and my skin chilled. I was no longer looking down at the scenes reflected in glass. My eyes glazed over and it was as if I were there, as if I were Lin.

I'm hurtling down a hallway, a dark labyrinth, being jostled by the other panicked girls.

"Hurry, hurry," shouts a guard from behind. He's dressed in the old Ming-style warrior's robe. I run faster, but Pei trips in front of me. I try to catch her, but we both go down. I scrape my knee, but am too scared to cry. A guard runs up behind us and scoops us up like sacks of feathers until our sandals once

again hit the stone floor. We run forever, it seems, until we reach the Palace of Heavenly Purity.

I hear the gasps and muted cries of horror from those who enter the tall templelike living quarters. I expect to see what I always see here: a half dozen private bed nooks made of dark cherrywood and partitioned by expensive embroidered yellow-and-turquoise silk curtains and elaborate murals made of precious polished stones and jade. I expect to see our sisters grooming themselves or playing cards as they always do when we go out to play. But what I see instead is almost impossible to absorb.

I see Pei's sister first. She is an angular eighteen-year-old with wide, pretty lips. For some reason she is asleep on the blue-tile floor next to the bed she and Pei share in the corner. Light streams in through long, narrow windows and in its beam I see blood on her sheets. Pei runs to her, then shrieks like a wounded animal, her body in spasms as if she's been electrified.

I run to the east side of the temple structure, pull back the curtains and there is my sister, brown-black hair splayed on a bloody pillow, eyes open a slit, her simple white blouse darkened with blood. She is dead. They're all dead.

"No!" I cry out. "Sister!"

A guard wraps an arm around my waist and pulls me away. She is all I have and I cannot even hug her one last time. Likewise, the other girls who live here with us are drawn away from their slain sisters. We howl in a dissonant chorus.

The scene changes suddenly. A moan stops in my

*throat and I realize I've been crying. My cheeks are
damp with tears. From a greater distance I see the
palace as we are leaving with the man called
Capone. Behind the palace, I see a big shiny building and American letters: F.R.Y. Barring. My eyes
blur and I begin to cry.*

*The sense of loss is indescribable. I can take no
more.*

I force my eyes open and find Lin still staring at
me. Her cheeks, too, are wet. But the distance between us is gone. It didn't matter that we'd only recently met. She knew that I knew what she'd gone
through. I understood the depth of her loss. I respect
it. In a way, it has become my own.

"You never saw your sister again?" I said in a
torn voice.

She shook her head and a new wave of tears
flooded her eyes.

"You don't know what happened to her? Why she
was killed?"

"I don't know," she whispered hoarsely.

An overwhelming wave of sympathy propelled
me to my feet. I pulled her up and lifted her into my
arms, clutching her tight. She was nearly too tall to
hold, but I was strong, and strength could be used
for more than fighting.

I sat in a chair against the wall and pulled her into
my lap, cradling her as best I could a—what, a six-
year-old? I didn't even know. And not knowing intensified my urge to protect and heal her. She had no
one.

"Oh, Lin," I murmured against her bangs as I

rocked her in my arms. "I'm so sorry. That shouldn't have happened." I kissed her hair and tasted my own tears. Grief shook from inside me in a silent, hammering sob. I held her and cried uncontrollably for all we had both lost. I mourned because she couldn't. Not yet. She was limp in my arms, unresisting. While I'd never allowed myself to cry for me, I could cry and rage on her behalf. She needed that. She needed someone to stand up for her. It didn't take the whole world to make a difference— just one person.

I held Lin until my tears dried and I was filled with a sense of peaceful acceptance. By then she was asleep. I looked in the corner and found Mike patiently watching us. I never had to explain anything to him. He understood without words.

I carried Lin to bed and tucked her in, stroking her hair away from her soft cheeks. I gazed down at her with a bundle of emotions that were new, exciting and a little frightening. Surprisingly, one of them was admiration for Lin. I thought that was a feeling triggered by someone who had accomplished great things in life. But, in fact, a child being courageous in the face of cruelty was a great thing.

By the time I left the room and quietly shut the door, I knew what task lay ahead of me. I finally had tangible evidence that even the most apathetic city officials couldn't ignore. Lin wasn't raised in Beijing. She had been kidnapped from a suburb of Chicago. The royal palace she called home was apparently nothing more than a replica built in the shadow of one of the newest landmarks and most glaring eyesores to hit the Chicago area in the last fifty years.

In my vision, when I viewed the past through Lin's eyes, the last thing I saw was the Friedman, Reilly & Young building in Barrington. F.R.Y. Barring was all I could see, but there was no mistaking the gleaming corporate icon. Apparently, Capone was no longer stealing girls from China. God forbid, was he breeding them now in the wooded suburbs of northern Illinois? If he sold girls who were literally homegrown, he couldn't be put in jail for international slave trade.

But he could be put in jail for murder, and that gave me something solid to give to the police. Before I did, though, I wanted to free the girls myself. I didn't trust the government to do it without screwing up.

That meant it was time to pay a visit to the only man in Chicago who had the guts to steal nearly a dozen girls from Corleone Capone. Vladimir Gorky. Like a Blue Dragon slithering out of the water, I would rise up and face the Russian eagle. The day of reckoning had come.

Chapter 22

The Headless Housekeeper

In the kitchen, Mike and I gathered to talk about our plans over a cup of tea. No sooner had we settled in than Lola came up the stairs and peeked her head into the kitchen.

"Yoo-hoo," she said in a singsong voice. "What time is it? Shouldn't you kids be in bed?" She sat in a chair, dark eyes bright with curiosity.

"Yes, Mrs. Baker," Mike said obediently, but he didn't get up to leave, and I smothered a smile.

I poured Lola a cup of tea and while she stirred in five teaspoons of sugar, I questioned her further about her visit to Gorky's mansion. I needed to know where she'd seen the girls. I had envisioned her chained in a dark basement. But while she was there, she informed me that not only did she dine on shrimp alfredo, she passed by a room with a bowed glass wall overlooking the lake, à la Frank Lloyd Wright, filled with adorable little Chinese girls eating chocolate cupcakes.

Apparently Lola had a far closer relationship with good old Vlad than she'd let on. And the girls were, at least temporarily, being well cared for.

Based on Lola's experience, I concluded that there was only one way to free the girls. I had to meet face-to-face with Gorky and strike a bargain.

To that end, I told Lola exactly what I needed from her. She had to call Vladimir Gorky and arrange for him to meet with me. She turned white when I explained my plan.

"Honey," she said, "don't go near that man. He's dangerous."

"I know," I said in a monotone, oddly calm inside. "I predict this is the job that will finally do me in. But I have to do it, because if I don't try to do what's right for those girls, no one will. I cannot stand by and let children be bought and sold."

"Don't make me do this, Angel. I'm scared."

"You owe me, Lola. If you do this for me, I'll forget about that whole adoption thing. I'll never mention it again."

She blinked with touching hope. "You mean that, honey?" When I nodded, she added, "Why?"

"It's not often that we get a chance for redemption. I have a lot of regrets. Not so much for what I've done, but for what I haven't done. I just have this feeling that if we help these girls, we can both start over."

This was starting to sound like a snake oil salesman's version of the Buddha's Noble Eight Fold Path. In reality I didn't know squat about redemption. But it wasn't like they offered a course on it at the local community college, so it was time to take some risks.

"I just know I have to do this," I said in conclusion.

Lola clutched my hand and looked into my eyes deeper than she ever had before. "Angel, baby, are you willing to die for those girls?"

"I'm willing to die trying to get them home. Everybody should be able to go home."

Lola slowly drew back, nodding with resignation. Then she smiled contentedly. "All right, honey. I'll call Vlad. You're doing the right thing, Angel. You always do."

Yes, irony sucks, but sometimes in a delicious way. Lola arranged a meeting between me and the head of the R.M.O. at Rick's Café Americain. Lola said Gorky had been to Rick's before. When I expressed concern about meeting so close to my two-flat, she waved me off impatiently.

"Honey," she said, "if Vlad wants to find out where you live, nothin' will stop him. He probably already does know. And if he'd wanted me back after my escape, I'd be gone by now."

We made a few last arrangements then went to bed. I woke early for a light workout, breakfast and then I took Lin to Evanston for safekeeping with Sydney. Lola was highly put out that I trusted my foster mother's care-giving more than hers, but I wasn't going to take any chances. Even if Lola had been Mary Poppins when it came to child care, I didn't want Lin caught in Gorky's net if he decided to scoop up Lola, his errant soothsayer.

By the time I arrived at Rick's in the early evening, I was feeling downright fatalistic. While Gorky was dangerous, he was also a quasi-public figure and would not risk his reputation by killing me in public. He would let his minions do that at another time and place. It was too hot to wear my millifine steel suit anyway, so instead of dressing in a defensive mode I decided to try to look tough.

I wore short, pale blue shorts, a jeweled aluminum bra top and an easy-stick spiderweb tattoo that covered my cleavage and spread over my bare abdomen down to the low-cut line of my shorts. I heavily lined my eyes, generously colored my lips, slicked my hair back and donned my black stiletto ankle boots.

When I walked into Rick's at six, the place was already crowded. Dinner was served in the north end of the building. The bar area was filled with tourists and locals, plus the usual dozen or so compubots. Ilsa Laszlo was powdering her nose, as usual, at a table in the corner while Victor, her husband, talked to the refugee about escaping French-occupied Morocco. They sat at the bar, pretending to barter over a ring.

Through the distance, which was hazy with pungent, unfiltered cigarette smoke, I saw Rick in a white tux ordering a drink at the bar. He caught my eye and did a double take. I smiled and waved. He nodded and raised his glass in a private toast. I found myself waiting for his come-hither look, but remembered I'd stripped it from his program. He would never look at me like that again. From now on I'd only receive the wistful looks reserved for a fond former lover.

I looked around for Gorky but saw no sign of him, so I took a table on a dais in the back where I could see the whole room in relative privacy. I ordered champagne. I was about to give the most critical performance of my life and a slightly elevated mood might help. Gorky was no two-bit crook I could intimidate with the threat of bodily injury. It would be my vision of the world against his. And whatever happened tonight, I'd have to do a better job bluffing than I had with Tommy Drummond.

I'd had maybe two sips of the pink bubbly when Gorky walked in. He was tall with broad shoulders, more striking than handsome, with swarthy skin stretched tight over hard, Slavic features. Topping it all was a head of thick, distinguished-looking silver hair. He had to be at least seventy years old, but he had the body of a man thirty years younger and he could probably kill a man with a single punch to the heart.

Gorky spoke briefly and authoritatively to the Moroccan host, then strode confidently toward me in ivory slacks and a gray silk shirt. Heads turned his way and people milling between the tables parted instinctively to make way for him, in part because of his extraordinary presence and in part because many doubtlessly recognized him from news coverage.

"Ah, you must be Ms. Baker," he said in a gravelly Russian accent when he climbed the single step to the dais and reached my table. He smiled broadly with oodles of charm. His icy-blue eyes twinkled and he held out his arms in a where-have-you-been-all-my-life? gesture, saying, "It is such a pleasure to meet you after all this time. Lola has told me so much about you."

I stood and held out my hand. "How do you do, Mr. Gorky?"

He took my hand, undressed me with his eyes, and then kissed my knuckles with chivalry that took me aback. It reminded me of one of Lola's old phrases about men: just because there's snow on the roof doesn't mean there isn't a fire burning down below.

One kiss wasn't enough. He clasped his enormous paws on my arms, kissing each cheek without permission and with no recognition of my stiff resistance. "In my country, we greet people as old friends, Ms. Baker, unless we know them to be enemies. If they're enemies, then we make love to them."

"You make love to men?" I inquired, pulling myself out of his grasp.

"No, we just kill the men. But why kill a woman you haven't yet seduced?"

I pulled myself up, dignity restored, and motioned to the chair opposite mine. "You talk about your country?" I said, trying to steer the conversation away from sex. It was giving me the creeps. "That would be America, wouldn't it? You are a naturalized citizen, I thought."

"True. But in these wonderful days a person's allegiance is not to the land of his birth, but to great ideas."

Carl, the plump, white-haired, tuxedo-clad waiter, took Gorky's order with attentiveness I'd never received, I noted with irritation.

"What would you like, Mr. Gorky?"

"Vodka." The word was a burr in his throat. He pinned his powerful gaze on me. "For two."

"No, I don't drink vo—"

"Your very best," Gorky added.

"Very good, sir." Carl hurried off.

I realized with some pique that Vladimir Gorky was a man who didn't listen to women. I doubt he'd heard anything I'd said so far.

"So, you are Lola Baker's daughter."

He leaned back in his chair and crossed his thick arms. I'd bet a paycheck he had started out as a street thug and had risen through the R.M.O. ranks by brute force, as well as cunning. His manly charm and large size had probably been part of the equation, as well.

"Yes, I am."

He nodded approvingly. "You're very beautiful."

I took in a deep breath and felt self-conscious about the low cut of my metal bra. I was so supposed to be intimidating, not fetching. Men like Gorky prided themselves on finding everything a woman does sexy. It was a way to diminish any other platform from which a woman might assert herself. He was all about power and he'd gotten it by disregarding some basic rules of civilization, like don't kill, lie or maim.

"I'm not here to talk about me, Mr. Gorky."

"Please," he said with a cajoling smile, "call me Vladimir."

"I know that you have eleven Chinese girls in your safekeeping," I began diplomatically. "I trust they are in good health."

He frowned. "Who told you that? Oh, yes, Lola was there. Where is she, by the way?"

I looked at him and took a sip of champagne.

"Don't worry. I gave her to Cyclops to teach her a lesson. I think she has learned it. I would never hurt her, Angel *moy.*"

As I recalled from my encounters with the Sgarristas, *moy* was Russian for "my." My Angel. What a presumptuous jerk.

Carl returned with two shots of vodka and a chilled bottle for refills. Gorky slid a glass toward me, then raised one in a toast.

"To the beautiful Angel Baker." He tossed back the liquor and exhaled contentedly. "Please, Angel, drink. It is the best vodka my homeland has to offer."

"What lesson did you want Lola to learn?" I said, ignoring his entreaty.

"That she should not play me for a fool."

I chuckled softly. "I wouldn't think anyone could play you for a fool."

"Only when I let them."

"Vladimir," I said in conciliator tone, "I want you to give me those Chinese girls."

He laughed as if I'd just told a hilarious joke. "Just like that? They're worth one hundred million dollars." His inscrutable eyes hardened, then lit with curiosity. "What could you possibly want with them?"

"I want to return them to their rightful parents."

His frown deepened. "Why do you care?"

I slowly turned the clear glass stem of my champagne flute. "Because I know what it's like to be torn away from your parents. Because it's wrong. Whatever you plan to do with them, it's wrong. Children should not be bought and sold."

He poured himself another shot, swilled it and put the glass on the table with a quiet thud. "So how long have you been working for Corleone Capone?"

"I do not work for the Mongolians," I hissed. "That's ridiculous. I'm a Certified Retribution Specialist."

"I know what you are," he shot back impatiently. "You do kung fu. You're stubborn and independent."

My jaw parted and I forced it shut. "Who told you that?"

He shrugged. "Why, Lola, of course."

"How discreet of her," I said tightly.

He raised a bushy gray eyebrow and looked at me pointedly over his large, arched nose. "There isn't a discreet bone in that woman's body."

I wouldn't deny that. "If you don't hand over those girls, I'll have to report them to the police.

You'll be put behind bars for slave trade, just like Capone was a few years ago."

His mouth parted with a coughing chuckle. "That's good, very good, Angel *moy*. You have an admirable sense of justice. But the police can't touch me. I haven't sold the girls, so I'm guilty of nothing. Capone is the one who kidnapped them. Besides, my people have been in Chicago a lot longer than Capone—the Mongolian Capone, that is. I have the police exactly where I want them."

"You have untold wealth, Vladimir, from untold shady businesses. Why do you need to sell innocent girls? Surely you're not that hard up for cash."

That elicited a spark of anger from his steely blue eyes. "Don't insult me. I have more money than the Illinois treasury. Of course I'm not doing it for the money. Leave that to the Mongolian bottom feeders."

"Then why?"

He looked around the room, as if noticing his surroundings for the first time. "I like it here. I'm a big Bogart fan. Did you ever see *The Maltese Falcon*?"

"Yes," I said tersely. So we had one thing in common—we were both fans of Bogie. "But it's not my favorite."

"I suppose you like *Casablanca*. Women always do."

"Yes," I reluctantly admitted, "I do like it."

"And *The African Queen*?" he inquired almost disparagingly as he tossed back another shot.

I refused to admit he'd nailed me again.

"I liked Bogart better when he was a character actor, before he wimped out as a romantic lead."

"I want the girls," I said through clenched teeth. "Why can't you let them go? I have my own connections in the police force who won't turn a blind eye on this."

He really looked at me for the first time, blinking in surprise. He probably wasn't used to women trying to direct the course of a conversation.

He poured another shot for himself. "I kidnapped the girls from Capone because he killed my cousin ten years ago. I have been waiting for a chance to pay him back. His organizatsia is not nearly as wealthy as mine. He needs the money. By keeping his girls, I can hurt him financially. But more than that, the Asians want to save face. You hear of this before?"

I nodded. Every now and then you'd see something in the news about a Japanese corporate executive who committed hara-kiri because his company went bankrupt. It was considered the honorable way to account for failure. In America, CEOs who bankrupted companies didn't apologize for their shortcomings. They waltzed into the sunset with billion-dollar buyout packages.

"So," Vladimir said, still showing no signs of affect from the alcohol, "I took these girls because Capone went to a fucking boatload of trouble to get them to market. He wanted to play the magnanimous godfather and sell them to the Chinese community here in Chicago to strengthen their bloodlines. So I'm going to make sure they end up with good boys from the motherland, just to embarrass him."

"You're going to sell them to your own people?"

"Or give them away. I don't know. But I want these girls to have children named Vladimir, Sergei and Natasha. And I'll do it just to see Capone have a heart attack over it."

Revenge. I was beginning to think it made the world go around. I took a long sip of my champagne. Every man had his price. What was Gorky's? If I knew a little bit more about him, perhaps I could make him an offer he couldn't refuse.

"So tell me, Vladimir, how did you and my mother get to know each other?"

He pressed his large hand over his heart. "She never told you? I'm crushed. She must be ashamed of me."

"My mother and I don't share secrets. She didn't raise me after the age of seven, so I don't know much about her."

He shrugged. "Oh, we've known each other for years. When I was a younger man and still involved in street activities for the R.M.O., I was in charge of the Rogers Park operation. At that time the Cosa Nostra was still a player in the gangland scene. This old hit man named Jerry Manetto got a shot off on me outside of Lola's parlor. I killed the bastard, but not before he plugged a wad of metal in my thigh."

He stopped and I leaned forward. "Really?"

"Lola came down and pulled me into her building. She dug out the plug, sewed me up and nursed me back to health. I couldn't go to the hospital or I'd be arrested."

My eyes nearly popped out of their sockets. "Lola operated on you?"

"She dug around a bit," he said, his eyes finally relaxing from the vodka. "Then she told me I was going to have a great future. I came back for more readings after that."

I blinked in amazement. What more had my mother done that she hadn't told me about?

"In fact, I say I owe all my success to Lola Baker. She has an uncanny ability to see the future and to advise me to make good decisions."

My heart started pounding. I couldn't believe how deep into this R.M.O. scene Lola had gotten herself. If Gorky really believed Lola's readings had helped him, he had a helluva way of showing his gratitude. I'd hate to see how he treated his enemies.

"If you're so grateful to Lola, why did you kidnap her? You slaughtered her cleaning lady, for God's sake!"

"I am sorry about that, *dorogaya moya*." *My dear.* Another inappropriate endearment. "The woman wouldn't cooperate and my Sgarristas got a little carried away."

"Were they trying to kill my mother?"

He shook his head with a look of benign regret. "No, Angel *moy*, I would do nothing like that. Lola just made me mad. She had some information about something I hold very dear, something I lost. And she wouldn't tell me where it was. You don't want to make Vladimir Gorky mad."

He poured another drink. The clear liquid

glugged from the blue bottle. His hands were cal-
loused and muscled, with tufts of gray hair curling
on the fingers. He wore two rings. One was a pinky
ring adorned with a diamond that was so big I wondered if he'd stolen it from the last tsar's crown
jewel collection. The other was a shiny, fat gold
monstrosity on his ring finger. Simple in contrast, it
was adorned with a three-dimensional silhouette of
the symbol of Russia—the two-headed eagle.

I suddenly remembered Mike's dream: *the eagle
soon comes for the blue dragon.* Typical of my luck,
it was now two heads against one.

I was beginning to glimpse the big picture here.
Lola was hopelessly enmeshed in Gorky's world,
and if she didn't somehow detach herself, she'd
probably end up like the headless housekeeper.

I had to find a way to make Gorky lose interest
in Lola the Soothsayer and at the same time give up
a one-hundred-million-dollar investment that was
guaranteed to satisfy his quest for revenge. What
dark human motive was stronger than revenge? Perhaps greed, but I wasn't in a position to buy him off.

Oh, if only I were Cosmo the Magnificent, I
could just make Gorky disappear. Right now sleight
of hand would be more useful than my psychic ability.

"What are you thinking about, Angel *moy*?" he
said. "You are so serious. I hope I haven't frightened
you."

Psychic. That was it! I could convince Gorky my
mother was a fraud to make him lose interest in her,
then find his lost treasure myself, thereby earning his

gratitude, which I could then parlay into the release of the girls. I could kill two eagles with one stone.

"Vladimir," I said, leaning forward and speaking in confidential tones, "I don't know how to tell you this, but Lola is a fraud."

He frowned skeptically.

"She doesn't know how to read the past, present or future. She's a con artist. She's been taking you for a ride for years."

"How do you know this?"

"I know. She's admitted as much to me. Her ability to tell the future stinks."

He gave me a knowing smile. "Ah, I see how it is. Children never want to admit their parents can do anything right. One day, *dorogaya moya,* you will see your mother's good points."

I shook my head. "When she mentioned your lost treasure, it was simply an accident. She was drunk. She made up something that just happened to be the truth. That's why she couldn't you tell where it actually was. She wasn't holding anything back. She simply didn't know."

"And how do you know all this? What makes you the expert?"

"Because I am a true psychic." This time I really meant it and I could see it made an impression on him. He was really listening to me now. "I was tested and scored off the charts. And speaking as a professional, Vlad, you need to forget about Lola. She's well-meaning, but a rank amateur. Yeah, she's a good old gal, but her advice can't be trusted. Just leave her alone."

He frowned at me, his inscrutable blue eyes scanning as his sharp mind whirled. I couldn't begin to guess what he was thinking.

"I hope, Angel *moy,* that you are not the one who is now trying to play me for the fool."

I reached out and gripped his wrist. He looked down at it in surprise. "Trust me, Vladimir. I will find your lost treasure. But on one condition."

He grinned slyly. "You want the girls."

I nodded, releasing his arm. I had laid out my best hand. It was time to sit back and see if he was ready to fold.

"It's a deal." He leaned closer to me and whispered, "But if you fail, *dorogaya moya*, I will throw you from my house into Lake Michigan where you will sleep with the fishes."

His soft purr sent a shiver of foreboding down my spine. I had just committed myself to having a vision on command. Not just any vision, but a very specific one that had to produce results. What if I failed?

"Sleep with the fishes?" I said with a forced laugh. "I thought that modus operandi died with the Italian Mafia."

He smiled and poured more vodka. "It is just a figure of speech. You know all too well how we kill our enemies."

"Yes, I know." And if I needed a reminder, all I'd have to do was ask the headless housekeeper.

Chapter 23

La Petite Morte

I arranged to meet with Gorky at 9:30 p.m. the next night at his lakeside compound. After walking back to my place from Rick's, I called my brother and asked him to check the station data bank to see if there was any information about Gorky's mansion. If I knew what I was walking into and how to get out, I'd increase my chance of survival.

I told Mike about the meeting and didn't even politely refuse when he offered to come with me. I simply nodded and heaved a sigh of relief. He and I then talked to Lola, picking her brain for every detail she could recollect about Gorky's spread. She told us a lot about the eighteenth-century Rembrants, the nineteenth-century Monets, twentieth-century Pollocks and twenty-first-century Joberts adorning the walls, as well as the hand-woven carpets and the handcrafted woodwork, all of which she knew to be expensive and therefore coveted, even though it wasn't to her taste. She hadn't paid much attention to anything else that might be helpful to us. And she had no idea what sort of lost treasure she'd unintentionally touched on in her reading. Personally, I hoped it was a cache of priceless jewels and not a stockpile of plutonium.

After grilling Lola, I went to bed around eleven. I would be walking into Gorky's place cold in less than twenty-four hours and would need to rely on my instincts. For that, I needed a good night's rest.

Unfortunately the air conditioner went into one of its off modes. It never failed to fail me when I needed it the most. I flexed my fists, tightening my muscles. They were covered in a sheen of perspiration. I tightened various muscles through my body as I mentally reviewed my best kung fu moves.

I shut my eyes, but after tossing and turning in bed for an hour, I dragged a pillow and sheet to the couch in the living room. I looked out the window and was disappointed not to see Marco as I had once before. I gripped the rough bricks outside the window ledge, straining to see his car in either direction, but he wasn't there.

A dull ache pounded in my chest. For the first time in my adult life, I was really scared and wanted him tonight. *Needed* him. I needed to hold him and to know I was alive before I faced possible death.

If I had to spend the night sweating, why couldn't it be in the arms of a man? A real man. One who couldn't get enough of me. One who could hurt me or love me, depending on my luck. One who could carry my heart safe in the palm of his strong, beautiful hands, if my luck was exceptionally good.

It was funny, but I hadn't missed Bogart at all. When you're over it, you're over it. Especially when it is an it and not a he. I'd been living in a fantasy for too long. In a way, I'd exiled myself from human contact and now I regretted it. I claimed it was because I didn't want to be used again, but it was much more complicated than that.

I blamed myself for being dumped by Peter. If I'd been dumped once, it would happen again, right? Peter wasn't the one who had been broken, after all. I was.

But that was so wrong. *He* was the dickhead, not me. He had used me, and I'm quite sure he never had a second thought or a moment of guilt. So, by God, I would not let him define the rest of my life. I needed and deserved love. Some lucky sonofabitch was going to experience love from me in return. So there!

I threw my arm over my forehead as I stared at the whirring ceiling fan. I was going to love some lucky bastard, yeah, but not Marco. I had sent him away. Not because I didn't want him, but because I did and I was afraid of being hurt. Did I really deserve someone as special as Marco?

Yes, a voice inside me said. But what if I was

wrong? Could I survive the pain of rejection again? *Yes,* the voice answered.

I'll bet Marco really knew how to make love. Could I call him up now and ask him to come jump my bones? I'd tell him no commitments. Of course, I wouldn't tell him I was afraid he'd break my heart. I'd just pretend I didn't really care, that I was simply mad with desire.

No, that was dishonest. He deserved more. So did I.

But I might die tomorrow. Would I die never having been close to someone who deserved my intimacy?

No, I couldn't die. I would have the vision Gorky demanded and everything would work out fine. No need to call Marco in a tizzy. He'd proven to me I had a special talent. I would simply have to use it.

Icy panic flooded my veins. My fingers felt numb. What had I gotten myself into? I didn't even know the girls I wanted to save. I might die for them without ever having fully lived myself. What was with this stupid savior complex I had? I couldn't change the world. I could barely manage my own world.

I held myself tight, shivering in spite of the blistering night heat. I rolled into a fetal position, hating myself for being so damned naive, yet knowing I had no choice because I wasn't going to back out of my commitment to those girls no matter how afraid I was.

I took a deep breath and propped my head on my arm. No, I wouldn't let Lin down. I would find her friends. And on some level I wasn't even afraid of Gorky. I wasn't afraid to die as long as I died standing up for what I believed in. I'd be pissed as hell to check out so early, but not afraid. I was more fearful of living in a world where men like Vladimir Gorky were never challenged. Then there would be no hope.

But, what if? What if this was my last night? What if I died never having made love to a real man? Peter Brandt didn't count.

My hand reached for the phone and I didn't stop it. I pressed the small handheld receiver to my ear and used speed I.D. to pull up Marco's number from the memory card. "Riccuchio Marco," I said, and after a second, the machine dialed his number. The phone rang four times. I almost hung up. My heart beat in my throat. Air escaped my lungs like steam vanishing from a hot pot.

"Hello?" His voice was groggy, deep and, as always, sensual.

"Hi." It was a breathy reply. "It's me."

Pause. "Hi." His voice was even lower. Warm and intimate.

It was exactly the reassurance I needed. I finally let out my pent-up breath and we shared a moment of knowing silence. When you're with someone who really turns you on, even silence is magic. "I was thinking about you."

Another pause. It seemed eternal. My throat tightened as I waited.

"Oh?" He sounded like he was smiling.

I smiled back. "Yeah."

"Good thoughts?"

"Yeah."

"I'm glad. I don't like to think you're thinking bad things about me, Angel."

For the first time, my name sounded right coming from him. This man knew me. He really knew me inside and out, and I didn't know how it had happened. "I guess I was a little hard on you. But you weren't exactly Officer Friendly, either."

"I'm not a cop tonight, okay?"

But he was. That was part of the problem. No matter how much I wanted him, or even how much he wanted me, his duty to his job would always come first.

The silence stretched on. Finally he said, "Don't you believe me?"

"No. But I know nobody will ever change you, Marco."

He didn't argue. "Are you scared?"

A little, I almost answered. Then I sat up slowly, my languor tightening with suspicion. He didn't know anything about my plans to visit Gorky. "Why would you ask if I'm scared?"

"I don't know," he said on a yawn. "You've been through a lot. You're not out of danger yet."

We'd been through a lot in a very short time together. If Gorky was going to kill me, there were things I wanted to clear up first with Marco.

"Hey," I said, "Marco, I want to explain about Bogie."

"Don't bother. What I think doesn't matter."

It did to me. I suppose if I were a man, I wouldn't

care. But I wasn't. And I did. "He was safe." Emotion clogged my throat. I swallowed and tried again. "That's why I...well, he was safe."

"Angel Baker, you are a fine woman and you don't have to explain yourself to anyone."

A fine woman. "Thanks."

I felt a little more relaxed. I enjoyed talking to him like this. We were on the same wavelength.

"What are you wearing?" he asked out of the blue.

I'd never heard dead like the silence that followed. *What does that mean?* I almost replied. But I knew what it meant. His voice was so husky goose bumps shimmered over my arms. Yes, it was one of *those* questions. An invitation. Do you want to have sex? he'd just asked. *Yes,* my silence replied, *but I can't admit it.* Not quite yet.

"Why don't you come see for yourself?"

"Great idea." Click. The phone went dead.

I sat there on the couch, frozen, contemplating what I'd just done. Then the doorbell rang. I frowned and glanced at the wall clock. Who would ring at this hour? I briefly considered the remote possibility that it might actually be Marco. But it had only been about forty-five seconds since he'd hung up. I went to the window and looked out. *Shit.* There was his S.U.V.

"Marco?" I called in a loud whisper.

He stepped away from my door and looked up with one hand in a pocket. The other tipped an invisible hat in greeting.

"What are you doing here?" I said sotto voce.

"Staking out your apartment," he whispered back. "I looked earlier but didn't see your car."

"That's the whole idea behind a stakeout." He gave me a cheeky grin. "Are you going to invite me in?"

In that moment, my decision was made. I didn't care what happened tomorrow. I didn't even care what happened an hour from now. I wanted him and that was all that mattered.

"Sure. I'll buzz you up." One could only hope, I mentally added with a smile.

I touched a code into the security pad on the wall, letting him in the foyer, then opened the top door by hand. At the bottom of the stairs, the cast-off glow from the street served as a backlight for his striking figure. The humidity had turned his thick hair into loose brown coils.

He wore skintight jeans that hugged lean hips that fronted what I knew to be a great ass, though I couldn't see it now. On top he wore a loose-fitting, white linen shirt.

I couldn't wait for him to reach me, so I descended and met him halfway. One step above, I was taller than him for the first time.

He looked up and down my petite form, breaking into a lopsided grin. "Beautiful," he murmured. He put both hands on my muscular hips where my small waist curved in at a sharp angle. His fingers pressed into my flesh, then smoothed over the mint-green tank top I was wearing.

At the same time I put both hands on the narrow stairwell walls, trying to resist the nearly overwhelming urge to molest him here and now.

Doing it on the stairs couldn't be easy. But by lifting my arms, I inadvertently raised my breasts closer to his face, and my back arched in a provocative pose.

He moved one hand up and over my tight rib cage, smoothing the cotton material with his thumb as he went. Studying my torso with almost analytical intent, he moved his hand up until it cupped one breast. As his thumb swooped up over the heavy fullness encased in his hand, he looked up into my eyes with the keenness of a hunter who has cornered his quarry.

I leaned forward ever so slightly and felt his breath on my neck. Yes, I silently told him, you're doing exactly what I want.

His forefinger dipped over the fabric and moved downward, his fingernails brushing my skin as he followed the V cut of the tank top. I reached out and grabbed his shoulders, digging my fingers into his flesh, bone and muscle, all perfectly proportioned in his *GQ* physique.

"Oh, Marco, make love to me."

He pressed his hips against my leg and the hardness I felt confirmed he was thinking along the same lines.

"Should I?" he whispered, kissing my breastbone.

"Yes."

With one fell swoop, he lifted me in his arms and, like Clark Gable in *Gone With the Wind,* he carried me up the stairs into my bedroom. Obviously he didn't have as many stairs to climb as Rhett Butler and I was no Scarlett O'Hara. But in the movie that scene faded to black and I was going to get to enjoy this one to the scintillating end. For once, I was experiencing my life in living color. And it was glorious.

"Hey, Baker, guess what?" he said a few hours later, pulling me partially out of a deep sleep.

"Mmm?" I stirred enough to nestle closer in his arms.

"I found out something interesting about that gun we pulled off of the R.M.O. assassin outside of Lola's apartment." He gently smoothed a strand of hair off my cheek and tucked it behind my ear.

"Hmm?"

"It's the latest creation from Trimara Corp, the weapons makers from Ireland, which has oddly given the weapon the whimsical trademark name of Radioart, as in radioactive artillery. Cute, huh?"

"Yeah, it sounds like a toy." I reached up and smoothed my hand over his cheek. I wanted every part of me touching every part of him, though I still didn't want to wake up.

"The damned thing shoots out a concentrated and specific beam of radiation so precise there's only a one-millimeter margin of error."

I managed to crack open one eye. "So the only person exposed to the radiation is the one who is shot?"

"Yes." He kissed my temple. "The radiation compound we saw glowing in the gut of the rifle is so powerful that only one shot guarantees the victim will suffer from radiation poisoning, eventually leading to a variety of fatal diseases. It kills so slowly that the assassin who pulls the trigger can't be connected to the death. I guess the R.M.O. uses it on people whom they want dead eventually."

"Sounds wicked."

"The bad news is that the R.M.O. is the first and only group to have access to the weapon. The good news is that not even the R.M.O. has yet to come up with a way to protect their own people from the radiation—should it fall into the wrong hands. That R.M.O. assassin you blasted on Howard Street will be checking himself into the hospital in the not too distant future."

"Can we play with the new toy?"

"We're not supposed to. It should stay in the evidence lockup."

"Department rules, eh? Doesn't matter," I murmured in his ear with a smile while my hands began to grope. "Right now I'd rather play with something else instead."

The next morning I woke with a luxurious, satisfied yawn, like Vivian Leigh minus the expensive satin nightgown.

Marco was gone. I reached across the bed, caressing the place where he'd slept, wishing I could give him one more hug. He had been as tender and powerful a lover as I had imagined he would be. I wondered if I'd ever see him again. I supposed I would in an official capacity if he was staking me out. But did he care enough to make love again?

More important, was he the kind of man who would go the distance?

I hadn't asked for any commitments, so I couldn't expect any. And until I came back alive from Gorky's mansion, I couldn't give any, either.

The sun beamed in with far more cheer than I felt. But I was surprisingly eager to get on with my mission. At least if I died now, it would be with no regrets.

I made a cup of coffee and went into the living room to call Hank. To my surprise, Marco had left three items on the coffee table in front of the couch. One was a bundle of architectural blueprints of Gorky's northside mansion, stamped with the logo of the Chicago Police Records Department. I held the scrolls in my hands and whooped with joy. This was exactly what I needed to know my way around Gorky's place.

The other gift was the Radioart weapon we'd confiscated from the R.M.O. assassin. It was supposed to be under lock and key as evidence in the investigation of the murder of Lola's cleaning lady. Marco had risked his career sneaking it out of the evidence lockup for me. I picked it up and turned it over in my hands. Marco hadn't made any commitments, but he'd put his butt on the line to make sure I would be safe.

And last but not least, he had left the ignition chip for his SUV. I suppose he expected it would be my getaway car. But how did he know I'd need one?

"Thanks, Marco," I said, wiping my eyes. "You're the best."

Then I saw a note he'd tucked under the weapon.
It read:

Dear Angel,
Thought you might need these accou-
trements when you meet with Gorky. I
bribed Carl, the waiter, to give me the low-
down. Sorry.
M.
P.S. Some rules were made to be broken.

Chapter 24

Showdown at the R.M.O.'s Corral

After poring over the blueprints and reviewing notes Hank had gathered for us, Mike and I climbed into Marco's SUV just after dark. I brought the Radioart, but hoped I wouldn't have to use it.

"Here's the ignition chip," I said, tossing it to Mike when we reached Marco's vehicle parked outside my two-flat.

Mike caught it in midair with a graceful snap of his hand, then stopped and frowned. "You drive, Baker."

"I don't have a license."

"Nor do I."

"What? I thought you bought one on the black market."

"No, I think about it. But since I do not drive, it seems pointless."

I sighed. "I usually subcontract getaway cars when I need them. We'll just have to use the Optical Guiding System. But you're sitting behind the wheel. If I get pulled over for driving without a license, I could lose my R.S. certification."

"Okay, but we won't get pulled over if we don't speed."

"From your mouth to God's ears." We climbed up into the hydro vehicle. "Gorky's home, James."

"My name is Mike," he said as he revved the engine.

"You're so literal," I said, chuckling.

"To read is better than to watch TV." He put the car in gear and it lurched when the O.G.S. kicked in. The great news about guiding systems is that you can sit back and relax without ever touching the wheel. The bad news is that you always do the speed limit. Unless, of course, you override the system. Not a good idea, in our situation.

We took Lake Shore Drive, following Lake Michigan's coastline north, which was a scenic route I could not appreciate for obvious reasons. By the time L.S.D. turned into Sheridan Road, I was nervous. By the time we reached the far north shore, I was sweating bullets.

It wasn't just my possible tête-á-tête with the Grim Reaper that bothered me. I couldn't breathe. The girls flashed in my mind. I felt their anxiety, their terror at being torn from their sisters. But they were in Gorky's mansion. Why did I feel the oppression coming from behind us?

"Someone follows." Mike looked in the rearview mirror, and I twisted around in my seat. Headlights stabbed my eyes with a rude glare and a vehicle I couldn't make out was soon inches away from our rear bumper.

"Oh, great. I hope this isn't Gorky's idea of a friendly escort," I muttered.

The low, black land vehicle rammed us from behind. Our SUV lurched forward. Suddenly two aerocars zoomed up beside us. Their windows rolled down, revealing the noses of automatic weapons and the Mongolian gunmen aiming them at our heads.

"Shit!" I cried out, grabbing the O.G.S. controls. "Burn rubber!"

That was one colloquialism Mike had never heard, by the look on his face. But he inferred my precise meaning when I yanked the controls, overriding the computer, and punched 80 mph into the hydroinjection program.

"Whoa!" Mike shouted as the force of our propulsion slammed our heads back. The Mongolian aerocars were momentarily history. We began to veer to the right and I realized Mike still hadn't taken over the wheel.

I reached out and grabbed it, awkwardly driving from the passenger seat. "Mike, you have to steer."

"No, Baker, we will crash!"

"We will if you don't steer! Now drive!" I looked back and our stalkers were gaining on us.

Mike protested, "The police—"

"Are nowhere in sight, unfortunately."

I released the wheel and Mike flung himself toward it as if it were a life buoy from the *Titanic*. We veered wildly until he gained control. I was beginning to feel seasick. Regaining my balance, I glanced at orange-and-green veins illuminated on the satellite mapping console. We were less than a mile away from the entrance to Gorky's compound, thank heaven.

What a difference a day makes. I now thought of the man who had been dubbed the R.M.O.'s "massacre mind" as my savior. If we could just pass through his electric gates, we could declare sanctuary.

With wheels squealing, we rounded a hairpin curve in the road and Gorky's Palladian mansion came into view with as much grandeur as Tara in the opening scenes of *Gone With the Wind.* I was beginning to think it was the story of my life.

"We're here!" I cried.

The huge, square home and white pillars had been built on the water just off the edge of the coastline. A high-tech security fence engulfed the footbridge, which was the only way to reach the house, except by boat. Landside, outbuildings dotted the property, including a twenty-car garage, stables, an armory, a lookout tower, servants' quarters—the usual fare for filthy-rich mob bosses.

Right now my focus was riveted on the computerized twenty-foot-tall electric fence that surrounded the entire thirty-acre compound. I prayed the gate had been programmed to open for us.

"We're close," I said when we were about a quarter of a mile away. But close doesn't count in games of life and death. The land vehicle zoomed past us, spun sideways and came to a smoky, screeching halt right in front of us. Mike slammed on the brakes. We stopped just as our front fender hit the car's side door. We both jolted forward.

We sat a moment, stunned. Then I began to slam my fingers into console buttons, opening the doors. "Let's get out of here before they blow our heads off." They probably would blow our heads off anyway, but at least we wouldn't mess up Marco's car.

As we jumped out, the chasing cars all came to wild stops like Pick Up sticks thrown in the middle of the road. Burned rubber clogged the air. Bullets whizzed near my head. I ducked and scrambled around the car. Mike went the other way.

I found myself next to the drivers' side of the black car. The driver was unbuckling. I shot to my feet and through his open window I punched him hard in the jaw. His gunrunner in the passenger's seat flew out his side, racing around the car's front end to pump me full of bullets. I crouched, waited, then used the Shaolin *hou tiao qian* technique—monkey jumping over a wall, or in this case jumping over the hood of a car. I jammed my boot into the short, black-haired triggerman's chest, taking him by surprise.

As he staggered back, I moved in, driven by fury over his role, however remote, in the kidnapping of innocent girls. Punching, kicking, crouching, twirling—*tou gu zhi*, the finger as hard as metal, into the eye; *Pi chai zhang*, the palm cutting wood, into the throat. I was *Jiao long nu kong*, the coiling dragon growling in wrath. Pumped by adrenaline like I'd never felt before, I hammered in a relentless and pure explosion of energy until the techniques Mike had taught me worked. Down the Mongolian assassin went, knocked out cold.

I whirled around. Mike was fighting off two attackers with twice as many moves as I had just employed. He was a blur of motion, but he couldn't stop all of them. Three others were heading toward him. I was about to call them my way—a suicidal tact—but froze when I saw a convoy of four gray Humvees, led by an honest-to-God armored tank. It was a compact model, to be sure, but still it was a friggin' armored tank. I had to say, I was impressed.

So were the Mongolian gangsters. They all stopped fighting and those who were armed dropped their weapons and raised their arms in surrender. When you have a twenty-foot-long cannon aimed at your nose, you don't really have any other choice.

Two people got out of one of the Humvees and surveyed the scene. Both wore black ski masks, but I thought I recognized the curvaceous figure of one of Gorky's operatives. It had to be the James Bond chick Marco and I had seen on Howard Street. She conferred with her masked companion, then jogged to one of the Humvees and drove back to the compound. The masked man stepped forward.

"You two!" he shouted, pointing at me and Mike. "Come with me."

Mike and I eagerly left the melee and climbed into the remaining Hummer. The driver pulled a U-turn, and as we rode away, I felt the vibration and heard the boom of a huge blast behind us. We turned in our seats just in time to see an orange-and-yellow fireball curling up to the sky. The armored tank had obviously taken out the entire scene with one blast. I saw no bodies and only a few chunks of the cars.

Mike and I looked at each other, then slowly turned face front. I knew I should feel sorry for the men that Gorky had just obliterated, and on some spiritual level I did. But I couldn't help but wonder how in the hell I'd explain to Marco what had happened to his SUV.

We were led by a series of employees from the vehicle, over the bridge and into Gorky's house. I was hoping to see the svelte Svetlana, as I mentally dubbed the masked female bandit who had ordered our rescue on Sheridan Road, but once again she had fallen off our radar screen.

By the time I reached Gorky's personal study in the back of the house, I had concluded that for the first time in her life Lola had not exaggerated. The place was gorgeous, and Gorky had incredible taste—at least his decorator did. We didn't actually see the various wings of the house—each apparently with its own architecture and style, but we glimpsed hints of the decor beyond by the lavish hallways that led off the main artery we traveled. We saw everything from old-style Russian to art deco.

When we reached Gorky's private quarters, I was amazed to see architecture that imitated some of Frank Lloyd Wright's famous houses. There was a two-story dining room with a long mission-style table that might have fit perfectly at the Dana

Thomas house. Outside, overlooking the lake, was a concrete patio with Oriental and geometric sculptures similar to those found at Taliesin West.

We found Gorky in a large sunken room with two walls made of etched glass, shooting out from the floor at a ten-degree angle and met with a low-slung roof of long wood beams. On the far side of the room, the floor actually had steps that led down to the lake some twenty feet below. I suppose that idea was taken from Wright's most celebrated house, Falling Water.

"Ah, here is the woman of the hour, and her good friend," Gorky said, rising from a wooden chair on the circular stone slab floor in the middle of the room. "Come in. I heard you had trouble. I hope you weren't hurt."

I am ashamed to say I almost found Gorky's European double kisses on the cheeks comforting after our brush with death. But if we were going to get out of here alive, I had to get my head together and have a vision.

"How do you want to do this, Angel *moy*?" Gorky asked.

"Oh, my God," I said as reality settled in. "Lola's crystal ball was destroyed." I didn't bother to mention that the Radioart weapon had been blown to bits, as well.

"Not to worry, *dorogaya moya*," Gorky said with a gruff smile. "Lola keeps one of her crystals here."

"She does?" Good Lord, was she shacking up with the guy?

"Don't be disappointed in her," he said, pushing a button on his chair. "Sometimes she does her readings here when I must keep a low profile."

An older woman wearing a floral scarf entered carrying a round crystal. She placed it on the table in front of me in a round stand.

"Thank you, Alexia," Gorky said. "Make sure no one interrupts us now."

The woman nodded and departed. When we were alone again, Gorky turned to me with anticipation. "Well? It's all yours, Angel *moy*."

I looked down at the cold, dead ball and felt a cold, dead feeling in my gut. Oh, shit. This time I'd really bought the farm.

"Where are the girls?"

"They are here." Gorky pressed the tips of his fingers together and sat back in his chair to enjoy the show. "You need not fear, *dorogaya moya,* I am a man of my word. If you produce information for me, I will give you the girls free and clear, as long as you promise to keep them out of Capone's hands."

"Oh, I can promise you that."

"Then we are agreed. Have your vision."

I looked up at him with a scowl. "Boy, you're not going to make this easy for me, are you?"

"It was easy enough for Lola."

"That's because she made things up!"

Gorky frowned. All humor vanished from his ruddy face. I had a good idea this was a man I didn't want to anger. "Do not be disrespectful to your mother."

I nodded. I was glad to know that "Honor thy mother and father" was a commandment he held near and dear, since "Thou shalt not kill" obviously meant nothing to him.

"I meant no disrespect. But my mother couldn't give you the information you needed, remember? That's why I'm here. But…I'm new at this. If you could just…hint at what you want me to find, we'd be way ahead of the game."

"I already told you it is an object inside of which is hidden a priceless thing."

"Well, that helps." Not. "Can you be more specific? Is it, say, bigger than a bread box?"

"Smaller."

I sighed. "Okay. I want you to picture it in your mind. Try to remember every detail and I'll see what I can come up with."

I shut my eyes and breathed deeply. I was surprised how quickly random thoughts faded. I felt energy drawing me toward the crystal. Heat sizzled in my palm.

Whoomph. I felt a bird flutter around my head. A breeze from its wings cooled my temple. My eyes flew open. I looked around, but there was nothing.

"What is it?" Gorky asked, moving to the edge of his chair. "What did you see?"

"Quiet," Mike said. "Let her concentrate."

"I saw a bird." I looked questioningly to Mike. "An eagle?"

I focused on the ball and smelled gunpowder. "Someone has been shot. A man with silver hair."

"Where was he wounded?" Gorky said in a low voice.

"Below the heart. He's going to die… He—no, he's okay."

"That was me," Gorky said. "Where did it happen?"

"On a cliff overlooking water. It's snowing. I see the bird, but he's not flying."

Gorky let out a raspy baritone chuckle. "No, he wouldn't be flying. It happened in Wisconsin. You have seen it all exactly as it happened. You are right, Angel *moy*. You have a true gift." He gripped the arms of his oak chair and pulled his strapping body to the edge of his seat. "Now, to get those girls and yourself out of here alive, you must tell me what happened to the bird."

I shut my eyes, trying to lure back the fading vision. I saw snow, even felt the cold flakes on my cheeks, heard the shot and smelled the blood that splattered the white ground, but I could not see the bird. It would have flown at the gun's report.

"There is no bird," I said, opening my eyes. The spell was broken.

"Look again," Gorky urged me. "Sometimes things are not what they seem."

I licked my lips and willed myself to try once more. I touched the crystal ball. It had cooled and was lukewarm at best. Then a tickling sensation scratched at my palms. I placed them firmly on the round glass. Heat poured from my lifelines. The glass glowed and I was stunned by what I saw— Humphrey Bogart. I blinked, waiting for the vision to pass, but it was still there. He was talking and I could tell somehow that I was watching a movie.

"I see Bogart," I said, half-afraid Gorky would laugh me out of the house, but I remembered that he was a Bogart fan.

"What do you see?" the mobster asked in a prodding, sly voice.

"It's a scene from a movie."

"What is he saying?"

I shook my head. It was as if someone had muted the film. This wasn't *Casablanca*. Bogart was too intense, almost mean. Then suddenly I heard, "It's the stuff that dreams are made of." And I knew.

Risking the loss of the vision, I looked at Gorky as I said, *"The Maltese Falcon."*

His wide mouth broke into a slow, satisfied grin. "Excellent, *dorogaya moya.* Yes, it is the Maltese Falcon that was stolen from me."

I almost burst out laughing. Was this guy for real? I tried to remember what I could from the film. It had to have been shot in the 1940s. It was Bogart's first roll as a leading man, but he was antihero material. It was a film noir, almost clichéd, and certainly nothing remotely like a true story.

"There was no real Maltese Falcon, Vladimir. The film was based on a novel by Daschiel Hammett. Pure fiction."

"True, but I am a film afficionado, and I chose such a statue to carry my treasure, which I assure you is very real. It was stolen, and you still haven't told me where it is."

I glanced almost casually at the ball, and there I saw a vision so clear it took my breath away. "There is a farm with rolling hills," I said in a monotone as if I were merely translating a message. "And a covered bridge over a small stream."

"Yes?" Gorky whispered.

"There is a two-hundred-year-old house at the

end of the road. An old woman lives there. She has had a stroke—her mouth is pulled down and her one foot drags behind her."

"Yes?" he said in a strangled voice.

"She has hidden your treasure under the floor-board in the dining room."

And just like that, the scene I had described vanished. The ball emptied of images. I was fully back in the room. But I still hadn't told him where he could find the farm.

"I'm sorry," I said. "I can't tell you more."

"You told me enough." He leaned back in his chair, his big knees half blocking my view of him. He stared sullenly at nothing in particular. "You described a place I know in Chechnya. I would not have thought it would be there. This is a great knife in my heart, but I now know it's true. You could not have made that up."

I shot Mike a look of relief. Then my mind raced over the details of the movie. As I recalled, no one ever found the priceless Maltese Falcon. It was said to be a statuette made of pure gold, covered in jewels. It had been disguised with a black covering. But the bad guys had stolen a counterfeit version made of lead. Everyone in the movie had fought over a fake and they'd all ended up empty-handed.

"What if it's not there?" I asked. "What if it's not what you think it is?"

He gave me a wily half smile tinged with darkness. "Then I'll come back for you, Angel *moy*. But for now, you are free to go."

He left us, and his servant lady brought us tea.

Mike and I drank, anxiously waiting to see what would happen next. After an hour, we were ushered back into the Humvee. I protested, but the driver, who had scarred cheeks and surly lips, cursed and told me to be patient.

He drove us without further explanation about ten miles down the road. When the driver turned down a dark, unmarked dirt road, I gripped Mike's hand and dug my nails into his flesh. I was certain we were about to die, execution style. We would probably be dismembered.

When the vehicle stopped in a clearing, our headlights illuminated a big, unmarked white van. Standing in front of it was Marco. My heart literally leaped with joy. Then I frowned. What was he doing here? Was he part of this whole operation? Had he been an operative planted in my life not by the police department but by the R.M.O.?

We stepped out of the Humvee, and I approached him cautiously, shielding the glaring light from my eyes with a hand over my brow. He wore some kind of uniform. He looked like a bug exterminator or a house painter. Nevertheless, he was drop-dead gorgeous in his undercover garb.

"Hi," I said. I stopped about ten feet away from him. He leaned against the white van.

He crossed his arms. "Hi."

My mind whirled. I was confused, tired, relieved and still scared. "I—I wrecked your SUV. I'm sorry. It was…an accident."

"I thought that might happen," he said, and one of his sculptured cheeks dimpled with a wry grin. He patted the grill of the van. "That's why I borrowed this."

"I don't understand." I shoved my fingers through my hair, tired of pretending I knew what I was doing.

"I figured I'd have a big load of pint-size passengers to bring back to the city. See, I've always had faith in your talents, Baker. Even more than you have."

I heard Mike chattering away in Chinese. The sound came from inside the van. I walked slowly toward it, stopping when I was close enough to see in the open sliding door. Sitting there on two long seats, all safely buckled and hugging cute little backpacks, were eleven adorable Chinese girls. Mike stood next to me, rattling away in his native tongue. The girls, absorbing every word, barely spared me a glance.

I heard him mention Lin's name and the girls' frightened expressions changed. Their eyes lit with anticipation and the oldest of the girls asked questions, then chattered at her friends. All broke into smiles.

"I tell them they will see Lin soon," Mike said, giving me one of his rare smiles. "They are very happy to hear they are safe now."

Overwhelmed, I pulled Mike into my arms and hugged him tight. Together we rocked back and forth, and tears rolled down my cheeks onto his black ninja tunic. "Oh, Mike, thank you so much. We did it. We really did it."

"You did it, Baker," he said, pulling me away and giving me a tender look. "Like a blue dragon, you rise from the depths and defeat the Russian eagle."

Or the falcon, I thought. But I wasn't sure I had

defeated anything or anyone. All I knew was that the girls were safe.

I let him go and stepped away, not wanting to interfere with Mike's work as translator. There was a lot he'd have to explain to the children and a great deal more they needed to tell us, if they could.

The Humvee's engine rumbled into gear and I turned just in time to witness something that made absolutely no sense. The surly Russian driver called to Marco, spitting out incomprehensible words in his native tongue. And to my amazement, Marco responded in kind. He shouted out in fluent Russian. The driver nodded, laughed, and then put the Humvee in gear and tore out of the clearing, leaving behind a cloud of dust.

Marco turned back to me as if nothing had happened.

"You just spoke to that guy in fluent Russian."

"Yes."

I couldn't breathe. "Why? How?"

He folded his hands, looking contrite. "I guess I'd better explain. Come with me. We're close to the beach."

He told Mike we'd be back soon, then took my hand and led me down to Lake Michigan. Inky water lapped softly on the man-made beach. A round, blue moon cast its unassuming light on the lake as far as the eye could see.

"I love the water, don't you?" he said, sliding his hands into his jumpsuit pockets. A warm breeze pushed at his loose, dark curls of hair.

"Marco, what was that all about? What did you say to that Russian guy?"

He gave me a lopsided grin and stroked my cheek with one hand. "Ah, my lovely Angel, how can I explain?"

"I was wondering the same thing."

"That man who drove you to the clearing is my cousin."

"What?" When I took a step back, he grabbed both my arms and pulled me close.

"A distant cousin on my mother's side. Her maiden name was Natasha Petrovsky. She married my father, Luigi Marco, and then married Tom Black. I grew up speaking Russian. And for a while, I went down a bad path. Almost joined the R.M.O. When Danny was killed, I thought it might have been a belated payback for my decision to walk away from Gorky's organization. I needed to find out. That's why I came looking for you. You were the last one who saw Danny alive."

My heart beat fast as I tried to make sense of it all. "So you didn't really blame me for your brother's death?"

He let out a long sigh, then started walking down the beach, pulling me along with an arm around my shoulder. I put my arm around his waist and strolled beside him.

"I wasn't sure," Marco said. "I blamed myself most of all. After looking in your files, I realized you had nothing to do with his death. But then I saw another opportunity."

"An opportunity to use me," I said in a hollow voice.

He stopped and turned to me, tucking a finger

under my chin. "At first, yes. It turned out that your relationship to Lola gave me an unexpected entré into Gorky's personal life. And he was the man I was after. But by the time you and I made love, I was there because I wanted to be there. With you. Do you believe me?"

I sniffed the fresh lake air that came from some clean, faraway place. A memory of Marco's love-making flashed in my mind and I smiled. He certainly hadn't been phoning it in that night. "Yes, amazingly, I do believe you."

Clearly relieved, he put an arm around me again and we continued our stroll. "I decided to go after the R.M.O. when Dan was killed. I was assigned to a special team of investigators who reported directly to Mayor Alvarez. Remember? The first day we met I told you Alvarez sent me."

I chuckled softly. "That's what got you in the door, but I thought you were lying."

"Alvarez wanted to bust the R.M.O. wide open. Our team was working on various ways to get him. We've had undercover operatives working on this child-kidnapping case for weeks."

"You knew all about the Chinese girls?"

"I knew bits and pieces. Recently our operatives discovered that Capone was breeding kids like fish in a hatchery outside of Barrington. When Gorky stole the girls, Alvarez hoped we could nail the R.M.O. and the Mongolian Mob at the same time, for the same crime. I couldn't tell you what I knew about the case without endangering the lives of our officers working inside the R.M.O. As it turns out, you didn't really need my help figuring out how to rescue those girls."

I let out an indignant breath. "Well, I'm glad the police were planning on busting Gorky, but were your people ever going to bother to save the children? Or were they just pawns?"

"Of course the girls were going to be rescued. But I found out two days ago that the mayor got cold feet and decided not to bust Gorky for anything until after the next election."

"No!"

"Yes. Politics triumph again," he said bitterly. "I contacted my cousin tonight. He told me Gorky was going to let you and the girls go. I offered to pick you up in an unmarked van. Knowing that Alvarez had lost his spine, Gorky figured he had nothing to fear from me and approved our little rendezvous."

I digested this and nodded slowly. "But why, Marco? Why would you help me when I'm doing what a legitimate police officer should be doing? You demanded that I give up my profession."

We slowed to a stop and he smoothed a short tuft of hair behind my ear. His touch sent a delightful chill down my neck.

"Tonight you weren't a CRS," he said. "You were a guardian angel. Just as you were when you saved my life outside of the abuse shelter. That day I learned everything I needed to know about you."

"Uh-oh," I said with a sly smile. "That sounds ominous."

"You and I are a lot alike. We'll both fight for justice to the bitter end. And sometimes we'll do really stupid things in order to help others. The bottom line is that I trusted your commitment to those girls more than I trusted Alvarez's commitment to do the right thing."

I put my arms around his waist and looked up into his dark eyes. "Are you telling me we have something in common?"

"I'm afraid so, Ms. Baker." He wrapped his arms around my shoulders. "After Alvarez pulled the rug out from under my team, I began to understand why people like you take the law into your own hands."

"Now wait a min—"

He stopped my protests with a kiss. His lips were warm and perfect on mine. When he finally pulled away, he said, "I admire the hell out of you, Angel Baker."

"The feeling is mutual, Detective Marco," I replied breathlessly.

"And I need you."

My eyes widened. "What for?"

"I need you to help me bring down Gorky."

I smiled coyly. "You sweet talker. You are the most romantic man I've ever met."

He raised a brow. "How do you figure? It's not like I just offered you a bouquet of roses, kid."

"No, it was much better than that. You gave me hope. I love that! Who needs chocolates? We can do this, Marco. Together. I've got it all planned out." I tucked my arm in his and half dragged him back toward the van. "Not only were those girls kidnapped, but their sisters were murdered. We've got an airtight case, including a witness who saw the girls in Gorky's mansion. We'll go around the mayor if we have to, straight to the governor. But first we have to get the girls to safety. I know they'll be placed in good homes."

"But Lin stays with you, Angel."

I frowned. "I don't know, Marco. She deserves so much more than I could give her."

"She needs you. And speaking as a former psychologist, you'd be a great mother."

"It's funny. My mom said the same thing."

"She was right."

"You know, Marco, Lola was a lousy mother, but I'd bet she'd be a damned good grandmother."

When we reached the van, we found the girls curled up on the seats, sleeping contentedly. Mike sat in the middle row, cradling two girls in his lap, watching over them all like a proud uncle. He gazed at me in the loving silence and I knew we were thinking the same thing. The pieces of our strange and wonderful little family were pulling together before our eyes. I nodded at him and smiled, blinking back tears. Life was good. Very, very good.

Marco and I climbed into the front seats and we headed back to the city. My heart raced with excitement, confidence, hope and even faith. The world just might be okay after all. At least our little corner of it would be.

"Marco?" I said over the sound of the tires whirring on the pavement.

"Yes, Angel?"

I waited until he glanced my way, then I nodded approvingly. "I think this is the beginning of a beautiful friendship."

ATHENA FORCE

Chosen for their talents.
Trained to be the best.

Expected to change the world.

The women of Athena Academy
share an unforgettable experience
and an unbreakable bond—until
one of their own is murdered.

The adventure begins with these six books:

PROOF by Justine Davis, July 2004

ALIAS by Amy J. Fetzer, August 2004

EXPOSED by Katherine Garbera,
September 2004

DOUBLE-CROSS by Meredith Fletcher,
October 2004

PURSUED by Catherine Mann, November 2004

JUSTICE by Debra Webb, December 2004

**And look for six more Athena Force stories
January to June 2005.**

Available at your favorite retail outlet.

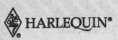

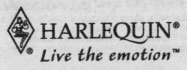